Dirty Diana

A Novel

Jen Besser
and Shana Feste

THE DIAL PRESS

New York

A Dial Press Trade Paperback Original

Published in the United States by The Dial Press, an imprint of Random House, a division of Penguin Random House LLC, New York.

THE DIAL PRESS is a registered trademark and the colophon is a trademark of Penguin Random House LLC.

LIBRARY OF CONGRESS CATALOGING-IN-PUBLICATION DATA
Names: Besser, Jen, author. | Feste, Shana, 1976- author.
Title: Dirty Diana: a novel / Jen Besser and Shana Feste.
Description: New York: The Dial Press, 2024. | Series: Dirty Diana; vol 1
Identifiers: LCCN 2023018537 (print) | LCCN 2023018538 (ebook) |
ISBN 9780593447666 (trade paperback; acid-free paper) |
ISBN 9780593447673 (ebook)
Subjects: LCGFT: Erotic fiction. | Novels.
Classification: LCC PS3602.E7828 D57 2024 (print) | LCC PS3602.E7828 (ebook) |
DDC 813/.6—dc23/eng/20230725
LC record available at https://lccn.loc.gov/2023018537
LC ebook record available at https://lccn.loc.gov/2023018538

Printed in the United States of America on acid-free paper

randomhousebooks.com

2   4   6   8   9   7   5   3   1

Book design by Debbie Glasserman

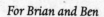

For Brian and Ben

The armored cars of dreams, contrived to let us do
so many a dangerous thing.

—Elizabeth Bishop, "Sleeping Standing Up"

Dirty Diana

Prologue

—

Outside our tent, the night is dark, deep, and absolutely clear. Inside, I close my eyes and try to sleep.

But the ground is cold and so hard beneath my back. I press my lips together to keep my teeth from chattering.

It *must* be warmer in your sleeping bag.

I shift onto my side so I can see you. It's a new moon and only the stars give off light. They paint you in a dreamy tint—your skin is smooth except where the stubble of three days in the desert has grown in. Your eyes are closed, your face turned up toward the tent's mesh opening and your lips, full and perfect, are arranged in a relaxed smile, as if you're stargazing in your sleep. You must not be cold because your arms are outside your sleeping bag, resting triumphantly by your sides. Your chest, naked and muscular, rises and falls in a steady rhythm.

We haven't had sex in hours, but it feels like years.

I was prepared for the desert days to be hot and the nights to be cold—or at least, I listened and nodded as you warned me, which I know now is different from being prepared. I underestimated the weather the same way that, earlier today, we had both underestimated the craggy hills surrounding us. "The peak isn't *so* high," we'd said. "Let's hike to the top." You climbed like the sun didn't bother you, and if I hadn't been with you, you would have moved much faster.

Near the top, we passed the entrance to a cave. I wondered aloud what lived inside. "Maybe a bobcat," you said and shrugged. So I shrugged, too, said, "Cool," and backed away.

I burrow deeper into my sleeping bag and wish for another layer of clothing. It *has* to feel different in your sleeping bag. I imagine crawling inside. But I'm not sure if you want to be woken up. Our relationship is so new that every choice feels weighted, like it could be gravely misinterpreted—waking you up might signal that I don't understand boundaries and the importance of a little space to balance out the intensity of our physical closeness. The infancy of this is intoxicating, but also slippery and uncertain.

It's been this exhilarating for the last three days, both of us set off by the smallest thing—a slow puff of weed, a bra strap that slips off my shoulder. We look up constantly from our work to catch the other one staring.

I pull my arms into the sleeves of my T-shirt for extra warmth and stare through the tent's mesh roof at the stars. I think of the steep, rocky trail, of the entrance to the cave. And the bobcat.

I remember the wool hat I left so cavalierly by the campfire. It's suddenly the solution to my sleeplessness. It will make me warm. I have to have it.

I slip out of my sleeping bag, careful not to wake you, and unzip the tent to sneak quietly into the night.

The air is so cold it's sharp. There's an owl close by; I can hear her, loud and watchful, as I grope for my hat near the dying campfire. The trees at the edge of our campsite have a bluish glow, and near my feet, some kind of lizard skitters by. I startle so easily I make myself laugh.

I take a deep breath and find consolation in the fire's last red embers, holding my hands out to warm them. As my shoulders relax, I drink in the stillness.

"Diana!" The sound of your voice makes me jump. You grab my shoulders and scoop me to your side. The beam of your flashlight illuminates the trees, dancing across them, until it settles on a set of eyes—shiny and bright and glowering right at us. "Get back in the tent."

I gasp, then step away slowly. She's watching.

Inside, we shine the light through the tent's window until her long, feline body skulks into the night, toward the hills.

"Do you think she'll come back?"

"We're fine," you say, but your heart still hammers against your chest and so does mine. In the quiet, we study each other—our eyes big and vigilant, our bodies frozen. My laugh breaks the tension first, then yours.

"That was terrifying," you say.

"Truly."

The tent is small but the distance between us is suddenly too far. Your eyes flit from my eyes to my mouth. I study your throat, the thick muscles of your arms, your face.

When our lips touch, I realize I'm shivering. Your mouth is warm and briny, and we kiss until we can both feel the heat radiating from my body. I pull off my T-shirt. You sit back so you can take in the curves of my breasts, soft and wanting in the pale light.

You unzip your sleeping bag and smooth it out as a blanket for us. We lie down on our backs, both of us naked from the waist up, only our hands delicately touching. We try to slow the ecstasy of this moment.

"I don't want to go back to the city tomorrow," I say. *When we do,* I think, *everything will evaporate, including us.*

I watch the night sky, but you're too distracting. When I turn to face you, you've already shifted to meet my gaze. We turn on our sides and you pull me into you. Your skin is warm, as if you've just been lying in the sun.

I pull the waist of your pants down over your hips then brush the bare skin of my stomach against you, feeling you grow harder.

I take you in my hand and you groan. "Where am I?" you ask.

I smile and hold you tighter.

"And what are we doing?"

I laugh. "With our lives or in the moment?"

You kiss me, biting gently on my bottom lip. "Both."

"We're camping." Then I add, "And we're also out here having sex. Lots of it."

"Mmm, right," you murmur, still kissing me.

"And maybe hiding out from the world." I drape a leg across you, then my whole body. "Or maybe no one's looking for us." Maybe it's only the owl watching over us.

Your hands move down my back, sliding beneath my pants. "We need these off," you say.

I smile and lift my hips so you can undress me. "And definitely these," you say, and together we slip off my underwear so we're both naked.

"Are you still cold?"

I spread my legs in answer, just slightly, so I can brush the warmest, softest part of me against your erection.

You tilt your head back in pleasure and grip my hips. "I like hiding out with you."

"Me too." I kiss the stubble along your cheek. You pull me even closer and your guttural moans fill the tent. *We're also falling in love,* I add, but not out loud.

I hook my legs around yours, then skim my body along yours. I need you inside me. It's no longer a desire, but a need. I inch my body up higher and I tilt my pelvis forward so the tip of your penis enters me. "Wait." You hold me by the hips. "Let me touch you first."

You gently ease on top of me, your forearms pressing into the ground beside us. I spread my legs wider. But you shake your head no. "Don't move." You pin my wrists above my head. A wave of heat rolls through me and I shift underneath you, hoping to feel your hardness inside me. You shake your head again. "No moving," you whisper.

You let go of my wrists and trace your hands down my sides. My hands are free, but I keep them exactly as they are. I close my eyes. We're both somewhere else now, floating in a kind of feverish dark where the only thing I can concentrate on is following your directions toward the depths of our pleasure.

Kissing the hollow of my throat where it meets my chest, you cup my breasts. Then you kiss my nipples. They're erect beneath your lips. You slip two fingers inside me and I know you can feel how swollen I am. I can't help it, my hand grabs for yours. "Please," I whisper. "I want to fuck you." But you keep your hand where it is, moving your fingers in slow circles.

"I want you inside me," I say.

"Trust me."

At the sound of your voice, deep and hungry, a fullness builds in me, a pressure that only you can release. Or maybe it's that no one has ever tried like you to become so intimate with the geography of my body.

The fuller I become, the more I want to wriggle away. I fight the urge to pull at your hand and a molecule inside me awakens. Will it evaporate or build, I wonder.

It flits away, and I take the time to catch my breath.

"Stay with it," you whisper in my ear.

I arch my back and push deeper into you. Your stubble scratches my cheek, leaving a sting. This time the molecule returns, and now it's multiplying. My mouth opens and I breathe faster and harder.

"Trust me," you say. "You're so close."

My hips move with your hand, urging you to press harder, stay longer, keep going until I can melt against you.

"You're so close," you repeat, as if you know my body better than I do.

I move against you until I'm about to shatter. "I'm going to come." Declaring it out loud gives my body permission. I let my head fall backward. I scream into the desert sky.

You smile, kissing me hungrily, and I know then that we are not done.

My body trembles. "What was that?" I ask.

You just smile, and in between kissing me, you ask, "Can I fuck you?"

My body is yours. You can do whatever you like with it. I nod and lie back into the warm sleeping bag, spreading my legs for you, my thighs still quivering. You enter me quickly and your thickness is even more pronounced. I tighten around you, as if begging you to stay. *Never leave.*

You grip my hands and we intertwine our fingers, digging into the hard ground.

"God, you feel good," you whisper.

I roll on top of you so that my legs are wrapped around your waist. You sit up, too, your hands on the small of my back. You take my breast in your mouth, biting my nipple and then sucking on it, as if to apologize. I raise and lower my hips as you push more deeply inside me. We move together, faster and faster.

I lean back and feel a strange tickle at my neck. It's warm. Too warm. I swipe at the sensation with my hand.

I sit up straighter and focus on you. I focus on our bodies, your skin against mine, the feeling of fucking you.

Now there is a tickle at my cheek. More like a cloying wind. I brush it away. I move against you, but the pressure of our bodies against each other has gone. I can feel the hard earth beneath me—but

I'm on top of you, I should feel you, not the ground. The strange, annoying breeze returns to my cheek, distracting me from you.

I look down, but you turn away. I can't see your face.

I press my eyes shut and will myself back into my body, into its rolling waves of pleasure. I desperately want to get back to the heat between us.

But I'm somewhere else now.

My eyes fly open. I'm staring directly into the face of my husband, sleeping beside me. I'm not in a tent or beneath the stars. I'm in my bedroom, between crisp pin-striped sheets.

The heat I feel is not my own desire but my husband's breath, warm and stale, against my face. Each time he exhales, he makes a noise like a tiny bicycle pump working hard to inflate an enormous life raft.

I sink my face into the pillow, willing myself back into the dream, to the tent, to the cold, starry night.

It's no use. I'm awake now.

Dallas, Texas

NOW

Chapter 1

There's a room in our house that we rarely set foot in. It's the third of three bedrooms, small and perfectly square, the room no one sleeps in. It's also the only room that still has carpet—thick, creamy white pile laid down by the previous owners.

Oliver and I have come here searching for wrapping paper, just enough to wrap the small plastic mermaid he and our daughter, Emmy, bought for her best friend's birthday. "They would have wrapped it for you at the store," I say. I can't help it. "For free."

He glances toward the overstuffed closet. "We had to hightail it out of there, before Emmy swiped anything."

"Oliver." I laugh. "That was *one* time. Almost a year ago." When she was five, our daughter stole a pack of Juicy Fruit from the grocery store checkout line, then feigned innocence in the car while trying to blow a bubble.

"She's a thief, Diana. A stone-cold klepto." Oliver smiles and backs out of the room, leaving me to hunt for the paper.

In the beginning, Oliver and I dreamed this room could be a work space for us both. It's too tight for him to set up a proper workshop, but it gets great afternoon light and could fit the kind of drafting table he's always wanted. And I'd have room for an easel and paints.

When we first met, I was twenty-six and living in Dallas with seven roommates in a run-down house we all tried to pretend was an artist commune. We called it "The Co-op" but it was more like a party house that no one ever cleaned. I once determinedly taped up a chore chart with a sign-up column, thinking this would fix things. Instead of marking down their own initials, my roommates penciled in *Matthew McConaughey* for toilets and *The Ghost of Sir Alec Guinness* for kitchen duty.

In the hottest part of summer, someone left raw meat in the broken garbage disposal and we got maggots, so I started stashing my food in my room. Some afternoons, I amused myself by sketching the house and my roommates, embellished and a little grotesque. I sent a handful of the drawings to my friend Barry, back in Santa Fe, and others to my best friend, Alicia, away at film school in New York. I signed them *"Dirty Diana"* because exaggerated stories of my filthy Co-op adventures horrified Barry and made Alicia laugh. They both sent back long, sweet letters, and once Alicia just sent a note that read, "Blink twice if I should send help," glued to a clean kitchen sponge.

Then one night I got food poisoning, probably from the family meal at my waitressing job, and had to hole up in the Co-op's downstairs bathroom. My housemates were having a party, and while I lay on the cold tiled floor, my long, dark-blond hair matted to my sweaty face, I prayed for the vomiting to end as partygoers stepped over me to use the toilet. Curled up near the bathtub, I noticed its edges had been graffitied in

Sharpie. Someone had drawn a pretty good Bart Simpson on a skateboard, and someone else had composed a limerick: *Now I sit, my buns a-flexin' / I just gave birth to something the size of a Texan.* My head was split open with a headache and in that moment I thought, *Nice rhyme. But the meter is off.* The next day I started looking for a new place to live.

I saw five studio apartments, all with leaks and strange smells, and then I walked up to the last place on my list, in a squat gray stucco building on a quiet street, with a cheerful row of pink rosebushes along the entrance.

A guy sat out front, calmly slapping at mosquitoes. "Ms. Reece?" He folded the paper he'd been reading into a perfect square and stood, tucking it into his pants pocket. He was dressed like someone much older, in pleated khakis and a mint-colored button-down shirt, so it was only when I got near him that I realized we must be close in age. He had thick brown hair, broad shoulders, and blue-green eyes that look the way I imagined a midwestern lake does at the peak of summer— no choppy waves, just warm, glistening water.

I apologized for keeping him waiting. "I got the wrong bus. Twice, actually. I got off the wrong bus to catch the right one and got *back* on the wrong one." I searched his expression, those kind eyes, and imagined how I'd sketch him: perfectly straight nose down, looking up at me from under furrowed brows, a thought bubble over his head: *Jesus, who sent this one?*

But in real life, there was no judgment on his face, not even a ripple in his calm eyes. I pushed my bangs from my forehead, wishing I'd washed my hair instead of twisting it into the messy bun at my neck. "And then the AC on the third bus wasn't working, so even though I was on the *right* bus, it definitely felt like—" There it was, a small but perceptive crinkle between his brows. "It was the right bus," I wrapped up. "But it felt like the wrong bus."

He paused, as if to let me catch my breath. "I'm Oliver Wood. You're here to see 4B?"

"That's right. I'm Diana."

We shook hands and I followed him to the elevator. The space was so tight that standing side by side my shoulder grazed his biceps and I could smell his aftershave, light and clean. When the doors shut, he leaned forward and pushed the fourth-floor button three times. Nothing happened. We waited in silence and he tried again. Still nothing. This seemed to fluster him, so I jumped up and down and the elevator jerked awake.

"Thanks." He cleared his throat. "Have you lived in Dallas long?"

"Not really, no. About a year."

"Are you in school?"

"No. I paint." The elevator was hot and silent so I added, "I just published a book."

"Really?" His eyebrows rose, like he was genuinely happy for me. "I'll have to buy a copy."

"It's kind of hard to find. It was published by a tiny local press."

"Oh." His disappointment surprised me.

"I could send you a copy?"

The book was the whole reason I'd landed in Texas, after an editor had been so encouraging of my work and even found me a room at the Co-op. I pictured what might happen if I did pull out a copy in the tiny elevator, and together this polite stranger and I leafed through my paintings, some of them of women in various states of sexual longing, framed by interviews I'd compiled about their desires.

"My aunt paints," Oliver piped in.

"Oh yeah?"

"Mostly portraits. Of her dog." He lowered his voice as if she were near. "They're a little frightening. But come to think of it, her dogs are pretty frightening so maybe she's more talented than I think?"

"Maybe." I smiled and felt his shoulders relax beside me.

Oliver showed me to the apartment door, then pulled a gigantic ring of keys from his satchel and tried one after another, the tips of his ears going pink. Finally there was a click and he sighed. "High security, right? Even the tenant can't get into their own apartment."

The apartment wasn't much: a square room with two small windows, one overlooking the parking lot and the other overlooking the roses. A small kitchenette with a half-size refrigerator, an electric oven, and a sink. Oliver consulted his sheet of paper and said, "All new appliances!" And then he opened the refrigerator and found a half-empty bottle of ketchup, a jar of mayonnaise, and a Coors Light. "And look at the amenities!"

When I laughed, he looked relieved. "I'd give you more of a tour but you really just have to spin around," he said. "Not that that's a bad thing. Less to clean?"

I remembered the Co-op's Sharpie poetry and sticky bathroom floor. "I like it."

"Water and trash are included. Do you like baths?"

"I do."

"Good. I like baths too." He swung open a door just opposite us, and then paled when he saw the size of the bathroom, which barely fit a toilet much less a tub. "I really am horrible at this."

"It's actually the nicest apartment I've seen today."

"Yeah, but you deserve a bath." The intimacy of this took us both off guard and Oliver blushed.

"The kitchen is *definitely* the best I've seen today."

"Do you cook?"

"Not at all." Then, because I got the impression neither of us wanted the house tour to end, I opened the fridge and reached for the Coors Light. "I do appreciate the amenities."

He smiled again and took the bottle from my hands, opening it with one of the many keys on his ring. The beer was cold and delicious and I handed it back, offering to share. "I'd get you a glass, but . . ." I gestured around the empty kitchen. "We could sit on my imaginary couch?"

He considered the invitation, or considered me, and while he did I pictured the Manga-style sound effect for *deafening silence* appearing over our heads. Oliver rolled the beer bottle in his hand. Then he waved toward the wall where a couch should be. "I didn't expect you to go for the cherry-red leather, but it looks nice in here."

I laughed. "Matches the coasters you macraméd for me."

We sat on the floor and passed the beer back and forth. The last of the orange sunlight dipped below the west-facing window, but neither of us moved to turn on a light and the room grew dim.

I ran my fingers along the neatly vacuumed rug. "You can tell the carpet was just cleaned. Thank you."

His expression was earnest. "I have to tell you. I'm not really the broker. This building belongs to my parents. Connie, the woman who usually shows the place, had to pick up her kid, so I said I would do it."

I was relieved that we both had something to confess. "To tell the truth, I can't really afford this apartment. I have enough for the first month's rent and the security deposit. But I can't afford the last month's rent up front." I leaned my head against the wall. "Also, my credit is terrible."

As I talked, his gaze flitted between my eyes and my lips. "Do you have a job? I mean, aside from painting?"

"I'm a waitress. At Momo's."

"That thirties-gangster-themed place? The place where they make the waitresses say 'fuhgeddaboudit' every time a customer says 'thank you'?"

"That's me." I put up my hands, like it was a stickup. "You've been there?"

He shook his head. "I saw it on the news. The owner's a sex offender, isn't he?"

"Mmm." I considered this. "That would make sense."

"Well." Oliver looked down at his lap. "I will now be dedicating my free time to finding you a new job."

"Thank you."

He leaned close, gently nudging my shoulder with his own. *"Fuhgeddaboudit."*

Eight years later, when we moved into this three-bedroom house in our Dallas neighborhood, I was already pregnant with Emmy. We spent the next few months getting ready for the baby, deciding on paint colors and puzzling over IKEA instructions for her furniture. Oliver, who could make beautiful wood furniture from scratch, was as confused as I was by the assembly instructions. "That can't be right," he said, turning the pages upside down and back again. "Are we missing a piece?"

Then Emmy arrived, and so did sleepless nights and bouts of crushing anxiety, sandwiched between pure joy and unending loads of laundry.

Now Emmy's six, and this room is full of plastic storage bins jammed with toddler toys she's too big for, clothes she's grown out of, and an enormous collection of Madame Alexander dolls that Oliver's too afraid to tell his mother give Emmy nightmares. We've labeled the bins "DONATION" and we promise ourselves, again and again, that *next* weekend, we'll clean them out. It's now a running joke. At night, when we fall into bed and one of us is thirsty but too lazy to move, we'll say, "If you get me a glass of water, I swear I'll donate the bins. *Tomorrow.*"

What these bins don't have in them is a single scrap of wrapping paper. I wind through two plastic towers to get to the closet at the back of the room. I turn on the overhead light and survey the shelves. I find extra blankets, a deflated air mattress wadded into a ball, and an old tackle box that holds spare paintbrushes. A few old canvases are stacked against the wall—an oil painting of bluebonnets, and a beach scene, both of which I painted in a night class years ago.

I make my way deeper into the closet. Behind the tackle box, I spot a battered red shoebox. I had forgotten it was in here. It's sealed with painter's tape, so I find a scraper and slice it open. Inside is an old minicassette recorder and two rows of minicassettes. Each cassette is labeled with a first name: "Jess," "Claudia," "Brynn," "Theresa," and so on. A familiar feeling returns—like I'm getting away with something. Underneath the shoebox is an old portfolio crammed with sketches, all portraits of the women on the tapes, intended to be paintings in a second book one day. They had been sketched hastily in thick charcoal pencil—the profile of a woman staring out the window, another reclining in her chair, her hand pulling at the back of her neck.

When I moved to Dallas, the editor I worked with on my first book liked to take me out to shoot pool and get drunk on light beer. Through heavy eyelids she'd pitch my own book to me, as if I'd never heard of it. "The perfect intersection of chronicle and art," she'd say and I'd nod along, unsure what to add.

A few weeks after the book was published, she moved to Michigan and never returned to work. Her assistant, a young guy with a quiet voice, took her place, but he was shy and awkward and not up for meeting in person. I sent him some rough ideas for a second book and he told me the sketches were nice but too soft. "Try to find the grit. Really *mine* for it, you know?" The day Oliver showed me the apartment, I'd been mining, very slowly, for months.

Now I take the box of tapes out of the closet and sit on the floor between two storage bins, a space big enough to stretch my legs out in front of me, but small enough to feel hidden. I flip through the tapes, one by one. All these interviews I'd packed away and never returned to.

I pull out a tape labeled "Jess" and put it in the recorder. I hit play and hear her voice:

He was tall. And, like, that's all it took for him to have confidence. That's it. He was tall. Can you imagine? Women have to have their shit so buttoned-up to feel even a little bit good and I swear all it took for him was some height. Tall, good shoulders, and all of us girls were like "okay, yeah, I'd sleep with him."

But really, honestly, I didn't actually think I would. Have sex with the bartender. I'd never had a one-night stand. But then like, here I was, newly single—okay, recently dumped—cocktail waitressing in a strange city, and acting like I was so cocky. It was easy to be confident at work because the place was always packed and everyone there was desperate to order drinks so even though you were technically waiting on them you had a kind of power. If a customer was shitty, you just ignored them all night, and you got the other girls to ignore them too. Anyway, this guy was a decent bartender and he flirted with every single waitress in the place. He could have sex with any of us, even the hostess and she had a boyfriend. All night as I was working, carrying tray after tray of drinks, I kept thinking, yeah, I want to sleep with someone I don't know. Someone whose body will be a total surprise. And when he touches me, I won't know what it's going to feel like or what's coming next.

And so, when I handed him my tables' orders I'd write, like, Vodka soda. Scotch rocks. Let's get out of here.

It was a joke between us all night. And my notes got bolder each time. Martini up, twist. What's your place like? Want to show me?

Then, like, Two Stellas. Margarita, rocks. Sex on the Beach—oh, that one's too easy. Stupid, silly stuff, you know? But it made us both laugh.

And then it was 2 A.M. and our shift was over and the music stopped. They flipped on the bright overhead lights and I thought for sure the mood was gone. But as I was cleaning up, I could feel him still watching me. He had these bright blue eyes and they were playful even with the lights on. And as soon as I finished cashing out my tips I felt his hand on the small of my back and it sent a kind of charge through me, like, I'm really going to do this.

When I turned to face him, he took me by the hand and pulled me out onto the street. It was raining but somehow we got a cab so maybe it was meant to be. And we jumped in the back, so fast, and in the dark, my hands were down his pants and he was up my shirt . . . I don't remember his name—I honestly don't—but I remember how his hands felt under my bra. They were cold, but it felt good, like my whole body was waking up. I wanted to take off all my clothes right there so I could show him. So he could touch me everywhere. So I could see how he felt. I wanted him to touch every part of my body—

"Diana?" Oliver calls from the hallway and I jump. I hit stop and shove the recorder in my pocket. Then I shut the lid on the shoebox of tapes and bury it deep inside a bin of Emmy's baby clothes.

Oliver appears in the doorway. "Any luck with the wrapping paper?"

"Nothing." I shake my head. "I'll pick some up while I'm out."

He hands me a travel mug of coffee and wraps his arm around my waist.

"Thank you."

"Of course."

He nuzzles my neck. "You smell good."

I feel my body tighten when it should relax.

He pulls me closer and eyes the door. "Emmy is still sound asleep."

I scan every part of my own body and wish for the right feeling—but any longing to return his affection feels just out of reach. I pull away and smile.

"What?" he asks.

"What do you mean, 'what'?"

"You're looking at me funny. Staring."

"No, I'm not." Yes, I am. I'm staring specifically at the hair curling out of his left nostril. *Don't focus on the hair. Focus on the kind eyes. The coffee mug, those hands, the steam.*

Oliver wipes at his chin like maybe there's food on his face.

"You just have . . . this hair." I point. "There."

"Shit." He laughs. "I'm turning into my father. I'll use that trimmer you gave me, I promise." He swipes his nose with one finger, trying to push the hair back into place. "Better?"

L'Wren is honking outside. Three quick blasts.

"I wish I didn't have to go." I slip from his arms with a kiss on the cheek.

He gazes around the room at all the cleaning out that needs to be done.

"Next weekend?" I smile.

"Sure." His eyes aren't on me, but on all the mountains of discarded stuff.

Chapter 2

"**I** don't know which is more depressing, a fifty-seven-year-old man trying to be twentysomething, or a twenty-four-year-old who still lives at home." L'Wren sighs and swerves into the highway's carpool lane. She's terrible at talking while driving. I grip the side of the beige leather seat.

"This is my family but they're like *roommates*," L'Wren says. "Plus Halston. My baby girl is six-going-on-sixteen. She keeps asking me to google 'Harry Styles, no shirt.'"

"L'Wren! Don't make me laugh!" Jenna shouts from the back seat. "My filler will mess up." She presses her hands into her cheeks as if to hold them in place.

L'Wren peers at Jenna in the rearview mirror. They have been friends since high school, and now we all have daughters the same age. "You're allowed to laugh after you get Botox."

"It's not Botox, it's *filler*. The derm said don't exercise or move your face too much for twenty-four hours or the filler could shift."

"Jesus. Are you getting your filler in the H.E.B. parking lot?"

"No. Stop it." Jenna almost snorts. "Dr. Laredo. She did Raleigh's lips that you loved so much."

At the mention of Raleigh's name, the three of us go quiet. We sit in the hum of the air-conditioning as L'Wren speeds down the highway. We're on our annual trip to Roundtop, a massive antiques show south of Dallas. Our first trip was five years ago when we were all in the same Saturday morning Mommy and Me class. L'Wren surprised Jenna and me with a babysitter. She suggested we ditch class and take a mini road trip instead.

Jenna clears her throat. She pokes her head between us, blond curls bouncing. "You could have worse roommates. At least Liam's like a live-in babysitter, right? He must help y'all out." Liam is L'Wren's stepson and is usually too stoned to be of any real help. He's more of an affable presence. "And at least your husband still has all his hair."

"Oh, that's so cute, do you really believe that?" L'Wren asks. "That Kev hasn't lost hair? Do I need to remind you about last summer? The hair plugs?"

I stifle a laugh.

"Diana, do *not* feel bad for laughing." L'Wren turns to me, fully taking her eyes off the road. "True, he can't help that he's losing his hair. But. *Nobody made him wear that beret.*"

"*Ohh,*" says Jenna. Things often occur to her a few beats late. "I forgot about the beret. Huh. I thought he was going through like a European midlife crisis."

"What the fuck is a 'European midlife crisis'?" L'Wren asks.

Last summer, L'Wren's husband, Kevin, wore a hat for every occasion. Oliver and I even spotted him wearing a hunting cap while taking an outdoor shower at their Memorial Day pool party.

"He did kind of made it work," L'Wren says, tenderly. "But, poor thing, he had to change the bandages on all the little follicles all the time."

I flip my mirror down and look at my face in the morning sun, studying the skin beneath my jaw, something I've never paid much attention to. There are circles under my amber eyes, but at least my hair is cooperating in long, tamed waves. I pull my skin tight to my ears like a homemade facelift and imagine painting a smoother version of myself with a shiny strip of forehead and a pair of newly puffed apple cheeks. I crinkle my nose, smiling at my own ridiculous expression, then drop my hands, but not before Jenna catches me. I pretend to check my lipstick, dabbing a finger across my mouth.

"And now *good luck* getting Liam to cut his," L'Wren says.

I flip up the mirror. "Who cares how long Liam's hair is?"

"I think it's why he got fired."

"Who got fired?" Jenna asks.

"Liam," says L'Wren. "Honestly, I didn't even know you *could* get fired from an internship. Don't they have to pay you something before they can fire you?"

I happen to know Liam wasn't fired. He just stopped showing up. But I don't say this. I shift in my seat and feel the recorder still in my pocket. I quietly slip it into my purse as L'Wren continues to vent.

"I thought, it's an ad firm, it's creative, maybe he'll like it? He was miserable. But, lord, we all hated our jobs at some point, right? That's why they call it 'the Sunday Scaries,' right?"

When Liam moved in with them a year ago, I thought L'Wren's head might explode. For someone like L'Wren who has a habit of collecting strays—cats, rabbits, lizards—having her stepson move back into the house was remarkably disruptive. But L'Wren quickly formed a deep affection for him. He confuses her, but in a way she seems determined to decode.

She sighs loudly. "I want him to be an artist, if that's what he wants. I just want him to be an artist with *ambition*, you know?"

A red Maserati cuts us off. L'Wren lays on her horn but doesn't slow down. "Maybe I'll just buzz that head of hair in his sleep . . ."

Out the windows, gentle rolling hills covered in bluebonnets and dotted with grazing horses give way to fields of towering sunflowers and I'm only vaguely aware of my friends talking around me. My mind drifts to the old canvases I'd found in the closet. Those poor bluebonnets I tried to paint. They really looked like something had chewed on them. Then I think of the box of tapes and the sketches I'd found. I can't remember if I've ever shown the drawings to anyone. Even Alicia. For a while, both she and Barry would ask how the new book was coming every time we spoke. But eventually they both seemed to forget about it too.

As if her ears were burning, my phone rings and it's Alicia. I hit decline and send her a quick text.

Call you tonight!

I wonder if I should play her one of the tapes. Or just mail one to her out of the blue for fun.

"How about you, Diana?" L'Wren asks.

"What's that?"

"How often do you and Oliver have sex?" L'Wren says this so flatly she might be asking me how often I floss. "My mother called to tell me all about an interview she read with Madonna, who says the key to a healthy marriage is sex three times a week."

"With your husband?" I ask.

"Diana!" Jenna giggles from the back seat.

"No—" I can feel myself blush. "I just meant, is Madonna even married?"

"Every magazine in my mother's house is a *Good Housekeeping* from like twenty years ago. But you get the point," L'Wren says. "How often?"

"Mmm." I narrow my eyes, as though I were working it out. A prickly hot sensation spreads down my neck at the memory of the last time Oliver and I had sex. A date night. It was an unseasonably warm evening, so we sat outside at Delmonico's and then quickly regretted trying to eat pasta in the heat. We pushed around the food on our plates, drank too much white wine, then fumbled with our cash when it came time to pay the babysitter. Upstairs in our bedroom, we peeled off our clothes and had quick, sweaty sex. Oliver felt good inside me, he always did, but still I felt a need to speed things along. "I want you to come," I whispered in his ear. "Now?" he asked. "Like this?" "Yes, just like this."

"Jenna . . ." L'Wren taps my thigh to be sure I catch this. "Tell Diana how often you and Charlie do it."

Jenna counts off the days on one hand, flashing her lavender-tipped French manicure. "Four times a week, unless one of us or the kids is sick. Every Monday, Wednesday, and Friday is sex, and Sunday is a hand job because I'm totally spent."

"Wow," I say. "Four times."

"You know blue balls isn't a real thing, right, Jenna? No man in his fifties needs to climax that much!" L'Wren says.

"Well, Charlie is *forty*. Plus, it's like exercise," Jenna says. "You don't always want to do it, but then you do it, and you're glad you did. And Charlie is so much easier to be around afterward. It's like wearing out a puppy."

"Ha." L'Wren laughs. "True."

"Should we stop and pee before Roundtop?" I ask her.

L'Wren looks at me, then presses her turn indicator. "Jenna, feel free to take Mondays off from now on—you're making the rest of us look bad! Kev and I are every other Friday."

"We're about the same," I lie.

"But you and Oliver don't have to schedule it in. You're an artist, it just happens . . ."

"Spontaneous sex," Jenna shakes her head. "Can y'all imagine?" Hard to tell if the idea excites her or horrifies her.

"It's what you do, right?" L'Wren crosses two lanes for the off-ramp. "What happens if you stop having sex with your husband? *Somebody else* starts having sex with your husband."

"Mm-hmm," Jenna nods her head solemnly. "Like Raleigh. So sad."

Again, the car goes quiet at the mention of Raleigh's name and I'm not sure what I'm missing. "I thought Raleigh cheated on her husband, not the other way around?" I say. Why do I want to score a point for Raleigh? I hardly know her, beyond seeing her at school dropoff and birthday parties or making small talk on the sidelines at our kids' soccer games.

All I can think is no one talks about how mysterious marriage is. The three of us in this car have bonded over every intimate detail of pregnancy and motherhood. "I know you're not supposed to look at your vagina right away," Jenna confessed about giving birth, "but I couldn't resist. I took a mirror into the hospital bathroom and almost *passed out*. It wasn't even the right color, y'all." But I have no real idea of what it's like inside either of their marriages. How do they fight? What's Jenna like when she's really angry? Now I know exactly how often she has sex, but what could I learn that's not jotted into her iCal? Does she enjoy sex with Charlie? Does she orgasm?

I know how important sex is to a marriage—there is no shortage of essays about this topic—but it's like, the more important I'm reminded it is, the less enjoyable it becomes. And these days, when I think about sex with Oliver, I get a fluttering, panicky feeling, like I'm inviting trouble. Like I'm knocking on the door of a haunted house and waking up the ghosts inside. Oliver and I have never talked about having a sex life. We just had it—*have* it. And maybe Oliver likes sex more. And wants it more. So I try to not overthink it. And then I overthink thinking about it until it becomes like a living thing that I alone am draining the blood out of.

"I heard she didn't cheat just once," Jenna says, still talking about

Raleigh. "I don't know if it's true—*so don't say I said it*—but apparently it was ongoing, like five different men."

L'Wren lets out a low whistle. "Sweet Jesus, I can barely get on my Peloton and she has five different affairs?"

"And Dustin's getting the kids in the divorce," Jenna warns. "Sole custody. And the house."

The antiques show grounds are muddy from days of rain. There are swampy puddles to pick our way around, and half the SUVs in the parking lot seem to be using their four-wheel drive for the first time. There's usually a sort of uniform among the shoppers—this year's most stylish, including L'Wren, are wearing knee-high boots with a rugged sole and an oversize buckle. The rest of the uniform is mostly unchanged—sundresses and denim jackets and cowboy hats. Oversize sunglasses. Heart-shaped charms on gold necklaces. I pull my own denim jacket closed against the late-morning breeze.

Inside the tents, the smell is strong, a mixture of cow poop and sharp, floral perfume. Other than finding a one-eyed senior cat a new home, nothing makes L'Wren happier than scoring a bargain. It's easy to get caught up in her joy. As a threesome, we wander the booths, sipping white wine from plastic cups, looking at beautiful things, feeling more and more buzzed and floaty as we go, even if most of the stuff is indistinguishable from all the other stuff and totally out of our price range.

L'Wren stops at a dealer selling nothing but farm tables. "For the kitchen? What do you think, Diana?"

"You told me not to let you buy anything bigger than a bread-box."

"But look at this one! Where is it from?" she asks the dealer.

"France," he says, looking bored.

L'Wren eyes the price tag and I take the chance to head to the other side of the show, where the deeper bargains live. Even the food is cheaper—corndogs and slushies instead of kale Caesars with overcooked chicken. I buy myself a funnel cake and eat it slowly. I run my hand across what Oliver has taught me is a Heywood Wakefield rocking chair. "How much?" I ask the harried young woman who is still unloading her truck.

"Sorry, I got a late start." She wipes the sweat from her forehead with the back of her work glove. "I'll take fifty bucks for it."

I peek under the cushion and find the Heywood label, which means the chair could easily fetch a thousand dollars, maybe more. I sit in the chair and rock gently, hoping for a minute that it'll share its stories—the books read in it at bedtime, the gossip shared over sweet tea on a wraparound porch.

"The chair is worth much more," I tell the woman.

"Really? I bought it at an estate sale. It was surrounded by junk."

"Ask for at least a thousand. You'll probably get it."

I stop to buy a pair of onyx and gold candlesticks for the dining room and a vintage Kantha quilt for Emmy's bed. I'm heading back to find L'Wren and Jenna when I see a picture that takes my breath away.

It's a black-and-white photograph of a tiny ski resort town in the summer. It's a ghost town, totally devoid of tourists and the locals who keep it running. In the foreground, there's a horse—a young dappled palomino, tied up outside an empty café. Something about the mood feels clandestine, like the secret beauty of this town happens when no one else is around.

"Excuse me." My mouth goes completely dry. "Hi . . . excuse me."

The dealer, a red-faced gentleman sweating through a plaid shirt, turns. "Can I help you?"

"That photograph. Could you tell me who the photographer is?" But I already know.

"You have a good eye. It's . . ." He stalls for time so he can remember the name. "A New Mexico kid, a real cowboy of a guy."

I smile. Jasper would love to hear himself referred to as a cowboy,

I'm sure. The dealer flips his reading glasses from the top of his head to the tip of his nose to make out the signature. "Jasper . . ." He can't make out the last name so he just mumbles something beginning with a G. "Do you know his work?"

"I do." My voice shakes. "Yes."

"It's signed," the dealer says. "Incredible opportunity, really."

"How much?"

He stares at me. "Six hundred," he says. "No charge for the frame."

It's more money than I planned to spend today but the photo is worth much more than he's asking. I pull out my wallet and when he hands me the picture, I'm surprised how heavy the frame is. I unpack the quilt I've bought, wrap it around the frame, and fit everything back into one bag.

I wander the booths aimlessly. I can't focus on anything but the piece of Jasper that I'm carrying. The tents are getting more crowded and hot and suddenly I feel woozy. A woman selling chandeliers pulls out a plastic folding chair. "You all right?"

"Thanks," I say, dropping my head between my knees. "I forgot to eat breakfast."

It was a mistake to buy this photograph. I've worked so hard to stop thinking about Jasper and now a piece of him is back.

After some deep breaths, I thank the woman and then find a stand selling bottles of water. I'm next in line when I hear L'Wren let out a high-pitched squeal. "Jenna! *Jenna!*"

Still holding the heavy bag, I push through the crowd in front of a row of booths. Jenna is doubled over laughing, holding two plastic cups and splashing wine everywhere.

"Help!" L'Wren calls. She has one leg straight in front of her and is using her heel to drag herself forward. Her other leg is stuck behind her, up to the buckle in mud. Jenna puts a cup in her mouth and tries to pull with her free hand.

"Diana!" L'Wren cries with relief when she sees me. "I'm stuck in the mud!"

I hitch my shopping bag higher onto my shoulder and drape one of L'Wren's arms around my waist and Jenna gets under the other one. "On three," I say. "One, two . . ." L'Wren grunts so hard she lets out a teeny fart. Jenna snorts and falls backward. She lands on her butt, then throws up her arms and cries, "My filler!" And then we all lose it, laughing until we're crying and covered in mud.

By dusk we're standing in the parking lot with a farm table, a pine armoire, three boxes of barn lighting, and two rugs. L'Wren is waving down a white cube truck. All three of us cringe as the truck scrapes a VIP LOADING ONLY sign. Liam leans his head out the window, his unwashed hair hanging over his eyes. "Sorry!" Then he takes out two traffic cones, honks twice, and pulls down on an imaginary rope, giving us a long-haul truckers' salute.

"Ladies." He hops out of the truck wearing a DEATH TO CAPITAL-ISTS hoodie with mismatched socks and Adidas slippers. Liam is somewhere between too young be the brother I spent my childhood praying for, and too old to be my misfit son, but since the day I met him, he's felt like family. Like the cousin you gravitate toward at the family reunion and together you avoid everyone else at the party.

He takes a long look at the three of us still caked in mud. "Jesus."

"Liam!" L'Wren hands him an armful of bags. "I owe you. You don't mind dropping off Jenna's armoire, do you?"

"Nope."

Two guys from the antiques show help muscle everything into the truck. Liam and I watch as L'Wren and Jenna buy the last of the wicker baskets from the dealer next to the parking lot and toss them into the back of her Range Rover. "A thank-you gift for Liam!" L'Wren hollers.

"Awesome!" Liam gives her a thumbs-up. "I definitely need more wicker in my life." He glances at me, then down at my muddy knees. "I have so many questions."

"I'll give you . . . two."

He doesn't miss a beat. "Was there, like, a mud-wrestling part of the day? And did you win?"

"Yes. And obviously, yes."

"Last question. Is any of this crap yours?"

I pretend to study him closely. "I'm sorry, are you trying to buy a wicker basket off me? How many is too many, Liam?"

He laughs and reaches for the bag holding Jasper's photograph. "I can put that up front if you want." I know this is the sensible choice. To place more distance between me and my ghost from the past.

"That's all right," I say. "It can ride with me."

We thank Liam for taking our stuff and pile into L'Wren's car. In the back seat, I pull out my phone and text Alicia.

You'll never believe what I bought today.

Before I hit send, I imagine our long back-and-forth. I quickly delete the text and decide to call her later instead.

I rest my head against the window, clutching Jasper's photograph to my chest the entire ride home.

Chapter 3

The next afternoon, two mermaids on fake clamshells are gliding in slow, easy circles around L'Wren's kidney-shaped pool. I recognize one of them as the teenager who works at the Subway shop near my office. It's a beautiful early spring day, crisp and cool. Emmy is in heaven, running in and out of an enormous bouncy castle, squeezing Halston's hand.

L'Wren's backyard is an explosion of pink and purple, with balloons tied to every chair, table, and tree. Each balloon is like a Russian nesting doll, trapped inside a bigger balloon, which is trapped inside another bigger balloon. At the perimeter of the lawn, her hundred-year-old magnolia trees are shellacked in rainbow glitter.

I spot Liam stationed near the bouncy castle's moat and feel a sharp pang of sympathy. He looks uncomfortably out of place and very bored. Last night after Roundtop, L'Wren texted me a video from an Australian news station—grainy footage of a bouncy house being swept off a front lawn, the children inside carried away with it.

Should I cancel the castle??? she texted.

For a brief moment, I thought she was kidding. But then I remembered how anxious she is about anything to do with Halston.

I typed: *The weather's supposed to be beautiful tomorrow. I say keep it!*

Ok, Okkkk. You're right. Thx!!! She replied. And then: *I'll have Liam stand next to it and make sure it doesn't blow away. He can be bouncy castle security, right? He needs a job anyway—LOL.*

I bring Liam a purple cupcake with a jaunty unicorn on top. He eats half of it in one bite.

"Are you here all day?" I ask.

"Sadly, no." He shoves the other half of the cupcake in his mouth and then wipes the excess frosting from his fingers onto his jeans. "I'm crazy in demand these days."

"Oh yeah?"

"Yeah. Apparently Rockgate has high winds and a million Kardashian-kid wannabe parties so . . ." He gestures to the castle behind him. "I'm booked pretty solid."

"Liam." L'Wren appears at my side. "Don't get so distracted by Diana's sparkling conversation that you forget about your one and only job."

Behind me, Emmy darts out of the castle and shrieks, "Mommy!" She grabs my hand. "Jump with me! Please!"

I slip out of my sneakers and follow her into the castle. The air is thick with little-kid sweat and screams of joy. It's also strangely calming. The party noise is hushed—I can make out voices but not what anyone says. I don't need to mingle, all I have to do is try not to fall into someone smaller than me.

When someone yells "CAKE!" Emmy scrambles out of the castle. I follow, hot and red-faced, and find Oliver at the open bar. He looks into my sweaty face. "What'd you do, find the Peloton?"

"Kevin and I did a quick HIIT workout in his garage." Oliver brushes a strand of damp hair from my face.

"Right," he says. "I should have known." After seeing Kevin enough times by the pool, Oliver and I decided that we knew what it felt like to hang out with Jeff Bezos on his yacht—no matter how many times Kevin rips off that polo shirt, the abs beneath are *always* a surprise. We also like to pretend we would work out as much as Kevin if we were semiretired, too, but we both know this isn't true.

Oliver hands me a purple fizzy drink. "Kir Royale?"

"Very on-theme." We clink glasses and spend the rest of the party mingling with other parents and talking about the weather. Every once in a while, I catch Oliver's eye and we exchange subtle smiles and tiny eye rolls at the insane level of detail of the party, especially the high school cater waiters dressed like real knights, in actual chain mail.

"A vodka tonic for m'lady." At home, Oliver hands me a drink, and I sit up in bed with my back against the pillows. He pulls off his half-zip and his T-shirt, then strips down to his boxers and lies down next to me. "I was going to do a whole routine, juggling the vodka and the tonic, but I decided against it."

I laugh and take a long sip. "Thank you."

He does the same, then sets his glass down. He pulls me into him, so we're in a perfect and familiar spoon. "This was a good day," he says into my shoulder.

When I turn to kiss him, I recognize that familiar hungry look in his eye and I force a smile. I know there should be desire—a feeling of warmth or a fluttering somewhere in my body—but there's nothing. Like my limbs have turned to smooth, immovable stone. Instead of longing, I suddenly feel very tired.

I had quietly hoped we could turn on *Law and Order* and cuddle in bed until we fell asleep, the perfect end to the day. *Not tonight, dear, I have a headache.* I only say it to myself. Bad jokes are always depressing, but especially when the only audience is yourself. I take another sip of my drink before Oliver pulls it from my hand and sets it down next to his glass.

And then here it is. His hand on my hip. As he touches me, my mind wanders in the way it likes to do after a long day, where only the most literal and obvious thoughts seem to take shape—like wondering if any woman, throughout history, has ever legitimately, deep in her bones, wanted to have sex with her husband only to pump the brakes because she had a headache. I try to picture this faceless woman, curled up in her bed, hugging only her crushing disappointment—not for her husband, but for herself, as she's then forced to drift off to sleep, her desires unmet.

The poke of Oliver's optimistic erection against my thigh brings me back to the moment, to our king-size bed that feels too small, in our bedroom that feels too big. Why can't his penis ever read the room?

I exaggerate a yawn, but Oliver either doesn't notice or doesn't care. He drapes a leg across my own, heavy, and kisses my neck. This time the voice in my head doesn't joke but only asks, *What the fuck is wrong with you?* Why do I make this so difficult? It's just sex. With my husband. My kind, loving, attractive husband, with whom I've spent a perfect afternoon. He nuzzles deeper into me and my body stiffens. *What the fuck is wrong with you? Whatthefuckiswrongwithyou?* His right hand moves from my hip to my stomach in its familiar dance.

"Think of it as a love gift" I once heard on a relationship podcast. The woman's voice was raspy as she leveled with her listeners about sex: "Let's face it, some occasions call for giving and *not* receiving." But I'm not in the mood for giving or receiving. Last time, when Oliver curled up against me just like this, I pretended to be asleep. I faked a light snore until finally he rolled away and began real snoring.

Now his hand slips up my T-shirt and across my bare skin, lightly squeezing my breast. His mouth finds mine and we kiss, his familiar tongue moving in its familiar ways. I can't play the exhaustion card.

His hand moves down my bare stomach where I know it will pause, for a brief moment, at the hem of my underwear. I know because it's always the same. We've been having the same sex, with the same five-minute foreplay and in the same positions, for what seems like a lifetime. So why is it suddenly so hard to play along? *What the fuck is wrong with*—I arch my back and moan the way he likes, the way that gives him permission to slip his fingers inside me. I watch as he licks his hand first, because he knows I'm not wet. Then he moves his fingers in slow broken-record circles, the same broken record he's never repaired in the years we've been together. I bite down on my lip.

He moves his body on top of mine and slides his other hand beneath me, grabbing my ass. I close my eyes and try to picture his sweet face, his easy smile. He's handsome and loving. And clean. So clean. I run my fingers through his hair and breathe in the smell of his soap. Kind of woodsy and citrusy. I wonder what the soap makers were going for. Maybe they wanted the scent to remind us of the outdoors, like a waterfall, or that nice mineral scent of dirt just after the rain. This is not sexy, thinking about soap scientists. I moan again and try to bring myself back to the moment, back to the feel of Oliver's skin on mine. He responds with his own guttural sound and an excited thrust of his penis against my stomach. I pull down my underwear, inviting him in and hoping to move things along. He accepts the invitation, kissing me hard on the mouth as he pushes inside me.

I look up at his intent face then close my eyes and moan a little more.

"Does that feel good?" he asks.

"Uh-huh." I moan again, but my delivery is off. Instead of boredom, I feel something more dangerous begin to warm beneath my skin. I try to push it away, but I can feel my anger building. I resent Oliver for enjoying my performance. Why does he buy it so easily? Or maybe he doesn't even need me here? I stop moving my hips, to see if he notices. He keeps up his steady rhythm, moving inside me. I take it a step further and in the voice of a tired phone-sex operator at the end of a sixteen-hour shift, I purr unconvincingly about how rock hard his cock is, something I've never said before. Then I open my eyes and sneak a peek at his face. I expect him to laugh. Or to be confused. Or repulsed. We can't be so disconnected that he isn't startled by the flatness in my voice, by the uncharacteristic line of dirty talk. But his eyes are closed and he seems lost in ecstasy. "Yes," he says. "Mmm."

I stay quiet. I shut my eyes tight and decide in this very moment that I'll stop pretending to be present, stop faking my own pleasure. I'll consider this an experiment. Like making soap scents. Will he stop? Will he finally ask me what's wrong?

He doesn't.

My T-shirt is pushed up around my chin when Oliver groans, then shudders, his eyes so far back in his head he can no longer see me at all. "God, I needed that," he says. He rolls off me and sighs.

I pull my T-shirt down while Oliver pads off to the bathroom, yawning, and turns on the shower. He doesn't pause to kiss me or to look back. The warmth under my skin is now a prickly fire. For a moment, I think about curling into my pillow and crying, how maybe that would bring some relief. But I'm not sad; I almost long to be sad—then maybe Oliver could come back from the shower and comfort me, and I'd sheepishly smile to myself about how overly dramatic I'd been, and we'd fall asleep holding each other. And in the morning, we'd both feel better. But it's not sorrow under my skin. It's rage. The feeling is so uncomfortable I want to run into the bathroom and jump into the cold shower. But I don't want to be anywhere near Oliver.

I get up and pull on my jeans. I grab my keys and purse, slip out the front door, and then I'm starting the car without letting myself wonder what Oliver will think when he steps out of the bathroom and finds my side of the bed empty.

Nothing. He'll think nothing except that I got up to check on Emmy, like I always do. He'll climb into bed and fall asleep, satisfied and snoring.

Chapter 4

While my house sleeps, I back quietly out of the driveway and drive out of our neighborhood. It has somehow gotten hotter since the sun went down. Even with the air-conditioning on, my T-shirt clings to my chest. I wipe my eyes with the back of my hand—the tears do finally come, heavy and hot, but they don't bring relief or sense enough to turn around and go home. I don't know where I'm going. I'm tired and crying and this is stupid. It's not like I'd run away. I'd never leave Emmy. Why isn't Oliver in that sentence? He should be. An oncoming car's headlights shine too brightly in my eyes. Is this how people get into accidents? Whenever I think about dying, I think of what people will say.

I heard she was running away from sex.

With her husband?

I should turn around but I don't want to go home, not right now.

I drive past competing outdoor shopping malls with giant furniture stores. Everything is closed at this hour. I pass a Cheesecake Factory, a Taco Bell, a mom-and-pop liquor store and then I'm onto a long stretch of nothing, just a two-lane road hugged by empty fields. After driving for a long time, I find a strip mall with an unlit nail salon, an Authentic Italian Pizza To-Go, a few empty storefronts, and a bar with no name, just *Live Music* in red neon script.

I pull in to the parking lot and turn off the car. The AC cuts off and it's quiet. I think about reclining my seat and resting my eyes. They feel heavy after crying. But when I close my eyes, I think about Oliver and how far I've driven and how late it is. I open my eyes, then the car door, and hear the din of music across the parking lot.

It's mostly dark inside the bar, except for the twinkling strands of rainbow-colored lights hanging like spiderwebs from the ceiling. The smell is familiar—the stench of old beer that seeps into bar mats and never comes out, no matter how many nights you spend dragging those mats outside after your shift and hosing them down with bleach.

I find an empty stool and order a vodka soda. I drain it faster than I mean to, the icy liquid going down like water. I watch a woman in a yellow silk dress feed the jukebox while the rest of her group shouts suggestions. She is beautiful—her shoulder-length light-brown hair and long limbs catching the light as she leans over the jukebox. I notice her tattoos, a murder of crows running up the inside of both arms. There is a pause in the music, and she looks up expectantly. At first nothing happens, so she gives the jukebox a shove with her hip and suddenly Rodney Crowell fills the space with his gentle voice, crooning "Shame on the Moon."

I feel two men close behind me, trying to catch the bartender's attention. One of them drums his long fingers on the bar. He orders six margaritas and leans over me to pass them back to his friend. The bartender slides another vodka soda toward me and tilts her head in their direction. "They bought you one too," she says. I raise the glass to them and smile, careful not to make eye contact. Soon a young man with tousled brown hair and small white teeth slides in next to me. "I hope you don't mind," he says, and I shake my head. We make small talk. Their group has all come from a wedding. "College buddies," he says.

"How was it?"

"Beautiful, very nice," he smiles, nodding. "But only pink champagne to drink, so the more determined drinkers have all ended up here." We talk about the hot weather, and a local swimming hole, and I lie, telling him that I'm just visiting from California. I feel too tired to have so much of his attention, so I thank him for the drink and wander out to the patio.

Here there is a second bar, just as crowded with customers. There's a small stage but no band, just a lonely microphone and a guitar leaning against a vinyl stool. Music from the jukebox is pumped in through large speakers. The woman in the yellow dress is easy to spot, dancing with her partner near the stage. They keep their eyes locked on each other. He slides his fingers underneath one of the thin straps of her dress and then pulls her close, pressing his cheek into hers, then closes his eyes. They are certainly at the beginning of something, I think, to be so intent on each other. Watching them, I feel comforted by the fact that they have nothing to do with me. I think of what it would be like to record this moment, to somehow bottle this evening to take with me, like one of my minicassette tapes. What would I pick up? The ambient noise of the crowd, the faint sound of the Texas night in the backdrop. What if I were brave enough to approach the woman in the yellow dress? To ask her how it feels to be her, to dance with her partner? To listen as she tells me what she honestly desires. But I'm not as brave as I used to be.

My lids have started to feel heavy and I leave my second drink mostly untouched and make my way back through the bar. I think of asking the bartender to make me a cup of coffee, but decide it will take too long. The moon is pale orange and it is hard to tell the lights of the stars from the lights of the city. I float in the soupy dark back to my car.

I don't get far before pulling over. The road is deserted and dark, and I have to use the light of my phone to search my bag. But I find it quickly, the recorder, shoved to the bottom. I press play and Jess's voice fills the car.

And the more he touched me, the more I thought, yes, this is exactly what I want from a one-night stand. Everything about his hands was unfamiliar. He touched me and I couldn't guess their pressure or where they'd go next. My shirt was pulled up around my neck and I was fumbling with his zipper when the cab stopped. I'd forgotten where we were headed. And now we were in front of a building I didn't recognize. I was really going home with him.

On the way up to his apartment we almost had sex right on the stairs and I probably would have but he breathed in my ear, "c'mon" and pulled me into his place.

Inside was just like I imagined. Boring furniture and an unmade bed with plaid flannel sheets. But I was impressed he lived alone. Thank god.

Then he asked me if I wanted a drink, some water or something. But I didn't want to talk. I was afraid I might slip out of character and lose my nerve—I could already feel it happening now that we were inside his apartment. It made him feel more real, somehow, like he had this whole backstory, but I only wanted to be here, in the present, so that I didn't get to learn anything about him. If I looked around too much, I'd know him suddenly, just by the stuff in his apartment, and I might see that he was ordinary.

So I pushed him up against the wall. He was so tall, you know, like a foot taller than me, and I had to stand on my tiptoes to reach his mouth. I kissed him, long and hard, and he told me, "You're so hot." His voice wasn't sexy, like it was underneath the music at the bar, so I told him to be quiet and I unbuttoned his shirt. He liked this.

"Don't move," I told him. And he nodded.

I stood back and admired his body. I tried not to look too impressed, but he was gorgeous. Those muscled valleys where his stomach dipped down into his hips. I could tell by the way his jeans hung that he was naked underneath. He reached for me, but I pinned his arms to his sides. "Don't," I told him again. Then I pulled off my shirt and unclasped my bra and let him watch as I took it off.

His eyes went wide and he reached for me again, but I shook my head. I told him, "I'm going to take your clothes off. We're going to suck each other and fuck each other for the first time and then I'm going to leave."

And he just nodded, silently, and I almost laughed. And when I smiled, the playfulness came back into his eyes and I liked it. I told him to keep quiet while I undressed him.

His shirt was already unbuttoned so I slipped it off his shoulders and let it drop to the floor. This was exactly what I wanted, arms that I didn't recognize, rippled and strong, that came without having to sit through all the boring gym stories a boyfriend would tell you.

I traced his unfamiliar tattoo, some kind of constellation on the inside of his biceps, and I heard his breath catch. He liked the way I touched him. I unbuttoned his pants and slipped them off his hips. I was right. He was naked underneath and fully erect, and bigger than I expected. I held him in my hands and stroked him, taking my time. The tip of his penis was wet and so I told him, "Not so fast. Slow down." His whole body trembled when I said this, like he was fighting to obey.

"You can come closer." I tell him to take off my skirt. "But you can't use your hands." He looked confused for a second, then totally eager, and then he focused in on me. I was wearing my black cocktail miniskirt. There was no button or zipper; all he needed to do was get down on his knees and use his teeth.

He bit my skirt at the top and peeled it off, down to my feet. I slipped out of my heels and when I did, he was suddenly the perfect height—kneeling in front of me, his mouth lined up with the hem of my underwear. He tried to reach inside, but I batted his fingers away. So he used his mouth and when my underwear fell to the floor, he couldn't help but return his lips to me.

I let him lick up my inner thighs, spreading me open and slipping his tongue inside me. He circled my clit and it felt so good I pushed his head into me for even more pressure. He got every signal I sent and sucked gently, then harder as I moaned in approval.

I curled my toes and told myself this is our one and only night together, so let's take it slow.

I pulled his face away from me and he looked up at me kind of pleading, waiting for my next move. He was breathing heavy and his erection was throbbing, like it was reaching toward me and happy to touch any square inch of my body as long as it could press against my skin.

I want his hands on me again, everywhere. I wanted him to pick me up and throw me on the bed and fuck me on those soft flannel sheets. But I also wanted this to last. And I liked being in charge, just like at work. I would dismiss him if he stepped out of line. So I told him to stand.

I lead him to the bed and he reached for a condom. Then we were both on our knees on top of the bed, kissing and our breath heaving. He groaned and we were both so ready I thought we could come just like this. But I pushed him onto his back and straddled his legs. He grabbed my hips and I let him. I let him hold on tight as I guided him into me and we both gasped. And when I thought I couldn't feel him any deeper, he lifted his hips to meet mine and plunged into me and I let out a cry.

Then I closed my eyes and all I could think was how good he felt, this guy I barely know. Who I don't want to know. And I grabbed ahold of anything I could reach—the sheets, his shoulders—and I kept thinking, the girls at the bar will love this. I braced myself against his chest and squeezed myself around him so tightly, riding him while he holds on to my hips and my orgasm built and neither of us could slow it down.

I felt this scream rising in me, and I can't help myself and I shout, "I'm fucking you and it feels so good and I can't remember your name!" And he bucked into me, harder, my whole body clenched around him. We both shuddered as we came, spent and sweating.

There's a rustling sound on the tape, followed by the sound of my own voice from years ago, asking Jess a question. And what did it feel like after, to be with someone for the first time?

There's a long pause. And then Jess's voice. *That's just it. I didn't want it to be the* first *time. Or the beginning of something new. I didn't want a next time. I just wanted it to be this one night.* Jess laughs. *I do wish I could remember his name, though.*

I stop the tape. It's quiet and still except for the duet of crickets and katydids outside my car.

I don't need to be at the beginning of something new. Oliver and I are where we should be. We have our own kind of intimacy, I tell myself. So what if it doesn't look like what I thought it would? We aren't at the end, for sure. More like the beginning of the middle of something, maybe. I have no plan, but I can make one. Oliver is happy like this and so why can't I be too? Tonight I'll go back to Levitt Drive to I-30 East to Kings Road and curl down Moorpark to my driveway. I'll climb the stairs and sneak in next to Oliver and have a good four hours of sleep and reset before it all starts over again.

Chapter 5

The next weekend, I spend most of Saturday catching up at the office. I join Oliver and Emmy at the kitchen table for an early dinner. Emmy is eating buttered noodles and Oliver is scrolling on his phone.

"What'd I miss today?" I ask.

Emmy sighs. "Errands. Grandma's house. More errands."

Oliver says, "Ice cream. Tea party. More ice cream."

Emmy grins and finds the box of paints I bought for her. Her eyes light up. "For me?"

I nod, and Oliver shoots Emmy an impressed look. "Your mom finds you the coolest stuff." He does this a lot lately, complimenting me to Emmy, but never looking right at me. He kisses the top of her head.

I pick up Jasper's photograph, which has been leaning against a wall since I brought it home, and try to find a place for it. "I thought maybe for the living room?"

"Nice." Oliver hasn't even really looked at it. Or even noticed it sitting there all week.

This annoys me, and now I'm annoyed at myself for feeling this way. Why do I want Oliver to admire Jasper's photograph?

"I spent more than I should have," I say. He looks up. "But it can be my birthday present."

"Well, we do have an early birthday surprise for you," he says.

"Really?" My birthday isn't until tomorrow.

"Close your eyes and hold out your hand."

Emmy climbs onto my back and covers my eyes with hands that smell like butter. "No peeking!"

They lead me upstairs, stopping at the door to the overflow room. Emmy removes her hands and I open my eyes.

The room has been cleaned. It's nearly empty. No baby swings piled on the thick carpet, no more plastic storage bins marked for donation. It's not a room full of junk anymore. And it's not a work space either. It's a guest room, the way the house's layout always intended it to be. Oliver has even pulled our old bed from the garage and hung my painting of bluebonnets above it.

"No sheets on the bed yet or anything like that," he says.

"Wow." My heart plunges toward my stomach.

"My mom took Emmy most of the day, but she did ride with me to the Goodwill."

"Two times," Emmy says.

I try to swallow my rising panic. The plastic bins. I stuffed that old shoebox full of minicassettes into one of those bins. I never got it back out. All those interviews. "You took everything?"

"All of it," Oliver says proudly. He scratches his arm, looks around. "Except for the air mattress." He opens the closet. "That seems in good shape still."

My throat is closing with rage. "Oliver." What do I say? "My stuff . . ."

Oliver looks confused. "Are you upset?"

"You should have asked me—"

"We've been trying to get rid of this junk forever."

"No, I know. But maybe there was something we wanted to save. I haven't checked in so long—"

I want to scream at him, but I shut down. *It's not his fault. It's not his fault.* My level of upset takes my own breath away. I can't look at him, I can't speak. But how is he supposed to know what those tapes mean to me? I've never played him a single one. I think of how I shoved the shoebox so carelessly into a bin, and now all the cassettes are gone. Hours of interviews and stories from years ago that I'll never be able to replicate.

"Diana," Oliver says and puts an arm that might be made of lead around my shoulders. I could topple backward. "All that stuff is off to a better home."

My smile is obviously pained. He has no idea that he threw out years of my life—years of other women's stories. Oliver looks hurt and confused. Of course he can't understand what he's thrown out. "Diana, I don't even know what I did wrong here."

Over his shoulder I see that Emmy is studying us, her fingers twisting in the hem of her pajama shirt. I smile at her. "Let's go brush teeth, okay, bear?"

"I haven't had dessert yet!"

"Diana," Oliver says, softer this time. "What's going on?"

I try to sound bright. "You know me and old junk. I get nostalgic."

Oliver wrinkles his forehead and looks like he wants to say something more, but he lets me go.

"Damn, Diana. Try taking a little heat off that serve. Give a girl a chance." L'Wren is laughing but I can tell she means it. She hates to lose, and I just beat her in straight sets. I should probably have let her win the last one, but it's my birthday and it feels good to push myself to total exhaustion. I think about reminding her that it's my birthday just so she doesn't realize later and feel bad, but that seems even weirder? I'm forty-one. This birthday should float quietly by.

We're zipping up our rackets and heading to our cars in the parking lot of Rockgate's public park. This is where we spend most weekends—either at the playground or the tennis courts or the town pool. Some mornings, Emmy and I stop here before school so she can watch for the deer that graze on wild strawberries at the park's edges.

"I'll buy you a lemonade at the snack bar? I have an hour before Emmy's swim class."

"You owe me something stronger than lemonade to make up for whipping my ass. Seriously, Diana, how many lessons a week do you take?"

"Just two," I say. I don't add that one of those lessons is two hours long. I never thought I was a competitive person but tennis brings it out in me.

L'Wren's phone starts ringing. "Liam?" she says. "I can't come pick you up, I have an appointment. . . . Yes, a hair appointment."

"What's wrong?" I whisper.

She puts her hand over the phone. "Liam's car broke down. His father is in the middle of eighteen holes of golf and isn't picking up." She mouths, *Why me?*

"I'll go get him," I say. "Where is he?"

"Oh my god, Diana, you're a literal angel."

Liam is standing in front of the gas station when I pull up. He's dyed his hair a deep midnight blue. "Thanks," he says, climbing into the passenger seat. "I owe you."

"Consider it payment for driving our stuff back from Roundtop. Where to?"

"You can take me back to the park with you and I'll wait for Pops. He likes it when I heckle him from the greens."

"Is that your car? The gray one?"

"Yeah. That's Rosie. I left a bagel with cream cheese on the roof a few months ago and it stuck. It's easy to identify now."

"Liam. Gross."

"I know. I kinda just do it to see L'Wren's face when I pull up next to her."

"Have you ever asked them to help you out with a new car?"

"L'Wren's offered. She hates seeing Rosie parked in her driveway. But once again . . . It's kinda nice to see her face." He grins. "I know, I'm a dick."

I pull onto the road heading back to the park. "She loves you, you know."

"You don't have to say that, Diana."

"I'm not just saying that. It's true." Why does my voice sound so hollow? "Maybe there's something you can do together sometime? Just the two of you."

"Sure. Maybe I'll book a his and her Fraxel."

I try not to laugh. "What about helping her cook dinner?"

"Dad cooks dinner."

"I know she likes to walk in the morning. You could go with her?"

"She calls that her 'me time.'"

"Fine. But you get what I mean. Because what's the other option, really?"

"To be the black sheep of the family permanently?"

"Come on, Liam. You're not the black sheep."

The car is quiet for a long minute. Liam cracks his knuckles, then finally speaks. "When I was a senior in high school, I was supposed to go to my mom's for the weekend but she ended up going to Florida so I had to turn around and go back to Dad's. When my cab pulled into the driveway, Dad and L'Wren and Halston were in front of the house dressed in red and green, taking the family Christmas card picture.

Even my racist grandma who tried to poison our gardener was invited. My dad pretended he knew I'd be coming back and told me to get in the picture, but it was obvious they had scheduled it for when I'd be gone. It's dumb even talking about it. I didn't want to be in the stupid Christmas card picture . . ."

"But you wanted to be in the picture."

"Ha. Clever, yes." He smiles. "I still want to be in the picture. I guess. I don't know, it's dumb. Besides, I almost have enough saved to move. So . . . soon."

We pull up to the golf course, and I park in the same spot as before. "Want to hit some tennis balls?"

"Very funny," he says.

"Just with me."

"Diana. Never." He looks at me in earnest. "Not even for your birthday."

When I was eleven, this would have been my dream—to lie by a glistening pool in a well-fitted, two-piece bathing suit. Instead, my mother and I lived in a dumpy apartment at the bottom of the Hollywood Hills, where we'd moved after her last breakup. She had been in community theater productions before she met my father, and once he left, when I was three, she decided it was time to pursue her dream of becoming a working actor.

Most afternoons, while my mother was at an audition or working behind the Clinique counter at the mall, I would knock on our landlord's door and ask him again when the pool in the building's courtyard would be filled. He was a tiny man named Chad with a thick head of sandy-blond hair and he always shrugged the same answer, "I called about the leak." I knew he was lying, that the pool would most likely never be fixed, but I asked anyway. Then I'd sit at the edge of the deep end in my bathing suit, the sun beating against my back, and let my bare legs dangle over the murky water at the pool's bottom. I'd swing my legs back and forth and say a quiet prayer for my mother's audition. I prayed to the patron saint of Los Angeles for callbacks and booked parts.

One hot summer day, after an audition that didn't go her way, she stormed past me, snapping, "Come on, move. *Move*." I hurried to stand, my bathing suit peeling off the hot concrete like Velcro.

Inside our apartment, Mom yelled for Chad, something about there being fleas, and he made his slow way upstairs and sprayed something on the carpet, then gave us instructions on when to vacuum. The entire time he was there, my mom complained about how difficult it was to get anything done—she couldn't even run lines, the fleas were *too distracting*. With a blank expression Chad told her, "Try to use the pain in your process," then winked at me as he left. Our apartment building was teeming with out-of-work actors.

The fleas persisted, but we were also out of money and overdue on the rent, so Mom stopped calling Chad to come back, and I quit asking him about the pool. Most days we stayed inside and pretended not to be home whenever he knocked on our door looking for our rent check.

But today, here I am, my nails are painted pink and I have a glass of iced tea in hand, from a snack bar only ten feet away. And on the other side of my cold drink is my handsome husband, and together we have a perfect, healthy, brilliant daughter who is standing at the edge of the pool, watching her instructor demonstrate a dive.

"Look at her," Oliver says, his eyes wide with pride. "She's so strong. When did she get those muscles?"

"I know!" I say. "Maybe we should get her into gymnastics. A lot of Olympic divers start out as gymnasts."

Oliver looks at me with a grave face. "That won't distract from her pursuit of the Nobel Peace Prize?"

I laugh. It's Emmy's turn to dive and Oliver gently squeezes my hand. I squeeze back, tighter. Emmy steps to the very edge, her arms stretched over her head. Then she gets up on her tiptoes and launches into the deep end.

We're not supposed to clap for individual kids—this is just a class, it's not competitive—but Oliver lets out a hoot as Emmy climbs from the pool. Other parents laugh, because Oliver is too nice and too popular to be chastised for cheering on his daughter. Emmy beams at us and then slaps on wet feet back to her classmates.

Oliver and I sit in silence for the rest of the class. Times like this are what I try to remember when I feel lost. I'm forty-one and I have finally let my guard down. I've outrun the chaos. I'm not worried about being evicted from a crappy apartment or avoiding debt collectors. I have a job, a beautiful daughter, and a husband who makes me laugh. When I check out at the grocery store, I don't worry they'll ring me up and I'll have to put things back. I have days, like today, when the quiet feeling of being loved and feeling safe washes over me. *This is a kind of desire, too,* I tell myself.

Class ends, and I stand to take Emmy a towel. Oliver puts out a hand to stop me.

"You'll see," he says, pulling his shirt over his head. He takes a Bluetooth speaker from his bag and presses play. Now Stevie Wonder is singing "Happy Birthday," loud enough for the whole pool deck to enjoy. Oliver dives into the pool and then motions to Emmy, who cannonballs in after him.

"On three, Ems!" he shouts. Other poolgoers gather around me and we watch Emmy and Oliver do an incredibly clumsy father/daughter synchronized happy-birthday swim. Lots of jazz hands and popping up to the surface at mismatched times. *Notice the way the water holds them up. See the way they look at each other, trying to remember the moves and laughing when they can't.* My face hurts from smiling and tears sting my eyes. Such a sweet gesture. I try not to let myself wonder why I'm instructing myself to enjoy it.

Emmy finishes the routine with a flip off Oliver's shoulders and I clap loudly.

. . .

On the way home from dinner, Emmy falls asleep in the car. Oliver carries her upstairs and while he gets her settled, I quickly get ready for bed. I wash my face and brush my teeth and hurry under the covers. By the time Oliver comes in, the lights are off and my eyes are closed. *I'm just so tired*, I tell myself. From the sun and the wine at dinner. It's okay to just want to sleep. Oliver sits down on his side of the bed, and I can sense his disappointment. Here is where I should reach for him. Initiate a moment of closeness. Once we get started I'm sure I'll find it pleasurable. The more I tell myself what to do, the less I want to do it. So instead I pretend to be asleep and avoid "birthday sex" until finally we both drift off to sleep for real.

Chapter 6

The first time Oliver and I had sex, it didn't feel like fucking. It wasn't the kind of sex that made you wonder, while you were having it, if this person was going to call afterward, or if you'd even *want* to see them again. It wasn't performative. I didn't move my body to put on a show and neither did he.

Two days after we met and he had shown me the apartment, Oliver called to tell me my credit was indeed terrible, but by that point I'd found a room in a two-bedroom with a friend of a friend who was in dental school and very quiet. A week after that, Oliver called again, this time to tell me that his father's company was hiring a new front-office person. "It's a lot of answering phones, but the hours aren't too bad. I've managed to survive it," he said. I could tell he felt bad about the apartment falling through. He mentioned he knew of a unit in his girlfriend's building that might be free. I told him again that I'd already found a new place. I was pretty sure he was mentioning a girlfriend to convince me there was nothing creepy in his job offer.

"How do you know I'd be good at the job?"

"You answered *my* phone call pretty well."

"Ha ha."

I started work the next Monday. It was an easy job at his father's wealth management firm. I sat up front and answered the phones, "McKinnon, Wood, and Bloom." I circulated mail to each of the three named partners by dividing it among their female assistants. Two of the senior executives—Messrs. McKinnon and Bloom—were ancient-looking, gray-faced men and were mostly indistinguishable to me, holed up in their offices behind closed doors at the other end of the hallway. Oliver's father, Mr. Allen Wood, was the second name on the masthead, and of the three men, the only one I ever saw outside his office among the assistants, making an effort at social interaction.

When the phones were slow, I used sharp No. 2 pencils and every other free office supply at my desk to draw new sketches for my old friends Barry and Alicia—mostly of the irritated, very wealthy people I pictured on the other end of the calls. This time I signed them *D$rty D$ana* to make Alicia laugh. And instead of sending me sponges, Alicia sent me back a tightly rolled joint, which I quickly stashed in the back of my desk drawer. She couldn't believe I was working with finance people. Then, years later when I became a financial planner, she said she knew I could do it and that it was good to have one in the family.

Other times when I drew at my desk, I tried to picture Oliver's girlfriend. I imagined her with a chestnut bob, an oval face, and rosy cheeks. In my drawings she said things like, *Y'all are too cute!* while looking at Oliver with large watery eyes. Every night, Oliver would exit past reception, sometimes letting his hand linger on my desk, and wish me good night. And every night, over that first two and a half months, my crush blossomed.

On my eleventh Friday afternoon of work, something in me

snapped. Without giving myself time to chicken out, I found an empty envelope marked *Personal and Confidential* then got to work drawing a map of our office floor. Over Oliver's desk, I wrote, *You are HERE,* and over the back stairwell I drew a star and wrote, *I am THERE.* And then at the bottom of the paper, a question: *See you THERE?*

The joint Alicia mailed me was still in my desk. I placed it in the middle of the map and folded it in half. I emailed my officemate, Glory, subject line *UH-OH:* "You were right. I *never* should have trusted that taco truck!! Cover my phones? Might be a minute . . ." I forwarded my incoming calls to Glory's number and walked the envelope over to Oliver's desk. I made sure he saw me drop it, then kept walking toward the stairwell.

The heavy door slammed shut behind me. I sat on the stairs and waited. After several long minutes, I thought about slinking out. I'd just slipped the boss's son a joint and an unsolicited invitation. Then the door to the floor below me creaked open and Oliver ran up, two stairs at a time, a huge grin on his face. "I had to go to three break rooms to find this."

He pulled a lighter from his pocket and lit the joint. He sat down next to me and we passed it back and forth.

After a while, he asked, "What do you think of my dad?"

I laughed because I thought he was messing with me, asking about his dad while we got high in the stairwell of the office his father runs. But Oliver looked so earnest. I told him his father seemed nice. The truth was, at that point, Allen had never spoken to me. I had only ever interacted with his assistant, Cindy, who called me when she needed office supplies. Every time I brought her something, she held up a bowl of mints, and when I took one, she croaked, "Don't let 'em catch ya!" then winked. I asked Oliver what she meant.

"I'm not sure, but she's been making that same joke since I was a kid. It might even be the same bowl of mints."

The weed made this hilarious and provoked fits of laughter in both of us.

"Do you want to meet him now?" Oliver asked, wiping his eyes.

"Who, your *dad*? Are we still talking about your dad?"

Then we were laughing again, even harder, until our faces were so close our foreheads nearly touched. I asked, "Are you still dating someone?"

His eyes were a summery blue green. "No. I like someone else." Oliver leaned in close, until his lips were on mine. The kiss was briefly delicate. And then it broke over us both, a wave that held all the stored energy of our monthslong crush. It was a kiss between two people flushed with relief, a kiss that said, *I was beginning to think you would never show up.*

Desire rushed through me with an intensity that made me shiver. Oliver assumed I was cold in the over-air-conditioned office, so he pulled me close and wrapped his arms around me. Maybe it was the weed, but the warmth of his skin just then was the greatest sensation I'd ever felt.

I turned and straddled him on the steps. He groaned with happiness and I lifted my skirt, hitching it high around my waist. Only my underwear and his jeans separated the heat between us. His hardness, the feel of him, made me ache.

He looked up into my face and whispered, "Okay?" and when I nodded, he slid his fingers inside me. We gasped at the same moment, which made us both open our eyes and laugh. Just when I almost lost it to another fit of stoned laughter, he pulled my face toward his with a conviction that surprised us both. We kissed even more deeply. He tasted like marijuana and peanut butter cups from the office vending machine.

We dated for close to four months before we slept together. Oliver wanted me to know that I meant a lot to him, and no matter how much I teased him every time we kissed, how often I moved my hips against his jeans or sucked on his earlobe, he would always whisper, "not yet."

It became a game between us, and I loved watching Oliver try to steady his breath, willing his erection to settle.

By the time Oliver was ready, we were both overcooked. The buildup had become monumental, and I feared both of us would be disappointed. Oliver's parents were out of town, so he took me to the home he grew up in for a nighttime swim. The pool was Olympic-size with a lit up sea-blue bottom. There were four chaise lounges with cabana-striped fabric and a perfectly folded white towel laid on each cushion, as if his parents had known we were coming. I giggled as I watched him undress then cover his penis with two hands before jumping into the pool. I stood on the diving board and tossed one piece of clothing into the pool at a time, while Oliver watched me quietly from the shallow end. It was a hot, humid Texas night and I remember worrying that I would freeze when I jumped in, but the water was the temperature of my body, warm and inviting. I dove underwater and swam until I reached Oliver, surfacing inches from his face. "You're so beautiful," he said. I just smiled; I felt beautiful with Oliver.

As we ran toward the house, naked and dripping wet, Oliver grabbed a Coke from the fully stocked fridge in the outdoor kitchen. Then he led me up the back stairs to his childhood room, which had a poster of Cindy Crawford in a black bikini that was only visible when you closed the door. His bed was full-size, covered with an emerald-green duvet, which matched the shades Oliver now pulled down one by one.

"Who's this?" I held up a framed picture of Oliver and a striking redhead. Oliver's room raised hundreds of questions and I wanted answers to them all. How many times have you read *Dune*? Who picked out your clothes? Did you ever sneak girls through your bedroom window?

"That's Alex," he said. "She was my first."

"Where is she now?"

"Married with three kids. Lives in Houston. Happy, I think."

"Were you in love with her?"

"Kinda," he said. "I'm not sure I knew what love felt like."

"Do you know what it feels like now?"

"Yes." He entwined his fingers in mine. "This."

This is what love feels like, I thought. The softness of his childhood bedroom carpet on my feet. The sweet taste of Coke on his lips. The smell of chlorine still on our damp skin.

Oliver held my face in his hands. He kissed me deeply, then sucked my lower lip. I closed my eyes and he put a hand on my back, guiding me to the floor. We cuddled, my back to his chest, on the thick carpet and Oliver kissed the back of my neck and gently circled my nipples with his finger. I felt his erection against my back and raised my leg slightly, allowing him to push himself inside me. He held me tightly while he moved in and out of me. "God, Diana. You feel so good."

I grabbed his hand, forcing him to squeeze my breast. I wanted more of him. More friction. More pressure. More fucking. But we were making love. I turned my face to his and Oliver's hands traced my lips. I took his finger into my mouth and started to suck on it. Oliver moaned with pleasure, as if this was the most erotic thing a woman had ever done. "This is everything to me," he said. "Being inside you."

I slipped away from him briefly and shifted onto my back so I could watch his face. I opened my legs and pulled my knees to my chest.

"Diana." His voice was strong and deep and I wanted him back inside me so badly my entire body trembled. When he entered me again, I knew I could never let him go.

Oliver brushed the hair from my face. He kissed me slowly, his mouth open wide like mine until we were no longer kissing—just lips pressed against each other, breathing the same air.

"You feel too good."

"It's okay," I whispered into his ear. "Come inside me."

Oliver's entire body shuddered, and then he collapsed onto me, burying his face in my hair. All I could think was, *Who cares if I get pregnant? Because this is who I want to be with forever.* My desire was for something so much bigger than sex. With Oliver, I could picture an entire life—time moving in breezy, gentle circles, the air around us always soft and sweet-smelling.

"Did you come?" he asked.

"Yes," I lied. Then I curled up against him and we both drifted to sleep.

Chapter 7

'Wren stands on my welcome mat holding a hairless rescue cat with goopy eyes and a hangdog face. "He comes with free antibiotics!" she offers. "The eye thing is really no big deal. It's kitty herpes, if you can believe it."

"Is it contagious?" I take a noticeable step back.

"No! Not to humans. God, Diana. Look at him. He's a gift. A belated birthday gift!"

My birthday was a month ago. "I didn't think you were actually serious."

"I have three litters of kittens in my catio right now. Kevin is a patient man, but I think I may have pushed too far. Listen, if you like him, I'm waiving the adoption fee. It's a great deal."

"What if Oliver's allergic?"

"This one is hypoallergenic," L'Wren lies. "And if he isn't, Oliver can take some Claritin with his vitamins. You look great by the way."

"Thank you." I've dressed up for tonight. This black dress I've had since before Emmy was born, but I like the way its thin straps make my shoulders look. And on my lunch hour, I bought new heels that give me three inches. When I put them on, even in the overcrowded shoe department of Macy's, I felt like someone else. I also spent real, concerted effort on my hair so that it looks more like L'Wren's, smooth and purposefully placed.

"Here." L'Wren, still holding the kitten, pulls a red lipstick from her purse and blots some on my lips. "I'd die to have your full lips." She stands back to admire her work. "Ooh, perfect. Keep it. It looks much better on you."

As soon as I had mentioned that Oliver and I might try for a night away, L'Wren jumped in and insisted she'd stay overnight with Emmy. At first, I was more embarrassed than grateful—was it that obvious how much Oliver and I needed this? That we'd been trying and failing at a kind of intimacy that should come so much easier? Or maybe it was shame at feeling like a bigger person would own it. *Oh god, sex with my husband—help!!* is what I imagine someone more evolved would lament. I take the lipstick from her and squeeze her and the kitten into a hug. "Thanks for doing this."

"*Please.* Halston's at my mom's all weekend and Kevin's working late. And Liam refuses to watch Bravo with me. Emmy will be way less judgy company." She slips off her boots. "Where are you off to?"

"I'm not sure. Oliver's going to text me." After my birthday, I decided what we need is a change of scenery. When I suggested the idea of a night away, just the two of us, Oliver took over the planning, telling me he wanted to surprise me.

"Hmm, well," L'Wren narrows her eyes. "I have faith in Oliver. If you were Jenna, I'd say change your outfit 'cause—surprise!—you're one hundred percent being dragged to nosebleed seats at a Mavs game. But Oliver . . . he won't let us down." The kitten meows in

L'Wren's arms as if to agree. "Emmy!" she calls up the stairs. "Come look what Auntie L brought you!"

My phone chimes with a text from Oliver. *Rosevale Hotel. See you soon.* I kiss Emmy good night and L'Wren shoos me out the door.

At the hotel, I park the car and call Oliver's cell. "I'm here."

"Good, good. I'm upstairs."

"What's the room number?"

"Oh, right." I can tell from the smile in his voice that this is exactly what he wanted me to ask. "When you get to the front desk, tell them Hugo Drax left you a key."

"Who?"

"It's my code name."

"Why do you need—Oliver . . ." I trail off, laughing.

"Sounds like a pretty cool guy, right?"

It used to be that when one of us was excited, it spread to the other, like a welcome contagion. But recently, the opposite is true. It's as if when one of us is excited, the other person feels they have to balance things out, temper the excitement with caution or reason or just throw ice-cold water on the whole thing . . . or what? What will happen if we're both happy?

"You're Fiona Volpe. I left the key under your name, Fiona."

"Wait, what?" But he's already hung up.

The lobby of the Rosevale has vaulted ceilings and pink marble floors. It's loud tonight, with a bar full of conference attendees drinking in their badges. At the reception desk, an older gentleman in a well-fitted gray suit and purple tie squints into his computer screen.

As I cross the lobby, Alicia calls. If anyone would love this assignment it's her. She'd waltz to the desk and announce "Fiona-Fucking-Volpe."

"Hey." I answer her call in a whisper for no good reason. "I'm about to meet Oliver in a hotel room."

"Please tell me you're wearing a trench coat."

"Totally."

"Dirty." Alicia laughs. "Call me tomorrow?"

"Of course."

At the reception desk, the well-dressed man says, "Welcome," with a practiced smile.

"I'm picking up a key," I say. "For Ms. Volpe."

Outside of room 1406, I take a deep breath. This night is exactly what we need. No strained intimacy or fake orgasms or hurrying things along. An entire night, just the two of us.

Before I can knock, Oliver opens the door. I'm not sure who I thought might be behind the door—of course it would be Oliver—but I startle anyway. He's wearing the blue button-down shirt I gave him for our anniversary.

"You found it," he says.

"I did." Oliver looks unsteady and I want to reach out to him and tell him, *we got this.* We do. We're going to slip into the best versions of ourselves and be better, together, closer.

"Well, come, come," Oliver says to me, like calling a dog in from the cold.

"Thank you."

Oliver's sprung for a suite, which has its own living room. I follow him through the sitting area, past the huge bay windows to the bedroom that I imagine is decorated to look like one of Laura Bush's guest rooms—silk drapes, ornate headboard, and very southern touches. The overhead lights are off, but we're bathed in candlelight. So many candles. "Wow. Flower petals."

"Two dozen red roses. I did it myself." Oliver's smile is easy.

"Two dozen? Really. Looks like more." A lot more. It's a churning sea of dead roses.

"Don't worry, I'll clean it up." Oliver flops onto the bed and looks up at the ceiling, his hand tucked behind his head. "Is it too much?"

"No." I lie beside him and drink it all in. How nice it is to be away together. I rest my head on his chest and close my eyes. "But maybe the candles? They're a bit. . . . strong." I can taste them in my mouth, like an unripe pear rolled in cinnamon potpourri.

"I got them on Amazon. They claim to be *aphrodisiacs*." He rolls the word. "Four and a half stars."

"How can a candle be an aphrodisiac?"

"Maybe all the effort is?" he asks hopefully.

I smile, remembering that I brought a gift too. I reach into my purse and pull out a wrapped box.

"For me?"

"Yeah, for us," I say. "Open it."

He lifts the lid and inside, lying on its own satin bed, is a very large, neon-orange vibrator. It glows cheerfully in the dim light.

"Hmm, I didn't realize how bright that color would be," I say. Oliver and I have never talked about using toys together.

"Maybe it glows in the dark?" he says.

I lift it from the box and it hums so loudly we both startle. The old us would be doubled over laughing by now, but tonight, we're earnest and focused. The only sound in the room is the vibration. Almost like the rattle of a small lawn mower.

I switch it off. "It was hard to tell how big it was, at the shop."

"You went to a sex shop?"

I nod.

"Did anyone see you?"

I try to read his face. "Just Emmy's teacher. And your mom . . . I think they were together?"

"Ha ha. I meant, did anyone working there see you and offer to help?"

"I was kind of in a hurry." I think about my hopeful shopping day—new shoes, new vibrator. Now I say, "I don't think it's for us."

He turns the vibrator over in his hands, genuinely curious. "Who is it for? It's got straps." He loosens one, then tightens it again. I watch his hands, strong and gentle. "It feels a little . . . advanced? Doesn't it? I wouldn't even know where to put it. I mean, aren't I enough?"

"Of course you are." I smile. "It was just an idea." Clearly not a good one. I was moving too fast, forgetting who Oliver and I are.

"I think I'm a little scared of it," Oliver says. "What if it turns on us?"

I'm already putting it back in my purse. "I bought the wrong one."

"We could try it."

"Is that what you want?" I try not to sound annoyed.

"I don't know. Maybe. Not really, no." He looks up. "I just want to connect with you."

In my head, the word *connect* has never sounded so dull. Yes, that's the whole point of tonight—*connection*. But when Oliver says it out loud, I feel like I'm sitting on the edge of the bed next to an octopus, his tentacles wrapping around me and pulling me underwater.

I brush the hair from his forehead. "I do too."

"Do you?"

His question makes me more annoyed. Of course I do. Don't I? Why does an easy night have to turn hard? The longer we go without sex, the harder it is going to be to get back to each other. And it does feel like a place I have to get back to, somehow—like an island that my boat keeps drifting away from, farther and farther. I'm never sure where Oliver is in this tired metaphor. On the beach? In a boat of his own? Underneath my boat, one tentacle draped over the hull?

I lie back on the bed and pull Oliver toward me. He kisses my mouth, gently. I close my eyes.

Oliver shifts beside me on the hotel bed and asks, "Why don't we take a bath?" his lips still touching mine.

I open my eyes inches from his. "Good, yeah. That sounds really nice."

"You get in first. I'll order us some room service. What would you like?"

He's pulling away, I realize. I hug my arms to my body. "You decide."

In the white marbled bathroom, I find the switches and play around with them until the fluorescent light isn't so harsh. I kick off my heels, and the floor is cold beneath my bare feet. In the mirror's reflection, I see Oliver has already run the bath. The bubbles are quickly evaporating so I hurry to unzip my dress.

I stand in front of the hotel mirror and smile—Oliver isn't the only one trying. I'd put on my best underwear, red and lacy, an impulse buy one Valentine's Day. They're six years old, but so uncomfortable that they've hardly been worn. I like how pretty and ridiculous they are. There was once a matching bra but it disappeared long ago.

I hear something like "Lite Jazz" drift through the wall. I inhale, suck in my stomach just slightly, and watch my small breasts rise and fall in the mirror. I trace my fingers down my naked stomach and across my C-section scar. I slip my hand beneath my underwear and think of gliding my fingers inside myself. I imagine inviting Oliver in to watch me masturbate. I feel myself pulse with a familiar, warm sensation, then pull my hand back. It falls to my side.

I turn away from my reflection. I dip a toe into the bath, then take off my underwear and climb all the way in. As I reach for the hot water tap, I spot a lone hair, so short and curly it could only mean one thing.

"Eww. Oliver, did you wash out the bath before you drew it?"

It is not, in fact, a lone hair. Its companion drifts toward me and I hurry out of the tub. I grab a towel. Louder this time, I call, "Did you wash out the bath? There's something floating—are these your hairs?"

"I don't know," he answers over a saxophone solo. "I don't think so."

"It's a hotel, Oliver. You have to wash the tub out first."

I pull on my dress and drain the tub.

"Want a bite?" Oliver comes in holding a plate of strawberries. "They're organic."

"Oliver . . ."

"I'm trying, Diana." The plate clangs against the marble sink. The effect is louder than he intended and his cheeks go red. "Please. Just take a bite of the goddamn strawberry."

I take a bite, but zip my dress first. "Now what?"

"Try not to look so bored, for one." He looks down at our feet and mouths the word *fuck*, which makes me smile.

"I'm sorry." I take his hand. "It's just—I feel like this is how a sixteen-year-old girl in a Netflix movie would want to lose her virginity. It feels almost silly. Rose petals?" I had to say it out loud. It was impossible to keep in any longer.

"Ouch," he says. But he takes my other hand.

"Maybe let's not make such a big effort . . ."

Oliver grins. "Lose the candles?"

"Please."

"Sorry."

"Don't apologize. Let's just be us."

"You're right. God, you're so right." He claps his hands together, exhales. "This is embarrassing."

"It's not. It's sweet."

He looks at the empty tub like he wishes he could slip right down the drain. "I'm seeing it with horrifying clarity now. I have had sex before, I promise."

I lead him back to the bed thinking about how I used to masturbate in front of my ex, my legs spread wide. I imagine doing that now. I slip my dress off and dive beneath the itchy quilt. Maybe we both need to be shocked.

Oliver circles the room, blowing out the candles, one by one. "Better?"

"Yes. Although—" I cough. "The smoke is almost worse than the scent?"

"Just ignore the smoke. Come here . . ." Oliver climbs under the blanket beside me and slips my underwear down my legs, stopping at my knees. He smiles. "You shaved." He pulls me closer, pressing his erection into my warm skin.

But I'm still focused on the smoke. I know I should stay in the moment but it's impossible. "It's just a lot of smoke, Oliver."

"It's fine." He pulls the quilt up over our heads making a fortress around us. He finds my mouth and kisses me hungrily.

"I'm just worried . . ." I pull the covers off us.

"Ignore the fucking smoke, Di—" The high-pitched beep of the smoke alarm cuts him off. *Beep. Beep. Beep. Beep. Beep.*

"Oh shit!" I grab a pillow and stand on the bed waving it furiously. "Fan the smoke!"

Oliver runs to open a window. "Fuck. They're sealed."

The alarm keeps screaming. *Beep. Beep. Beep. Beep. Beep.* "Oliver!" I fan harder as the sound gets louder and louder.

Oliver's erection is gone, defeated by the alarm. "I'm calling the front desk," he yells.

Too late. The sprinklers come on and water rains down. Everywhere.

Chapter 8

"We didn't know what else to try. We both agree that we're sinking." Two minutes into therapy and Oliver already looks defeated.

"Is this how you feel, Diana?" Miriam asks.

Oliver and I found Miriam online, typing: *best couples therapist, Dallas,* into the search bar.

"What if we can't afford the best one?" he'd asked me.

"We'll go with like number four or five on the list."

That was Sunday night, two weeks after the hotel incident. We'd been out to dinner with L'Wren and Kevin, the first time Oliver and I had been together without Emmy around. When we got in the car, tired from a long night of pretending everything was normal between us, Oliver held his head in his hands and neither of us spoke until he said, "My mom suggested we talk to somebody."

"Your *mom*? Oliver."

He shrugged.

We didn't fight. We drove home, paid the sitter. We opened my laptop and searched and landed in Miriam's lap.

Oliver crosses and recrosses his legs on the couch beside me. I'm not sure where to look—at him? At her? Looking at both of them is impossible. I pick Miriam. From the neck down, everything about her is soothing to me—the way her many linen layers drape across her body, her hands resting gently in her lap. But her sharply angled bob and glossy dark-red lipstick suggest someone a little more severe, which confuses me. I scan her office for clues, but I don't recognize a single book on her shelf, and her hands are clasped in a way that makes it impossible to tell if she's wearing a wedding band. "Diana?" she repeats.

I clear my throat and rest my eyes on her red-stained lips. "I think our rhythm has been a little off. Yes."

"Well," Miriam says. "I want to commend you both for taking such an important step together. So maybe as a place to start, let's have you take turns and state how you feel around the other person."

I sneak a peek at Oliver. He looks so vulnerable, staring down at his own hands. It all feels like a performance. We're sitting on a couch together and not touching, like strangers. This is crazy! He's my person! I want to scoop him up off the couch and say *Let's get out of here. We don't belong here, right?* I will him to turn and look at me, too, but he doesn't.

"No accusations or judgments," Miriam says. "I just want you to tell me how you feel when you're around each other."

"Which of us would you like to go first?" Oliver asks.

Miriam smiles. "Since you asked, Oliver, maybe you?"

Oliver lets out a long breath. "Around Diana," he says, meeting Miriam's eyes, "I feel unattractive."

There's a prickly sweat at my hairline.

"Why is that?" Miriam asks.

"Because Diana doesn't touch me anymore."

"That's not true," I interject. "I touch you every day."

"Try to keep it about your *feelings*, Oliver," Miriam says. "Try not to accuse."

"It's just a fact," Oliver says, still not looking at me. "We don't have sex."

My phone rings in my purse and both their heads snap in my direction. "Sorry. Let me just . . . It might be Emmy's school." I peek at the caller ID. Alicia. Maybe she's calling to save me. I switch my phone to silent, setting it on the end table beside me. When I look up, all eyes are on me. "It's not *never*. We had sex a couple weeks ago." I realize how not great this sounds as soon as it comes out.

"Diana," Miriam says, "things said in here can be hard to hear. While it's important that we avoid accusations, it's also important that we make space for how the other is feeling."

"Right," I say. "Of course." I no longer want to scoop up Oliver. Instead I imagine walking out on them both and driving away. It's my fault that Oliver and I rarely have sex. At some point we'd gone from having sex all the time to having it once a week, then once a month. And then sometimes nothing for months at a time.

"Is that how you see it, Diana?" Miriam asks. I panic—I haven't been listening.

"How could you not?" Oliver asks quietly. "It was supposed to be fun. As soon as she walked through the hotel door, I had an erection. I can't help it. Just thinking about her naked does that to me. It always has . . ."

"Oliver . . ." Why is he doing this? I turn to look at him full-on. "Are we going to talk about everything?" Now I sound prudish about sex. How did this happen? I don't mind talking about sex. Is it our lack of sex I can't talk about?

"Why else are we here?" Oliver sounds more than annoyed, he's angry. I hardly recognize his tone.

"Fine," I snap. "Yes, we have less sex. I got tired of pretending that I liked it."

The words sizzle in the air. No one speaks.

"Have you ever told Oliver what you do like?" asks Miriam.

"No. She hasn't," Oliver says.

I wait for Miriam to tell Oliver that he shouldn't answer for me. Instead she asks him a follow-up question. "Is that something you'd like to know?"

So that was how it was going to be. I should have known that Oliver would be treated like the good guy. Everyone loves Oliver. But shouldn't he know what I like? Shouldn't he be trying to figure it out the same way I've always tried to figure out what brings him pleasure?

As quickly as this idea comes to me, my resolve to be angry at everyone in this room but myself evaporates. This residue left behind is shame. It's my fault for not showing him. For not talking to him. But that's not what Oliver and I do. We never have. And the sex is not bad, it's just . . . sex.

Oliver shifts in his chair. "I'd like to know," the anger has left his voice, "if Diana knows what it feels like to reach for someone and have them slip away."

My heart sinks. Oliver *is* the good guy.

"I've adored Diana from the moment I met her. She knows that."

After a long silence, Miriam speaks. "I'm going to give you two some homework before we meet next week." I'm already thinking about how to get out of coming back. "I want you to look each other in the eye, in a quiet place, and share a secret. You should each take a turn sharing and listening. And I want you both to receive that secret with love."

. . .

When we get in the elevator, I reach for Oliver's damp hand. I don't mind that it's sweaty, I just want to hold it. "What was *that*?" I ask, dramatically. I hope that he'll laugh it off with me. "That was insane, right?"

"Which part?" he asks quietly. When he doesn't look at me, it's like a slap in the face. I realize what's happening in there isn't incomprehensible to any of us. We all seem to be agreeing we're in real trouble.

At home, I replay the therapy session over and over, rewriting it in my head. There's a revised version where I don't say anything at all—I share zero grievances about our sex life or Oliver not knowing what I like. This version feels sickeningly familiar, so I discard it. I know there's a better, more honest version where we tell each other everything. But when I try to write it, I get stuck. Maybe, I admit, that's what Miriam is getting at with her homework—Oliver and I have to figure out this part together.

When we're both in bed and the lights are off, I ask Oliver, "Should we try it?"

"The homework?" He obviously has been thinking about it too. This is good. Maybe therapy will help. We'll go back and this time I'll be there with an open mind. We'll get everything out in the open. Disassemble it all and put it back together.

"Want me to go first?" I ask.

"Sure." His voice sounds small in the dark. I reach over to turn on the light just as my phone rings with Alicia's call. I still haven't returned her missed call from therapy. I make a mental note to call her on my way to work tomorrow and switch on the bedside lamp.

"My secret . . ." I reach for the tape recorder now stashed in my nightstand drawer. "I want to play you something, okay?"

"Like a song?"

"No . . . Something I recorded. A woman talking. Remember how I talked about the recordings I made? And used in my drawings?"

Oliver is looking right at me, really focused on me, and it feels nice. "In Santa Fe? You never really talk about that time in your life. I have to admit I've been curious."

I never expected a weird little book of my paintings to sell like crazy, but when I met Oliver, I was so deflated by not making much progress on the second book, and the first book had had such a small print run and short life, I didn't tell him much about what I was working on. Then we started working together at his father's firm and I liked fitting into his life. He was safe and steady and I wanted to be that for him too. Besides, when I did show him an old portfolio, I saw the way he skimmed over the nudes and stopped to admire a half-assed sketch of mountains I'd done.

"Would you like to hear some? Of a recording?"

"Sure."

I press play on Jess's tape. I study Oliver's face while he listens.

I stood back and admired his body. I tried not to look too impressed, but he was gorgeous. Those muscled valleys where his stomach dipped down into his hips. I could tell by the way his jeans hung that he was naked underneath. He reached for me, but I pinned his arms to his sides. "Don't," I told him again. Then I pulled off my shirt and unclasped my bra and let him watch as I took it off. His eyes went wide and he reached for me again, but I shook my head. I told him, "I'm going to take your clothes off. We're going to suck each other and fuck each other for the first time and then I'm going to leave."

As the recording continues, Oliver shifts beside me. His forehead creases and his eyes widen. I stop the recording halfway through. "What do you think?"

"What is it exactly?"

"Just a woman. Talking about sex."

"Do you want me . . . for us to be more like . . ."

"No." That good feeling slips away. "This isn't about us. It's just about . . . Things I was trying to figure out. Am trying to figure out. Maybe a new project."

"Sorry, Diana. But I think about art like something you could look at. Like a sculpture. Or your paintings. I love what you paint, I always have."

"Right." He means the mountains and the flowers. "And you know I made paintings from recordings like these?"

"You know me, Diana, a lot of art goes right over my head. This is . . . I didn't expect it to be so porny, I guess?"

My cheeks flush. "It's just a woman speaking. About her very normal longing."

"Depends on what you consider normal, I guess."

My stomach drops, and with it, my voice. It falls somewhere deep and I can't pull it up. I switch off the light so he can't read my face.

"Diana. You just said this isn't about us. This person you recorded has nothing to do with us. How did you get her to tell you all that, anyway?"

"Never mind," I say. "It was a long time ago."

"I'm glad you shared that with me." I can tell he's just trying to do the assignment now. *Receive that secret with love.* "I'll listen to more if you want me to." I can't imagine playing more for him. It would only make me feel worse.

"That's okay. Why don't you just tell me your secret?"

"Right. Mine. Sure." Oliver sighs. He's going to tell me about the time he snuck into the movies when he was eleven and pretended not to know better. Or about cheating his way through tenth-grade French. His secrets are PG-13 at best, and I already know most of them. But I can't deny he seems nervous to tell me this one.

"Okay." He looks away from me, up at the ceiling. "Diana?"

"Yeah?"

"I'm worried I'm falling out of love with you."

"Oh."

It's all I can think to say. My mouth is dry, my voice in my throat, my heartbeat in my ears.

We lie together in the dark for what feels like hours until finally I say, "I think I hear Emmy," and get out of bed to check on her. Really,

I sit outside our bedroom door until I hear Oliver's breathing turn to snoring.

With my heart still racing, I get up and take my phone to the kitchen to plug in to charge, then I wander down the hall to the guest room, now clean and emptied. I shut the door tight and find myself in the guest bathroom, running the shower. Inside, I let the water run hot and muffle the sound of my sobs. Our ground somehow got even shakier. I used to know exactly what to say and how to make Oliver love me. How to recover from a hurt and make up from a fight. How to make us both feel better and loved and happy. How did we get here?

I wrap a towel around me. I don't want to be in this room anymore, so I stand in the hallway and dry myself off, careful not to make too much noise. I'm tired, but I don't know where to go next, so I slide to the floor and sit for a while. Jasper's photograph is opposite me, leaning in its latest spot against the wall, still waiting to be hung. I wish I could recognize the town, the horse, any detail that might suggest I'd been there before, but none of it is familiar.

My phone rings from the kitchen and I hurry to answer it before it wakes anyone. It's Alicia calling, for the third time today.

"Hey. Everything okay?"

"Sorry to keep calling." Her voice is shaky.

"No, tell me—"

"He's gone."

My heart drops to my feet. "I'm so sorry."

"Me too." She sniffs. "What a fucker!"

"Alicia."

"What? Now I have to miss him all the time."

"I should have come sooner."

"I said goodbye for both of us. He knew. But you're coming now?"

"I'll be on the very first flight I can find."

Santa Fe, New Mexico

THEN

Out the windshield, the desert sky is bruised purple and pink, and I lean back against my headrest as if I have all the time in the world. I want to get so stoned tonight that my worries soften into clouds, my head fills with loose tufts of cotton candy, and I forget that it's my birthday.

"You feel anything? I don't feel anything." In the passenger seat, Alicia blinks at me from under a curtain of thick black bangs. "Sorry, Diana. I think I bought you dirt weed." Her eyes are so red and glassy she could play the stoner in an after-school special.

"You're baked," I assure her.

"I'm completely freakin' sober."

I take the joint from her fingers. She has painstakingly written *Happy 25th Bday!* on the rolling paper in tiny cursive letters. I suck gently and watch the writing disappear, then snuff the joint in the car's ashtray.

"Whoa—hang on."

"We're late." I angle the rearview mirror and fuss with my hair—last night, in a moment of prebirthday impulsivity, I cut my blondish-brown waves into a choppy bob, using kitchen scissors. Now the hair stops just below my ears in frizzy layers. Alicia watches me, then digs through her bottomless tote bag. She pulls out a small glass bottle and rubs a few drops of oil between her fingers, then runs them through my hair. The oil smells of magnolias and honey. My hair calms down and looks almost as shiny as hers.

"My dad's new lady friend sent it to me. I'm sure she got it for free."

My car's passenger-side door has rusted shut, so Alicia follows me out by gracefully unfolding two long khaki-clad legs over the driver's seat and hopping onto the pavement. I zip my hoodie to my chin and jump up and down to stay warm. The air smells of burning cedar. Across the parking lot, the art gallery glows warmly. At my side, Alicia does a chicken dance, like a hippie at a Grateful Dead concert.

"You're *definitely* sober," I say.

She rolls her eyes. "Could I do this if I were stoned?" She playfully humps the bumper of my Toyota Tercel. The rusted bumper heaves once, then falls to the ground. This sends us both into hysterics.

Alicia and I met in an Intro to Screenwriting course our first year of college. She used to sleep through class with a bundled-up Patagonia fleece under her cheek while the rest of us tried to give constructive feedback about one another's writing without hurting anyone's feelings. One day a classmate named Ross, who had annoyed most of us by always talking like he already knew everything, started in on my scene. "I don't buy it." He waved a dismissive hand. "A woman would *never* say that." I sat up a little straighter in my chair and tried not to blush.

Alicia chimed in without lifting her head. "We should be careful not to get warped by our own jealousy when critiquing," she warned.

"Sorry?" Ross snipped. "Did I wake you?"

Alicia propped her chin on her hand and stared at him. "Diana's pages are easily the best we've read so far. And whether or not a woman would *ever* say that . . ." She sighed. "Of course a woman would say that. Maybe you just haven't been listening to many women. Not to be petty."

After that, and for the rest of the semester, no one listened when Ross said anything.

"Seriously?" Alicia straightens up now and peers across the parking lot. On the other side of the lot, Barry slides the door of his catering van shut. Alicia and I warned him recently that his white van looked a lot like a kidnapper's vehicle, and today we see he has painted it purple with *Barry's Eats* stenciled across the side in friendly bubble letters. Alicia whistles. "Hot *damn*, Barry. Now you're just a stone-cold fox."

Barry laughs. He is one of the nicest humans we know, and by far the best boss we'll ever have. He knows how broke we are, and he tries to hire us every time he books a job, and to save the more lucrative weekend shifts for us. He didn't even make us buy new clothes when he hired us—one day he just pretended to find new uniforms in our sizes. He lied and told us they had been returned by former employees.

He does have one teeny management flaw, which is that he often falls in love with his employees. He has never acted on a single crush, but if you know him, you spot it instantly. He flushes, his eyes go puppy-wide, and his voice gets high when he tries to give instructions. He has fallen for Megan who only works on Thursday nights, Alexander from Taos, Alicia for sure, and most recently, Rod, who almost never says a word. "He told me he's studying *botany*," Barry told me once about Rod, like it was the most surprisingly sexy thing he'd ever heard.

Now he speed-walks toward us in white platform sneakers and long shorts, his curly brown hair backlit by the dramatic Santa Fe sky. He's only a few years our senior, but his stress levels make him seem much older. He folds his arms across his chest. "Is it too much to ask that you abstain for one shift?"

"Oh fuck, Barry." Alicia widens her eyes. "Did you forget?"

Barry goes still.

"Baaaaaarrrrrrryyyyyy." She shakes her head. "It's Diana's birthday! You forgot?"

He looks at me so sweetly, so full of regret, as Alicia piles it on. "Diana is *working* on her twenty-fifth birthday! Is that even legal?"

"Happy birthday, Diana." Barry hugs me, and I want to take a little nap on his shoulder. He's an inch or two shorter than me and my head fits perfectly into the crook of his neck.

"If we *didn't* get stoned," Alicia insists, "I'd be the worst friend in the world and you'd be the worst boss. Like, really cruel."

"Your friend is hilarious." He squeezes my arm affectionately and hands me a duffel bag of aprons and Sterno cans. To Alicia he says, "Drink some coffee. And *please* tuck in your shirt."

Alicia nods and does as she's told, unzipping her khakis and pulling them down far enough to reveal the lacy top of her pink underwear. Barry looks immediately at his feet.

He notices my bumper on the ground and picks it up, leaning it against the trunk. "There's duct tape in my van."

"Don't worry, Barry," I say. "We're on it." It's my voice, but it sounds like I'm in a tunnel. The weed is hitting me hard.

Alicia holds up Barry's hand and high-fives it. "We are so pumped, Bare."

"It's a big night," Barry says, and I want to hug him again. He says this at the beginning of every shift because he's legitimately worried he's going to fuck up, no matter how many parties he's catered.

He slings a big bag of linens over his shoulder and heads for the gallery's back door. "Just don't eat all the cocktail weenies. This crowd loves them. They're ironic hot dog eater–types!"

"You know I don't eat weenies that small, Barry!" Alicia calls after him.

He pretends not to hear. My head is officially a cloud of pink cotton-candy dreams.

In the gallery's back kitchen, I count and recount the serving trays, covering each one with a white doily, while Alicia sets up the coatracks in an office off the gallery's main floor. Barry hurries back and forth to his van, unloading supplies and grumbling about how dirty the kitchen is. Silent Rod is here, too, tall and lanky, with a well-groomed, rust-colored beard and arms so long it looks like he's wearing a child-size flannel shirt. He carries milk crates of alcohol into the main room and sets up the bar in a corner. I check the miniquiches in the oven, then head out to help Rod slice lime wedges. I like to imagine that the faraway look in his eye means he's lost somewhere inside the pages of his botany textbook.

Sylvia Cross, the gallery's formidable owner, is moving methodically through the main room, asking her assistants again and again for an opinion of where each photograph has been hung. They make several laps, then land in front of us at the bar. They decide that *we're* what's out of place. "This is all wrong here." Sylvia waves her hands at Rod, who nods politely, unfazed, and gets to work breaking down the bar and moving it to the other side of the room.

Tonight's show is for Jasper Green, a local photographer I've heard talked about more for his good looks than his work. Sylvia has left copies of Jasper's profile in *Aperture* magazine—"Santa Fe's Next Art-Throb"—all over the gallery. In the photo spread, he's sitting in the bed of an old blue-and-white Ford 250, looking exactly like a person practicing the art of appearing laid-back: oatmeal fisherman sweater, faded Levi's, worn-in work boots. He has a wide smile and dimples in both cheeks. His legs dangle off the back of the truck and his hands rest on his thighs. I would assume someone so good-looking takes photos of other attractive people, like naked supermodels posing in the desert, but looking around I see his photographs are mostly landscapes. Their mood is eerie and a little cold. Two images face each other in the center of the gallery: one shows a giant arched mesa dotted with snow, and the other shows a frozen lake surrounded by the desert sand, which is textured like a wind-swept toupee. The prints are massive, taller than human-size, so standing in front of them you feel overwhelmed, like you might fall into their desolation.

My buzz is giving way to sleepiness. I search the kitchen, find a jar of Nescafé, and make a coffee to share with Alicia. When Barry isn't looking, I wrap some cocktail weenies in a napkin and shove them in my apron pocket.

The office door is closed. I rap on it. "Alicia?"

I find her asleep on top of a bed she's made out of Barry's duffel coat. I give her a gentle nudge. "Wake up. Guests are here. And I have weenies."

With her eyes closed, she smiles.

Half an hour later, the gallery is packed with people and buzzing with conversation. "What's that?" a young woman asks, peering indecisively at the tray I'm holding. She's roughly my age, with long braids and wearing a silver-beaded dress that ripples over her like water.

"Cauliflower samosas lightly fried with a tamarind chutney dipping sauce."

I recognize her from an opening I worked last spring. It was a group showing of recent Santa Fe Art Institute grads. Her pieces were all stunning, elegant cameos made from intricately cut paper. "I love your work," I say, offering her a cocktail napkin.

"Thank you." She takes a delicate bite. "I'm just glad it's not my stuff tonight, I can sit back and enjoy the party, you know? No pressure."

"Totally." My voice comes out too chummy, like of course I can relate—me, half stoned in my dirty khakis, surviving the cutthroat career of a cater waiter. I give a peppy "Enjoy!" and leave to find Alicia.

She's in the kitchen refilling both her serving tray and a big glass of red wine.

"Eat something," I say, by way of warning. Red wine makes her weepy.

She stuffs an eggroll in her mouth and hands me one. "How great is this party? Ten points if you make out with someone in the coatroom." Our sophomore year of college, Alicia went to a frat party in Albuquerque one Saturday where she overheard a bunch of guys rating the wildest places they'd had sex and assigning each other points. She'd found it disgusting, if unsurprising, and later it became a joke between us. I told her I once gave someone a hand job on a Ferris wheel, and she sighed like that was the most mundane place a person could possibly go for a hand job. For a while, I thought she forgot about the joke, but then one Christmas she hooked up with an actor dressed as an elf at the Dillard's Santaland during business hours. They dated briefly but she grew bored and neither of us has managed to top that one, points-wise.

"Fifteen points," I say, "if you get me Jasper's number." It comes tumbling out and I immediately regret it.

"Done!"

"I'm kidding. No, don't." I sweep the bangs away from her face. Her eyes are alight with mischief. "Seriously. Don't"

Barry rushes in, briskly clapping his hands. "Friends! Less chatting, more serving!" Alicia takes a swig of her wine, grabs her tray, and evaporates into the crowd.

I'm searching the kitchen for the mini plastic spoons to stick in the tiny tiramisus, when Barry hisses, "Diana!"

He's ghostly pale. An enormous cockroach is crawling near the toe of his loafer. "I felt it *through my shoe.*"

"Deep breath. It's just a bug." It is not just a bug, it's enormous. It parts its wings and slices two long, spindly antennae through the air. "Step on it!"

"We can't kill it!" He hands me a plastic cup. "Just lure it in here and then take it outside."

"*Lure* it in?"

He nods.

"Barry."

I inch toward the cockroach, slowly, the cup in one hand, a paper towel roll in the other. Barry grips my sleeve.

"Don't miss!" he hisses.

I shake him off my shoulder and kneel on the floor, then sweep the roach into the cup and cap it with the paper towels. As I do, an antenna peeks out and Barry and I scream. He runs to open the back door and shoves me through.

In the parking lot, I crouch down and shake the cup until the roach scampers onto the asphalt. A cold wind whips through my shirt.

"That's bighearted of you." A man's voice makes me jump.

He moves into the light of the streetlamp, and I immediately recognize the Art-Throb himself. He's tall and slender, and he looks a little sheepish, like maybe I've caught him avoiding the party. He's dressed in a gray suit and crisp white T-shirt, and he's undeniably good-looking, with dark brown eyes and thick black lashes.

I straighten, dusting the gravel from my palms onto my apron. "My boss is the bighearted one. I wanted to crush it."

"Smoke?" He holds out a battered blue tin with something hand-rolled inside. "They're some kind of herbal thing to help me quit. They're terrible."

I smile. "That's all right. I have to get back. My boss is kind of a micromanager."

"That nice guy who lets you get stoned in your car?"

"You saw that?"

"Of course not." He smiles—his dimples even sexier in person—and holds out his hand. "I'm Jasper."

"Your work is beautiful. Congratulations." Is that what you say at an opening? It sounds clumsy.

"Thank you . . ."

"Diana."

"Sure you don't want one?" He offers the tin once again and I shake my head.

"It's a good show, they've done a nice job with it."

"Are you an artist?"

"Sort of. Yes. Working on it," I say. "I'm an assistant to an artist. Justine Loka."

He raises his eyebrows. "Oh, I know Justine." He laughs. "Tough job." His warm brown eyes are kind. He seems impressed. "You're a textile artist then?"

"No, I'm studying painting."

His eyes are searching mine, like he cares deeply about my answers even though we're two strangers in a cold parking lot.

"I'm working on a project where I interview different people and use what they say in my paintings, mostly in the margins."

"Like a comic?"

"Yeah, sort of like a comic strip. But they look nothing like that, graphically. I try to render the portraits romantic and intimate, but then the words are just ordinary . . . or petty. Plain and direct. Sometimes it's about that. I like the contrast."

"What do you ask them about?"

"All sorts of things." The streetlight flickers behind him. "I'm most interested in stories about things people find it hard to talk about. Things that make us uneasy. Like money . . . death, sex. Discomforting things."

"Discomforting." He extinguishes his cigarette with his boot. "Sounds really interesting."

Interesting. Ugh. I've clearly done a rotten job of articulating this. Things that *I* find discomforting: explaining what I'm currently working on. Lately I've developed an aversion to the way some of my fellow art students are too ready to sell everybody on their topic. This is why I started interviewing people before I painted them—then I could put their words in the paintings. It means someone else is talking and I'm just painting. Makes me less suspicious of what I might be up to.

"I start with charcoal pencil. Sometimes even pen," I throw in. He nods and I'm distracted by the way he moves—rocking from one foot to the next and never standing still. Even the simple way he hunches his shoulders against the cold is stealing my focus. "But most of the finished pieces are oil paintings—"

The door opens and I've never been so happy to see Silent Rod in my life.

"Um, Diana? I think we need to cut Alicia off?"

"Shit." I turn to Jasper. "Nice to meet you."

He raises his hand in a wave, and his smile is dazzling.

I find Alicia behind a table, serving coffee with fat tears streaming down her cheeks, flushed from too much wine. I slide in next to her. "What's wrong?"

"I don't know, Diana. I just keep thinking what if this is never us?" She gestures around the gallery. "We're getting old. What if we're always serving cocktail weenies? I mean, what if I have to marry Barry?"

I give her a playful shove. "Don't be a jerk."

"You know what I mean." She's gulping in air. "We know he likes me and I'd be willing to invite Rod or whomever into our marriage . . ."

"What are you even talking about?"

A woman in sparkling jewels comes to our table, her beautiful gray hair swept high in a bun. She notices Alicia's crying and eyes me. "Is she okay?"

"I'm fine." Alicia sniffs. "Just old."

I look into the woman's much older face and smile awkwardly. As she takes her coffee and leaves, I catch Barry making a beeline for us. Alicia pours a coffee for the next guest, her eyes going wide as a cockroach crawls right out of the spigot. In one fluid movement, she chucks the cup in the trash can behind her and pours another—

nothing like the way Barry and I panicked and tripped over ourselves in the kitchen.

"Hey, Barry!" He's materialized at my side. "Everything is going great." He ignores me, instead studying Alicia's mascara-streaked face. "Our friend here is working through a teeny existential crisis but in a really fun way. Coffee?"

"Clean her up," he says.

Alicia sits on the bathroom sink and I close the door behind us. She wets her apron and uses it to wipe her face. "Sorry."

"You're fine."

"Birthdays make me depressed."

"It's *my* birthday. You're still a twenty-four-year-old spring chicken!"

"Yeah, but you and me are, like, one soul, Diana." She peers at me through wet lashes. "Twenty-five. We're not babies anymore."

I blot her cheeks with a paper towel. "Van Gogh didn't start art school until he was twenty-seven . . ."

"Twenty-seven is, like, tomorrow for us. What if I never finish a film?"

"Judy Chicago didn't show her work until she was thirty-*nine*."

Alicia blows her nose and shrugs, takes some solace in this one.

"Grandma Moses was *eighty*—"

Alicia laughs. "Okay, shut the fuck up, I get it."

After we exit the bathroom, I'm so preoccupied watching Alicia, to make sure she hustles back to the kitchen, that I almost crash right into Jasper, who is now deep in conversation with a group of men in dark suits. He stops to look me in the eye, as if to say, *Everything okay?*, and I smile, my heart slamming in my chest. *What just happened?* I think, walking away. I feel the way I did the night a deer suddenly appeared in my headlights, and I swerved and managed to avoid it just in time.

For the rest of the evening, no matter where I am in the room, I can feel Jasper's eyes on me. I try not to notice. I have this idea that if

I acknowledge the attention, it will disappear. I'm careful to move in wide circles around him.

I have by now picked a favorite photograph and I linger in front of it. None of Jasper's images include people, except for this one. A young girl is running along an asphalt road, looking straight past the camera. She is surrounded by the strange desert landscape, almost like an alien planet around her, the road she's on the only trace of a human-made feature. Her legs are skinny sticks and two knobby knees.

"Do you like it?" Jasper is beside me. Standing so close that our shoulders almost touch. "I think it's my favorite. Is that okay to say about your own stuff?"

"I love it," I say.

He stays very close to me, and then moves even closer. I feel the entire left side of his body against mine and realize I'm holding my breath. He's as terrifyingly beautiful as his photos, and everyone here seems to be a little in love with him.

"It's so striking that she's the only person in your show."

He looks around the room, a slight blush on his cheeks, then waves at a photograph of a cow on the front porch of a house. "I guess we can't count Junior?"

"Ah, of course," I say. It occurs to me, a little late, how unnerving it must feel to have all your work on display like this. I regret trying to make any kind of penetrating comment. "We can't ignore that handsome face."

Jasper turns his body toward mine. "Want to get some fresh air?"

"Me?"

Jasper finds this funny. He reaches for my hand, resting his fingers softly on the inside of my palm. I open my hand wider and then lace my fingers through his, lightly. The feeling is electric and we hold hands like that, as if in secret, and make our way out of the party. Alicia looks up from the coffee station and her eyes go big. I stare at my checkered Vans and try not to laugh.

We're two feet from the back door when Sylvia descends on us, the first time I've seen her all night without her gallery assistants flanking her. Jasper and I immediately drop hands. She takes him by the arm. "A quick hello to the Wheelers then one more lap. We're nearly at the finish line." Her eyes flit across my body. "I'll take something dry, honey. The driest white you have."

"Of course," I say as Jasper is pulled into the thickening crowd.

For the rest of the night, it's like we're trying to find each other again. I circulate with trays of food and brush against his arm. When he passes me, deep in conversation with another couple, he holds out his hand so that it grazes my hip. It's intoxicating. We're both working, and both so aware of each other. In the kitchen, I turn on the tap and run cold water over my wrists.

When I emerge, with a trayful of mini blackberry crumbles, I spot Jasper near the office, talking to Sylvia but watching me. When she heads back into the crowd, he slouches against the closed door, keeping his eyes on mine. He's alone in the hallway.

"Hi," I say.

"Why are you the only person here I actually want to talk to?"

I lean against the wall next to him, close enough that my leg brushes his. Our knees touch. Then our fingers as I turn to face him. I say, "Can I?" and then I touch his lips. As my fingers drop away, we fall into a kiss.

It's long and slow. An entire night of foreplay leading to a rush of excitement as our lips finally meet. There is no experimenting to see what the other likes, nothing tentative or unsure. He moves in front of me, his body facing mine, and presses his hands against the wall on either side of me. The sensation it creates is like being in a tunnel. We're protected here, shielded from the party, just the two of us and the echoes of this good feeling.

He's taller than me so when we kiss, he leans down and tilts my chin up to meet him. Then he pulls back and the corners of his mouth lift into a small smile. He runs his hands down the length of my arms and bends even lower to kiss my neck.

My senses are overwhelmed by the scent of his expensive shampoo, the sharp taste of vodka he leaves on my lips, the sting of his stubble on my cheek, and the press of his erection against my thigh. This isn't the first time I've made out with a boy I've met at a party or shared a furtive kiss near a crowd of people. I've had sex on a first date. I can hold my own in a game of *Never Have I Ever*. But this feels different. I'm not waiting to be kissed or even wondering if I should be here at all. Everything in me wants to take the lead, and nothing is run first through the tight filter of my mind. I clasp my fingers around the back of his neck and pull him closer, turning us until his back is against the wall. I lean into his muscular frame, pressing him to the office door. Then I reach just past his hip for the doorknob.

I crack open the door and for a moment, neither of us moves. I take his face between my hands, his eyes sparkling but hard to read. "Can you leave your own party?"

He kisses me again, tugging on my bottom lip with his teeth. "Yes."

Inside the office it is dark and cool. Standing in the middle of the room, I slide my hands under his jacket so that it falls onto the desk behind him. His T-shirt is thin and the bare skin of his arms is warm. He circles both of my wrists in one of his hands and lifts them over my head. When he lets go, I leave my arms suspended this way as he undoes the top button of my shirt. His eyes search mine, and I want to melt into him.

"Diana?" His breath is quick.

"Yeah?"

"It's really nice to meet you."

We both smile.

"Pretty great party," I add.

"Pretty great." He laughs. "Maybe the best." He kisses me more urgently and I imagine we're alone on an island, where we can stay like this, uninterrupted, for days.

He carefully undoes each of my buttons from top to bottom then pulls my shirt down my arms until it lands at my feet. He bites his bottom lip, studying me, and a heat spreads through my body. I watch his chest move under his shirt. I reach my hands beneath it and up his muscled back, pulling it off over his head. I touch his naked skin and his breathing gets harder. Faster. I press my mouth to his. His full mouth.

I take his hand and lay it against my chest. "Fast," I say.

He leaves his hand there for a long, easy moment feeling my racing heartbeat. He places my hand over his own heart. "Faster," he replies.

I run my hands through his hair as he leans back onto the desk, pulling me to him. I look into his eyes and we both smile, wondering how we got here.

"Jasper!" A hard rap on the door. A voice like daggers. "Jasper! I need you!"

He sighs.

"Jasper!" Sylvia knocks again.

"You better go," I whisper, laughing.

"Okay," he calls over my shoulder, still looking deep into my eyes. He sighs again. "I'm sorry."

He kisses me quickly and smiles his dimpled smile. He pulls on his T-shirt, then his jacket, and he's gone.

I stay alone in the office. Dressing very slowly. I should definitely get back to work, but first I slip into the bathroom where I splash my face with water. A smile breaks across my face.

Outside the bathroom, I hear a pop of a champagne bottle and loud cheering. When I come out, Jasper is standing next to Sylvia who grins from ear to ear. Silent Rod comes up next to me and whispers, "Sold every piece here. The big ones went for seven grand." It's the longest strand of words Rod has ever spoken to me.

Jasper raises a glass and looks at the small crowd of friends and staff who have gathered. "Thank you to everyone for being here. I was a pile of raw nerves earlier, but y'all didn't miss a beat. I went from not wanting the night to begin to not wanting it to ever end." He bows his head slightly. "This really has been about years of work for me and my fierce champion, Ms. Cross." Sylvia beams like a schoolgirl, clutching her heart and mouthing *thank you* for the crowd to see.

Then Jasper's eyes dance across his audience until they land on me. I can't help casually turning my head to make sure there isn't someone else behind me. But it's just an empty doorway. My gaze meets his and it's so startling that I look down and audibly exhale, as if my body is attempting to put out the fire he creates. Around me, the crowd shifts, waiting for Jasper to continue. When the silence goes on a beat too long, I lift my head and my eyes meet Jasper's again. He smiles and continues, "The night took many unexpected turns." Even the sound of his voice, easy and sure, turns me on. "One in particular that I haven't quite gotten over."

"The Desert Ten selling before we even served a single drink, maybe?" Sylvia laughs. If Jasper heard her, he doesn't acknowledge it. Instead he looks directly at me and says, "Pretty great party." My cheeks burn a deep pink. I smile and mouth, *The best.* Then Jasper clears his throat, releasing us both from his spell. His eyes fall away from mine and sweep the room. He showers his dazzling smile on the entire crowd. He's not just mine anymore. But he's still fun to watch. He lifts his glass. "Cheers."

Sylvia raises a glass toward the back of the room. "This was you too!" she says insincerely to the staff. "This entire night was perfect!"

"Cheers," I say quietly, suddenly realizing I don't have a glass to raise. I wipe my sweaty hands on my apron and try not to smile too big.

Then I watch Jasper as he's pulled back into a web of admirers, a sticky mix of heartfelt congratulations, kisses, and jealousy. There's no more eye contact and slowly, steadily, as the party wears on, what happened in the office seems like days not minutes ago. I have to remind myself it really happened and I didn't just dream it up.

So that it doesn't slip through my fingers completely, I take the feeling of being in that office with him—the surprising rush of desire and affection—and I imagine folding it neatly, like a cocktail napkin, and tucking it away. This way, I tell myself, I won't forget the feeling. Or maybe, folded away, it won't sting if we never return to it.

An hour later, after the gallery has completely emptied out, Alicia pulls out a quarter. "Heads, you take out the garbage, tails you warm up the car." To make up for being such assholes tonight, Alicia and I told Barry to let us handle the cleanup. We've already swept and mopped the floors, scrubbed out the oven, and wiped down all the kitchen counters.

She flips the coin in the air, and it clatters to the gallery's wood floor. Heads. I groan and hand her my car keys so she can warm up the car.

I'm doing a terrible job at not being disappointed that Jasper didn't find me in the kitchen to say good night, but staying busy helps. I roll out the big trash can for collection and throw two heavy-duty bags into the dumpster. The cold night air feels good on my face. *It was just impulse,* I tell myself. What really bothers me, though, is this feeling that I miss him. Is that even possible? Twenty-four hours ago, we'd never met and I hardly knew he existed.

When I get to my car, I see Barry has duct-taped my rear bumper back on. Of course he has. Alicia is curled up asleep in the back seat. I get in, and it's freezing cold, even with the heat blasting. I look out the windshield and see that someone has left a rectangular package against the wiper. I get back out to grab it, then flip on the overhead light. There's a note written in Magic Marker on the paper wrapping.

Diana, I think this is your car. And this definitely belongs to you.

—Jasper

P.S. If you're not Diana, then you're a thief and please return this to Sylvia Cross at Cross Gallery. Reward offered.

Jasper is long gone, I know, but I can't shake the feeling I've had all night, that he's watching me still. I carefully open the wrapping, my heartbeat picking up. And there it is, the photograph I loved so much. I've never been given a gift like this. I stare at it for a full minute before I grin into the rearview mirror, then I angle it down to watch Alicia breathing, fast asleep in the back seat. Nobody here but me to witness my reunion with the running girl. I set my gift on the passenger seat. Then I drive Alicia home, reaching out each time I stop to keep the photograph from sliding forward.

Chapter 10

It's two weeks of thinking of Jasper constantly, without end, and then one day, I show up for work at Justine's studio and find him pacing out front. My heart and stomach switch places. It has snowed overnight, a light April storm, and there's a dusting of untouched powder on every surface. At first he doesn't notice me and I watch him walking back and forth. He's in short sleeves despite the weather, and he runs his fingers through his dark hair, longer since I last saw him.

He exhales, leaving icy clouds in the air, and when he catches sight of me, he shoves his hands into the pockets of his jeans. He looks like an anxious teenager.

"Hey," I say. "How long have you been out here? It's freezing."

It's not clear to me whether he's here to see me or Justine.

"Diana. I hope you don't mind me showing up at your work." He blows into his hands and rubs them together for warmth. "But I'm totally fucked and I couldn't think of anyone else to ask for help." I'm thrown by his panicked look. I had expected the composed guy of the gallery opening, but now he seems genuinely distressed. His eyes are ringed with dark circles.

"Are you okay?"

"My assistant quit on me and now I've got no help and a huge shoot."

"Oh." I'm relieved it's just work that has him worried. Or am I? For a split second I had thought his unease was over me, somehow, and he meant to say, *I'm totally fucked because I haven't been able to stop thinking about you and so I tracked you down.* "When's the shoot?"

"I'm supposed to be in Marfa tomorrow; it's a magazine editorial and a cover. I screwed up and no-showed on an assignment for them last year, and they're making a big deal about giving me a second chance." Over his shoulder, I notice the vintage blue-and-white Ford from his *Aperture* photo. I was so sure it was just a prop, not his actual truck. "I need to leave in the next hour to get there before sundown so I can set up for tomorrow. It's a quick job, but a big one. I can't show up without an assistant." Jasper gives me a funny look. "Diana. Please?"

"Me?" I laugh. "I don't know anything about photography. Also, I have to work. And it's in Texas?" He looks down at his boots and traces an arc in the fallen snow. And we hardly know each other. Why me? When he doesn't say anything, I add again, "And I don't know anything about photography."

He looks up at me and smiles. "But you're an artist and I really just need someone with a good eye. *And* you work for Justine, which means you've already worked for an incredible hard-ass so this will feel like a walk in the park. Or the desert, I guess." He smiles again and all I can think is *Art-Throb, how fitting.* "I'd tell you where to hold the lights. You'd hand me lenses. Seriously, Diana, it might be fun. And I'll pay you double for any work you miss."

I take a step back, because I can't think properly when I'm standing so close to him. His explanation sounds reasonable. Cut-and-dried. Like it's just work. Which is for the best. I could use the extra money, and I've always wanted to see Marfa. Justine leaves tomorrow for two days visiting family, so if Melodie can fill in for me today, I could make up the hours next week. "Are you sure this is a good idea?"

"Maybe?" He laughs. "You'd be saving my life. And if you're worried that there are any weird kind of strings attached, please don't. You'll have your own hotel room, and I have a decent budget—we'll work hard, eat well, and you'll have a little time to see Marfa, if you haven't already."

Annoyingly, my body had said yes the minute he appeared in the parking lot, before he'd even asked the favor, but my brain is still trying to catch up.

"Let me make a call."

Jasper grins. "That's a yes?"

"Sure. It's insane, but I'll do it."

His eyes widen in surprise—and I wonder, then, if I should have said no.

The weather takes several huge swings on our seven-hour drive from New Mexico to Texas, much like the energy inside the truck's cab. At first, the drive is peaceful and we're both quiet for a while, calmed by the muted colors of the desert sliding by. Jasper smokes his herbal cigarettes, drumming his fingers to the music. I make an effort not to be noticeably quiet, but my mind is racing, trying to figure out exactly what we are to each other. Friends? Employer and employee? Friends who might have sex? Jasper gives me nothing but mixed signals on the drive. When we stop for gas he brings me a lollipop, like he's presenting me a bouquet of roses. In the next breath, he asks me to check the case at my feet and inventory his lenses, a painful reminder that I'm being paid to be on this trip. "And could you call the hotel," he asks, "to confirm our reservation?"

Halfway to Marfa, we pull off the highway for something to eat. Jasper's never hungry before a big job, he says, so we sit in the bed of his truck and he watches me eat a plate of nachos. The sun is high in the sky and the sharp piney air mixes with the salty food. It's windy enough that I have to tuck the hem of my dress tightly between my legs and sit on my napkins to keep them from flying away. By the time I finish, the weather has shifted again. The clouds are fat with coming rain and I wish I hadn't left my sweater in the cab. I take a sip of my drink and shiver.

"Here." Jasper drapes his jacket across my shoulders.

"Thanks."

"Of course." He pulls the collar tight around my neck and starts to button the coat from the bottom up. When he gets to the last one, our eyes meet. He drops his hands and looks up at the gray sky. "We should probably get going, anyway."

For the next hundred miles, we hum along to the Police and any weird tension slowly melts away. We can work together and still have fun, I tell myself. I begin to wonder, too, if I imagined the way he froze buttoning up the coat. By the time Little Feat's "Willin'" comes on, it's sunny again and we're singing along, loud and terrible.

Jasper turns up the volume. Instead of resting his hand back on the wheel, he places it on the center console, inches from mine. Both of us watch the road straight ahead. When I do glance at him, he bites his lower lip and runs a hand through his hair. Then he replaces his hand again, next to mine. Our fingers are so close I can feel the heat of his skin.

Long minutes pass where neither one of us moves. Jasper clears his throat and lets his ring and pinkie fingers rest on top of mine. My heart races. He traces my hand with his finger and looks at me. "No jewelry?"

"No," I say, quietly. "I've never worn it."

Jasper's hand lingers and he shifts in his seat. The late-afternoon sun beats through the front windshield. When it's too hot to ignore, he rolls down his window. I pretend not to notice and let the wind lift my dress high up my thighs. I hear his sharp inhalation and turn my head toward the window so he can't see my smile.

Close to Marfa, he tells me about his favorite restaurant in town and says we should have dinner there tonight. "You'll love it," he tells me, and I don't know what excites me more—the thought of being on a date with Jasper or the idea that he's already guessing at what I'll like.

I spend the last few miles of the drive quietly imagining Jasper is my fiancé and we take weekend getaways like this often. Packing our bags and heading out on the next adventure. I don't even realize that I'm smiling when Jasper pulls up to the location of the shoot.

The house we've come to photograph is a massive adobe structure with large circular windows facing out on a desert garden of prickly pear cactus and brilliant red salvia bushes. The walkway is lined with large agave plants and tall stalks of rain sage showing tiny lavender flowers. Jasper's subject—a country music singer named Annie James—opens the door to her house in bare feet. She is petite and beaming, with neatly made features and warm eyes. She is wearing a loose white cotton shirt and heavily beaded necklaces, which clack against each other as she wraps us in a hug. "I'm so happy you're here!"

Nothing about the home's plain exterior prepares you for the grandeur of the inside. We enter a large room like an atrium with a ceiling made of steel and glass. Sunlight splashes down on the white walls and cream-colored floors and catches each crystal petal of the two massive chandeliers. An oil portrait of Annie brandishing a guitar hangs on one wall, and there is a white grand piano on a furry white rug. A row of waist-high ceramic vases hold stalks of feathery pampas grass.

At a long wood table, a woman with close-cropped hair is arranging camelias in bowls of water, her long gold earrings brushing against her shoulders. A small man in a squat bowler hat is helping himself to a dish of strawberries and cream. "My publicists," Annie says by way of introduction. "We're in a bit of a crisis." She lets out a throaty laugh. I've never seen three people look less in crisis, but we just nod.

"Nothing Jeremy can't handle," says Annie pointedly, staring at the man in the bowler. "Let me show you around."

Maybe it's the long drive or the soft perfection of the light, but by the time we reach the upstairs I am wondering why a house like this would need to be photographed. If it were mine, I would not want it to appear in a magazine. I would wander these rooms in private, probably congratulating myself for whatever I'd done to acquire it.

"I spent so much time as an expat in Europe, I guess I really fell in love with Georgian proportions," Annie says. "It made me want a home that felt grand but still welcoming." She gestures to a massive fireplace in one of the bedrooms covered in mosaic for her by a local artist. In the next room, a handmade quilt, a gift, she says, from a Tuvan shaman she met in Russia.

The house is full of art and very few everyday objects. I'm lingering in a large bathroom, peering into a copper bathtub that shows no signs of use. There's toilet paper on the roll holder but no soap, no shampoo, nothing in the medicine cabinets. I hear Jasper cry out excitedly, "Diana, check this out!" and find them at the other end of the long hallway. There on the wall is one of Justine's pieces—a beautiful blue-and-gold tapestry. "How crazy is that?" Jasper grins at me with something like pride and explains to Annie that I work with Justine.

Annie looks genuinely starstruck, even though I'm only an assistant. "When I saw it, it reminded me so much of Marfa. I just had to have it." I know this tapestry—it used to hang in Justine's studio and was finished shortly before I was hired. I start to say that it was inspired by a Talking Heads song, but Jasper and Annie have already moved on toward the next bedroom.

Annie and Jasper find a million things to talk about. They discover two friends in common, and a mutual love for the now-defunct Panorama club in Berlin. Both attended the same performance piece last summer in New York City—oh, they must have been days apart! I can't shake the sinking feeling that I'm on someone else's first date.

By the time we head downstairs, Annie's two publicists are packing up to leave and I'm ready to follow. As everyone kisses goodbye, I stand woodenly nearby. Jasper notices and presses the keys to the truck into my hand. "Why don't you get some air. I'll be right out."

I'm grateful for a moment alone in the car. I slip low in my seat just as the sun is beginning to set and the intense beauty of the light makes me catch my breath. The horizon is like a child's painting, a strip of golden light under a strip of cobalt blue sky and above that a layer of moody gray-black clouds. Annie's not wrong, the blues and gold in Justine's piece match the Marfa sky exactly.

Jasper taps the window and I roll it down. "Hand me that black case behind the seat?" he asks. I slide it through the window. "Listen, I have to do a little bit of prep work before we lose the light, and Annie just invited me for dinner. Do you feel okay driving the truck to the hotel?" He reaches over me and fumbles through the glove compartment. "Here's the address. I'll call ahead and let them know you're checking in without me."

"Of course," I say. My stomach sinks at the thought of going to the hotel alone. "You don't need me to carry any more stuff in?" But he is already headed back inside.

At the hotel, I check into my room and collapse onto the bed. I'm swallowed up by the size of the room, with its big, brightly colored rugs, an oversize pink-striped chair, and an entire wall of floor-to-ceiling windows. How had I gotten this so wrong? There were no mixed signals.

Jasper wasn't using this shoot as an excuse to spend time with me or whisk me out of town. He needed an assistant. Plain and simple. I was an employee and it was convenient and, more humiliatingly, he knew I would say yes. Maybe I wasn't even the first person he asked. I flip onto my stomach and groan into one of many king-size pillows.

I cut myself a deal. I can wallow in my disappointment over Jasper bailing on me for the length of a hot shower, and then I'll get to work.

I have my tape recorder with me and the interview I've just done with a college friend named Brynn. I asked her specifically about her sex life because I remembered her as having been very embarrassed to talk about such things. She surprised me by taking up the whole interview with tales of sex escapades she'd had since we'd last seen each other. I decided I was going to use the interview's steamiest bits for a new series of paintings I would dedicate to Alicia called "Points."

The bathroom is also designed for more than one person with a generous clawfoot tub and a separate shower with multiple shower heads. I step inside and let the warm water run over my face and name all the reasons why coming on this trip was a dumb idea. I realize I would have said yes even knowing the trip was purely work, just to spend time with Jasper. Certain images of him are impossible to forget. Like the night of his show, the two of us in the hallway, pressed against the office door. Or his hand over my heart when we couldn't stop kissing.

I open the shower door and emerge in a dramatic billow of steam. I'm revitalized and I have an idea for how to paint Brynn. I pull on a pair of sweatpants and set myself up on the bed, sketching with charcoal pencil. I'm listening to Brynn talk about sneaking into a movie theater after it closed.

I should have known he didn't really work there when he pulled out a credit card and jimmied the lock.

In quick strokes, I draw a rectangle and place Brynn in the center of the movie screen dressed like a 1940s starlet. Then I run her dialogue like subtitles along the bottom.

I was too excited to care. Maybe more *excited because we might get caught.*

I take a break to check my phone, pretending—but failing—not to watch it in hopes that Jasper will call. I toy with the idea of texting him. Something friendly and upbeat. Casual, even.

How's dinner? Nope. Delete. I have never texted Jasper so why would I now breezily interrupt his night with Annie?

Unless it's just to let him know I got in okay? *Checked into hotel. Room is great.* It sounds less officious and more desperate. Delete.

To make myself laugh, I type, *Room 112. Fuck me senseless?* But instead of smiling, I roll my eyes and chuck the phone far away, to the end of the bed, where it bounces off a pillow and clatters to the floor.

Maybe I should just act like an actual assistant and ask him what time we start tomorrow. I pick the phone up off the floor.

And there it is. An envelope flying across the screen. And then: *Message sent.*

No. No, no. God no. I scroll to confirm that it did indeed send to Jasper. *Room 112. Fuck me senseless?* I scream loud enough to wake the entire hotel. There must be something I can do. A way to delete the text. There's no way. Do I drive to Annie's house and find Jasper's phone before he checks it? My face burns a deep crimson, imagining him gently chuckling with Annie over dinner, shaking his head at my sweet crush. Or what if Annie reacts more earnestly, "Be careful. She sounds a bit unhinged." I will leave. I will somehow find a ride back to Santa Fe and disappear.

I almost call Alicia, then reconsider. If I don't tell a soul, maybe I can block it out. I check the phone, apprehensively, for a reply, then turn it off, afraid to touch it ever again.

The woman at the front desk points me toward a small liquor store across the street and I buy a half-pint of vodka. My new brilliant plan is to drink until I fall asleep and tomorrow I'll blame it on the alcohol.

I pass a young couple holding hands, on their way to a night out, and I tuck the paper bag beneath my sweatshirt. I debate ordering room service, but it's so expensive and I can't decide what's a reasonable amount to spend on someone else's expense account. So I order a pizza with olives and turn on *Dateline*, slowly sipping on my drink. I turn my phone back on, praying for the off chance that Jasper thought it was a hilarious joke and responded with something equally funny. But there is no response. Minutes pass like hours and I try to lose myself in Stone Phillips and an unsolved murder.

A quiet knock on my door and I thank god for the pizza I ordered. I open the door, still searching my purse for my wallet, and look up to find Jasper standing on the other side. Too surprised to say hello, I just stare.

And then he holds up his phone, his eyebrows raised, and I want to sink through the floor.

"I was drinking," is all I can think to say.

He shoves his hands in his pockets. "Can I come in?"

"Sure." His expression is unreadable, his hair tousled and his stubble even darker. He's still dressed from the road, so he must have come right from Annie's.

"How was dinner?"

"Good. Ended early."

"Oh." My heart starts to pound in my chest. "Why?"

"I told her I was exhausted."

"Of course. Yeah, me too."

He grips the back of the pink-striped chair, then sweeps his eyes over the room. I'm painfully aware of my wet towel on the bed, my suitcase spilling onto the floor.

"They gave you my room."

"Sorry?"

"This is my room. I had the suite."

"Oh." Is that why he's here? "I can pack up my stuff. I had no idea."

He blushes. "No, no. You should stay."

Someone knocks on the door. I pay the bellman who's brought up my pizza while Jasper does a slow lap around the room. He notices my sketch of Brynn on the bed and picks it up. "You did this just tonight? It's beautiful." It's the way he looks at it so closely and holds the paper by the edges so delicately that feels especially good.

He looks up at me. "Did you get a tub? I requested a bathtub."

"I did, yeah." I look down at my sweats, bare feet, chipped polish. I've never so simultaneously wanted someone to stay and leave.

He takes the pizza box from me and sets it on the desk. "Let's take a bath."

"Now?"

"Yeah, now." He smiles. "If you want to?" I can't think of anything I want more. "Run the water how you like it. I'm fine with whatever."

In the bathroom, I turn away from him, filling the tub with mostly hot water. Behind me, I hear the pearl buttons of his denim shirt as they hit the tiled floor. I pretend to adjust the bath's temperature while I watch his reflection in the mirror.

As he undresses, I take in his toned arms, his biceps flexing as he pulls his belt through the loops of his jeans and drops them both to the floor. Steam begins to fill the room. Jasper stretches his ribbed tank over his shoulders exposing his taut stomach. A dark, narrow trail of hair runs from the center of his chest all the way down to his boxers. Longing flows through my entire body as I wait expectantly for him to take them off. I can't help myself. I turn to face him and his lips turn up in a crooked smile, knowing he's being watched. As he slips out of his boxers, his uncut penis rises. He's already aroused.

Jasper lowers himself into the water and tilts his head back. "You coming in?" Then he closes his heavy-lidded eyes, as if knowing I'm less sure about how to undress as casually as he did.

I lift my T-shirt over my head, tiny beads of sweat caught at my breasts, then slip out of my sweats. Completely naked, I step into the hot water. Jasper watches me now, making room for me as I ease my-self in. I sit facing him and pull my knees toward my chest. I lean back until I'm submerging my face in the water, taking a long beat beneath the surface. When I come up, neither of us moves. I can feel his gaze on my face, my shoulders, then lingering on my breasts.

"So." He finally breaks the quiet. "About this text. I didn't realize you were *also* a poet." He breaks into a smile and my face flushes red. Without thinking, I splash him in the face and he pretends to cower, laughing.

"Sorry!" He holds up both hands in defense. "Sorry. It was a very nice text. Maybe one of my favorites."

"Is that why you're here?" I ask, in mock offense.

"No. I would have knocked on your door regardless. The text just added a little urgency."

I smile. The air has been cleared. And now it's just us. Rugged, handsome Jasper naked and wet, inches away from me. It feels like a dream I never want to wake from.

He takes my foot in his hand and massages me with his strong fingers, then works his way up my calf. My whole body quivers. "And so you've come here to answer it?" I ask.

Jasper sits up and slips his arms around my waist. "I'll be honest. I was hoping we could fuck *each other* senseless."

Every morning since meeting him, I have lain in bed after waking up and tried to imagine what it would be like to be Jasper's lover. What would he say? How would he take my clothes off? Would he talk during sex? What would he sound like? What would he feel like inside me?

Now he's here in front of me, close enough that I can I feel the heat from his body. He pulls me close for a kiss. His tongue is so hungry for mine and I'm just as eager, wrapping my legs around his torso so I can get closer.

"I missed you all day," he tells me. "Even when you were right next to me in the truck."

I press my forehead to his. "What exactly did you miss?"

"This." He grips my hips with both hands and lifts me up out of the water. I hold the sides of the tub for support as he pulls me to his mouth, parting my lips with his tongue and entering me with a force I don't expect. He moves his tongue in and out and it feels so incredible I want him to slow down but I also can't imagine changing anything about the sensation. I press my thighs to his head, the warm water lapping against my back and onto my stomach, his stubble rough against my skin.

My head feels light and dizzy and I think he can read my mind when he moves his hands up my back and says, "I won't let you fall."

I open my legs wider and he slowly licks up my inner thighs, then takes his time stroking me with his tongue, varying the pressure and movement, which makes my nerve endings want to explode.

"More," I say, but it doesn't sound like my voice. I don't even know where it's coming from, somewhere so deep inside. Jasper leans back slightly, and gently pulls me with him. I'm spinning at this point but I need to feel him. I reach beneath the water and grab hold of his erection. As he sucks me, I massage him with one hand, feeling him grow even harder.

Our touches become frenzied, panicked, as if this kind of extreme pleasure won't last and we need to keep it all in. When he moans, his lips vibrate between my legs and I'm so raw, the sensation so intense, that all I want to do is come into his mouth. And then, without warning, I feel him pulsing in my hands and it sends me nearly over the edge. But we both stop at the same moment, knowing we are seconds away from orgasm.

I lower myself back beneath the surface of the water and when I come up for air, Jasper takes my hands in his and pulls us out of the bath. I wrap us both in towels and lead him toward the bed.

He lies still while I dry him off slowly, running the towel down his body and paying special attention to his erect penis, perfectly smooth and big enough to fill me completely. My body warms with excitement thinking of him inside me.

He pulls me onto the bed and I stretch my body close to his, resting my head on his chest. When he lifts my chin, his lips graze mine. A shiver runs down my spine. I close my eyes briefly, and when I open them again, he peers into them. The diamond cut of his eyes floats in my vision while his calloused fingers trace their way down my body back to my inner thighs. I climb on top of him and pull his arms over his head and kiss the hollow of his neck, his nipples—a trail of kisses down the skin that slopes from his shoulder blades. His breath goes ragged and the sound makes me want to swallow him entirely. I sit up, resting my hips against his. With the softest part of my body, I feel how hard he is. He slides a finger into my mouth.

"Diana," he says, his voice thick. "You feel so good."

"So do you."

"Tell me what you want"

I put my mouth to his ear. "I want you inside me. I want to sleep with you inside me."

"Fuck," he groans. I slip off him and he grabs for my hips. "Where are you going?"

I stand naked at the foot of the bed. "I want to show you."

"God, you're beautiful." He grips the pillow beneath his head with both hands.

I sit in the pink-striped chair and hold his gaze. Then slowly I spread my legs, opening myself up to him. I slip a finger inside me, and he watches it disappear, in and out, his mouth slightly open. I close my eyes with the pleasure of being watched, then open them again to see him stroke himself slowly. We find our timing together. As he strokes himself all the way down to the base of his erection, I plunge a finger deep inside me, as if he's making love to me.

"Fuck," he moans again. "Diana. I need to be inside you."

We've put it off for as long as we can handle. Our breathing fast and shallow. I walk to the bed and straddle his waist, pressing myself against the warmth of his stomach. He opens his eyes, pleadingly. "Please."

I lean down and kiss him, breathing him in. I take him in my hand and lightly tease his erection against my opening. We both moan, aching for the same sensation.

I let go of him and spread my legs letting him know I'm ready. He kisses me hard, and I lower myself onto him. He slides deep inside me, in and out, and I'm convinced nothing in the world feels better. Then he straightens his legs and lifts his hips, just slightly off the bed, longing to be closer to me. I give him what we both want, pressing my pelvis firmly into his. The feeling of fullness, of him inside me, makes me cry out in pleasure.

Jasper sits up and wraps his arms around the small of my back. He kisses my forehead then moves to my ear, biting me gently on the lobe before whispering in my ear. "I'm so fucking happy you said yes."

I picture myself in the snowy parking lot, trying to decide what to do. "Me too."

He thrusts deeper into me and I arch my back, grabbing onto his legs to keep from falling onto the bed. He slides in and out of me, and we move together like this, closer and faster, until we're both pulled under by the crashing pleasure—both our bodies climaxing then collapsing into each other.

Afterward, the room is quiet. Our bodies are still trembling. Sex shouldn't be this good. He offers me water from the nightstand and we both take a long drink.

In the dark he says, "I want to keep you in this room forever. And never let you leave." I smile as he drapes an arm over my belly and stretches a leg across mine. Within minutes, he's asleep.

It's a fitful sleep. I feel him toss in the bed, and when I finally begin drifting off, he shifts again. I open my eyes and he grins hungrily. I'm wide awake once more. He pulls me close and props himself up on an elbow. "Thank you for showing me how to touch you." He traces a hand down my stomach. "Can I try?"

"Yes." I spread my legs. Slowly, he moves his fingers in and out, exactly as I had done. I close my eyes and picture my own body curled around his. "I can't get enough of you, Diana." And then he's inside me, pushing deeper and harder, and we're fucking, but this time faster, with more urgency, my fingers digging into the smooth skin of his back. When I feel him coming, everything inside me tightens again with pleasure, and something bright and blinding creeps in at the edges of my vision, as though I might pass out. Then we lie back on the bed, panting and laughing.

At Annie's the next day I feel drunk. I can still smell Jasper on my skin. After he went back to his room, I showered but not with soap, hoping that his smell would stay on me. On the ride to Annie's house, he'd told me what we'd be shooting, which rooms in which order using what equipment. I was on the tour with him, wasn't I? I realize how little I'd taken in.

"Diana," Jasper says, "where's the twenty-five?"

I look around me at the sea of equipment spread around Annie's kitchen. We're shooting Annie in various casual-seeming positions around the room she probably uses the least. I peeked in her refrigerator and there was a carton of milk, some organic blueberries, and a jar of face cream made with manuka honey. Does she have another kitchen, I wonder, where the food actually is?

"Diana? The twenty-five?"

Recognizing my limitations, Jasper comes over to grab it.

I manage to finish out the day by thinking of everything as a tray of hors d'oeuvres that I need to pass out. It's a kind of meditation. This camera lens is any one of Barry's minicreations. The bounce boards are platters. This man asking me for a lens is the host. You don't talk to hosts. You just smile at them politely. That spectacular woman being photographed is just another guest at a party who won't eat what I offer her.

· · ·

"You were quiet today," Jasper says as we're driving back to the hotel late that evening.

"Was I?" He's clearly finding the delineation between work and play much easier than I am. Every time he gets near me I want to slip my hands under his clothes and feel his bare skin on mine.

Jasper nods. "Very quiet. You have this talent for making yourself invisible. I've noticed that. It's like you're getting smaller before my very eyes."

Maybe to seem bold, I place a hand on his leg and rest my fingers against his inner thigh.

He stares straight ahead, then slows and pulls to the side of the road, still a few miles from the hotel. There is nothing around us but the desert scenery and the deep black sky. I climb onto his lap and straddle his hips. "I've been waiting for this all day," I say.

"Me too."

I slip my hands under his T-shirt, feeling his warm skin. I unbutton his jeans and slide his erection inside me. We both exhale in relief—relief that it still feels this good, that he is finally back inside me where he belongs. I begin moving my hips, but he stops me, his voice rough in my ear. "I'm going to come . . . Don't move. Please. Don't move." So we both sit there, still, staring at each other like aliens dropped from the sky into a magical field. Neither of us moves an inch. We don't close our eyes or look away. Jasper teeters on the edge of orgasm—he bites on his lip as the pleasure rolls through him and I clench myself around him, tighter. That's when my own pleasure floods through me, meeting his, waves rolling over us both. Sweat drips from his forehead and down the middle of his chest.

After a quiet minute Jasper asks, "Are you a witch?"

"No," I say, laughing.

"Has that ever happened to you?"

"Has someone made me come just by looking at me?" I ask. "No. That's never happened before. Not even close."

"Good."

The boldness I felt on that first night at the gallery has never left my body. But there's an intimacy that has come to meet it tonight—and it has taken us both by surprise. I feel the hot prick of tears behind my eyes and quickly turn my head, looking out the window at the stars stretched across the night sky. I don't want Jasper to see me cry and mistake this feeling I'm having—a kind of happiness at the overwhelming feeling of our intimacy—for sadness.

He reaches for my hand and holds it in his. When I turn, he's looking out his own window. His voice comes out low and hoarse. "I was thinking about staying here in Marfa for a few more days. Maybe renting an Airstream at Cosmico, maybe even camping and checking out the Marfa lights. Would you want to stay with me?"

I don't think about missing shifts or how pissed Justine will be if I fall behind or any of the usual excuses. I don't wait for my fears to well up and spill over. I just say yes.

That night, we check into our rented Airstream. It's painted turquoise and pink and has its own small shower. We squeeze in together, and Jasper lathers my entire body with soap, working from my feet up to my shoulders. Then he gently shampoos my hair and wraps me in a robe. We lie together on the queen-size bed and I fall into a deep sleep, my head on his chest.

Morning is my favorite time of day in Marfa. The air is cold and the sun is just starting to burn. The sky is a light show, at first pale and moody and then, by early afternoon, beginning to slap on its makeup. We wrap blankets around ourselves and drink coffee by the fire in front of the Airstream. I tuck my feet under me and feel giddy. I don't need anything more than this. I really think I could stay for months, surviving on only sex and s'mores.

We visit the same spot each day for lunch, and then shop for supplies in the tiny grocery next door, which caters to a wide range of eating habits—bologna in the same aisle as organic tofu, boxes of Fruity Pebbles next to hand-labeled bags of heirloom grains.

Packs of dogs roam the desert during the day and one straggler makes its way to the porch of our Airstream. She's a chihuahua mix, with two milky eyes and a patch of mange on her forehead. Her nipples are dark and rubbery from countless litters and she has an underbite that makes her look as though she's permanently growling. I sit down slowly, and she runs into my lap, tail wagging. "Look at this!" I say, and Jasper startles when he sees her.

"Is that a dog?"

"Yes, it's a dog. She's cold, I think. And obviously not in the best shape."

"I thought it was an armadillo." Jasper takes a step toward us and the dog growls, warning him away. "I'm not going to hurt you, buddy."

"I don't think she likes men," I tell him.

"All dogs like me." He reaches out a hand and she nips him. A bright red drop of blood appears on his skin.

Jasper sits a safe distance away and snaps her picture, getting acquainted with her through his lens. She lifts her head regally, turning the most egregious spot of mange away from the camera.

He doesn't give up. He goes back to the grocery for a pack of hot dogs, and he breaks off small pieces and feeds them to her until he can pet her without her tensing up. That afternoon, we spread our blanket out by the fire, and she hops in between us.

"Is this our dog now?" he asks. I can tell we both hate the idea of her all alone in the desert. "Because let's be honest, no one else is going to love this dog. Ever."

I can't help it—my heart leaps at the idea of owning something with Jasper. I hold her up to the sky like a proud parent. "She's pretty cute. In a horrible way."

Jasper smiles. "She's got charm."

Later we give her a bath in the Airstream's tiny sink and do our best to get the prickers out of her fur. Jasper squeezes some of his expensive conditioner into his palm and rubs it into her skin. We name her Pippi. By the end of the night, she's sleeping on Jasper's face.

"I can't move. I live here now," Jasper jokes.

We move her gently to a spot on the bench. And then he kisses me deeply and I climb on top of him on the bed. I'm struck by the way our bodies fit together, two pieces of a clasp to a delicate necklace. His tongue explores my mouth and I bite down on his lip, lightly. He tastes like saltwater and smells like campfire and I want to stay here forever, breathing him in.

He moves his hands up my shirt and my body responds immediately, my nipples hard and wanting. I pull my shirt over my head, then remove his. I skim my naked breasts across his bare chest and he pulls me close. Pippi starts growling. We stop what we're doing immediately, laughing. Pippi calms down and closes her milky eyes, but as soon as Jasper pushes inside me she sits up on high alert.

"How does she even know what we're doing? She's got to be legally blind?"

"Pippi knows all," I say, laughing.

"Can we not talk about Pippi while we make love?"

Love. "Sure." I smile, an intoxicating mixture of happiness and desire running through my body. "Pippi, look away! Hide your eyes!"

Chapter 11

I accidentally jab my finger with an embroidery needle and suck on the tiny droplet of blood until it disappears. Some of Justine's other studio assistants wear thimbles while they work, but my fingers are too clumsy with them on. The jabs don't hurt, just an occupational hazard of working with a fiber artist.

It's been over a week since Marfa, and Jasper and I have spent almost every night together, meeting up at my place after I get home from catering shifts, and sometimes staying up until dawn. I'm grateful that today Justine's loft is quiet and empty. On Friday afternoons, it's just me and Henri, the bright blue betta fish who swims soundless laps in his burbling tank.

It had been Alicia's idea to apply for this job, which we did together, three years ago.

We came across Justine's flyer near the campus gym. Her listing read: *Must have nimble fingers. Strong wrists. Thick skin. Be savvy enough to leave your personal shit at the door and out of my studio. Only Good Energy need apply.*

"We have *very* good energy." Alicia pulled a tab from the flyer. "And if she likes us, she'll introduce us around."

This is the hopeful trade-off made by every artist's assistant in town: low pay, no raises, no vacation days, no health insurance. In return, the chance to be mentored by someone you admire and thrust into the orbit of art world connections.

Justine's space is sprawling, the second floor of a two-story building. It's above a microbrewery, so the stairwell always smells like hops, but the concrete floors are thick enough to drown out any noise from below. The small kitchen has a fridge, a coffee maker, and an endless supply of free green tea and raw almonds, the only thing I've ever seen Justine eat.

Justine's work is wildly beautiful, very popular, and hugely time-consuming to produce. She dreams up the intricacy of each piece, and once she's mapped it out, her assistants help to execute it. Some assistants last weeks and some, like me, last years. For the past several months, the same three of us have spent long days together working on a huge two-hundred-square-foot piece inspired by Elizabeth Bishop's poem "The Map": *"More delicate than the historians' are the map-makers' colors."* Justine's show is already scheduled, but this piece is not nearly finished.

Justine is using different textures of shaggy yarn in tufts of olive and golden yellow to represent landmasses, and these are surrounded by a mix of lapis and Aegean blues. I have been embroidering the tiny black letters meant to represent the names of territories labeled on a map. The words are supposed to look like something stamped onto the landscape, the ink waterlogged and bleeding into the sea.

When she's here, Justine carefully checks our work, and when she leaves us alone, which is most of the time, the loft is like a confessional. We tell stories about our lives and trade secrets about our families and complain about how little time we have for our own work.

About once a week, Justine's husband, Mark, trails her to the studio. On days when he brings his enormous St. Bernard, Jeffrey, whoever among us is quickest to react will grab Jeffrey's leash and take him for a very long walk. Those who remain are stuck with Mark's company.

Mark always looks ready to set sail on some expensive yacht. He wears shorts in any weather, blue oxford shirts that strain across his belly, and a large silver watch on his furry wrist. He likes to drag a chair into the middle of the workspace, cross his legs at his naked ankles, and regale us with mind-bogglingly dull stories of his adventures, liberally peppered with self-compliments and breezy chauvinism. There's nowhere to run. One morning, he spent what felt like an hour breaking down the difference between a New York bagel and the "bagels you get here." That was the day Alicia quit. She said she could handle jabbing herself with an embroidery needle, but she couldn't take being jabbed by Mark's toxic boringness. She said this to me. To Justine she said only, "I have carpal tunnel, sorry." She left after lunch and never came back.

I think about quitting, too, and finding a job that pays better, but I like Justine too much. If she's in the right mood, her stories of being a starving artist in New York City are inescapably romantic. Who cares if she actually spent a night at the Chelsea Hotel in its dingy heyday, or whether it's true she once pelted pedestrians with water balloons from an East Village fire escape alongside Björk?

I sit up straighter and exhale. Jasper is in my head. I focus on my stitching. I want to see him tonight. To feel his hands on me. I stand up and stretch and take a lap around the tapestry.

When Alicia first discovered how much one of Justine's pieces sold for, she hooted with laughter. "Holy shit! Fifty thousand dollars? Can you even walk on it?"

"It's not a rug, Alicia. It's tufted art."

She smiled. "Fifty points if you get down with Justine on her new tapestry. A hundred if you somehow keep embroidering while you do it."

I hear Justine coming up the back stairs, the familiar sound of gold bangles on her delicate wrists. I stretch out my fingers and get back to work. I haven't done anything wrong, but my cheeks flush anyway.

We call hello to each other as Justine slips off her shoes and pads across the loft. I feel her hands on my shoulders and I know she's peering over me, watching my fingers work.

She sighs. "I wish I could clone you."

I smile to myself but don't say anything.

She rubs my shoulders. "Are you cold? It's freezing in here."

She takes off the cashmere scarf she's wearing and wraps it around me. It's even softer than I imagined and smells like her tea rose perfume. "Thanks." I pull it closer around my neck.

"You look exhausted." She sits across from me and fingers the wool, flipping it back and forth to study the work. "Do you ever sleep at all?"

Justine looks healthy and well-rested. She's got to be at least twenty years older than I am, but her skin is smooth and dewy. I once asked Alicia how Justine managed to glow like that. "Snails and left-over penises from circumcisions," she said. When she saw that I thought she was joking, she added, "Seriously, she uses this crazy-expensive lotion with foreskin and snail slime in it. One of my dad's ex-girlfriends uses it too."

It's not just Justine's skin—it's also her hair, her smell, her posture. The way she moves around the loft in bare feet and no bra, her black T-shirt fitting so perfectly.

"Let's take a break," she says to me. "Have some tea."

I steal a glance at the clock. Only thirty-three minutes till I can go, and I really want to finish this square.

She walks over to the kitchen area and sits on a stool, her legs crossed, looking at me expectantly. I tap on the electric kettle and pull down a teapot and two cups, all made by a ceramicist friend of hers. I imagine Justine's home must be full of beautiful things like these.

I tip some Japanese sencha into the teapot, and then I fill a dish with raw almonds and set them in front of her. "Lovely," she says. "So what is it? Why do you look so tired? It's not just today. I don't think I've seen you lately without purple circles under your eyes."

Justine sounds as though she's hinting at something, and I wonder if Jasper has told anyone about us. It's a small circle, the art world in Santa Fe.

I burn my tongue on the too-hot tea. "Barry's had a ton of gallery shows. It's good to have the shifts."

"Anything good?"

Justine has a healthy competitive streak.

"Not really."

"Nothing?"

And then, wondering if she has heard something about us, and because Jasper has told me frustratingly little about what he thinks of Justine, just that he admires her work ethic, I bring up his name. "There was a photographer whose stuff I liked. Jasper—"

"—Green. Gorgeous, right?"

I'm not sure if she means him or his work. I blush and realize how much she can read on my face.

"Watch out for that one. He's trouble, I hear."

I flinch, like she's pricked my bubble.

"You really need to prioritize yourself, Diana." She puts a hand on my knee. "How can you nurture your art if you don't nurture yourself?"

Ugh. Sounds like something framed above my dentist's toilet, Alicia would have said.

"You're right." I know from booking her appointments what Justine's version of "nurture" includes—her Reiki healer only accepts (a lot of) cash, same with the woman who comes to her house to give her lymphatic massages and colonics.

I shift on my stool. "I've been staying up too late. It's just a money thing right now. I need both jobs . . ."

Justine's forehead is scrunched.

"You're very talented, Diana. You're the best assistant I have. And money isn't everything. What's money? I slept on floors when I was your age. I ate scraps. I did nothing but my art, and now look at me." She sweeps her arm around the room—and for a moment, her smile falters. She looks down at her hands, twists the ring on her finger. "Mark didn't build this."

She announces it like the answer to a question I didn't ask. "Of course not," I say. Is that what she thinks I think? That *everyone* thinks?

"No, it's okay, I see you eyeing it." She gives me a shy smile. She holds up her left hand, showing off her enormous diamond and ruby ring.

"When I first met Mark, I thought, No way. None of it's for me, marriage, compromise, none of it. But then, instead of getting harder, it all got easier. With Mark came a different kind of freedom."

She slips the ring from her hand. "Try it on. See how it feels on your finger."

"Oh, that's okay." It's as if she wants me to hold a thin glass vase and my hands are made of butter.

"Diana, don't be shy." Justine drops the ring into my palm.

I slide it onto my ring finger.

"You have to be practical, Diana. Yes, pour yourself into your work, but don't make yourself sick." Her gaze lingers on what I guess are the circles under my eyes.

"Right," I say.

I feel the flush return to my face. Sometimes I'm not sure what Justine is trying to instigate. She gazes at me benignly. She gets up and pulls my portfolio off the bookshelf, where it's been waiting since last month when she promised to have a look.

She places it on the counter in front of me and opens it. "It shouldn't have taken me so long."

"Those works are older . . ." I say as she flips through photographs of my paintings. I wish they were better lit, maybe they'd pop off the page more. Or maybe the colors I chose are just too muddy.

After several quiet minutes she stops at a painting of a woman named Clea, sitting next to a blank-faced man on a bench. They're in a garden maze, two figures in color against a black-and-white background. I painted strings of words in rose-shaped formations all around them—Clea's description of the fight they'd just had in the park. The type is so small, I'm not sure Justine can make it out. "To me, this one is the most interesting," she says. I peer at the image. It's one of the first in a series I'd done last summer, and the brushstrokes are too thick. Justine taps it. "This has all the energy of the others rolled up in it. Like they were all practice to get to this."

She flips through the rest with thoughtful nods and I watch closely to see which paintings she responds to, taking careful mental notes. Then, she shuts the book with a kind of finality. "I'm so glad we had this talk," she says. "It's important to me to be a good mentor to the girls who work for me. To take care of you."

"Thanks." I rinse my teacup in the sink. "We all really appreciate it." And by "we" in this moment, I'm pretty sure I speak only for me and Henri, swimming laps in his tank.

"Good," she says, nodding. "Well. You should get to the dry cleaner."

For a second, I'm confused. Does she think I work at a dry cleaner too? "Sorry?"

"You didn't see my note? I need you to pick up my dry cleaning. I leave for L.A. tonight. I need that silly dress for an opening." She's already on her feet. As she walks past me, she reaches for me and for a moment I think she's going to embrace me.

"One last thing," she says. Then she gently retrieves the cashmere she'd draped around my shoulders. "My scarf. I need it for the plane."

Chapter 12

That night I sleep at Jasper's place. I hear him get up in the middle of the night, and when he doesn't come back, I wander out to the living room. He's standing in his jeans and no shirt, his hands in his pockets, looking out the sliding glass door into the pitch-black backyard.

"Want to go for a walk?" I thought my voice might startle him, but he turns and smiles at me like I'm handing over the keys to a cage.

"Sure." Without bothering to put on a shirt, he pulls on his coat and boots. I dress quickly, and we call for Pippi, asleep on Jasper's bed, to see if she might want to come. She lifts her head, barely, then snuggles back into the quilt.

The New Mexico night is so dark that it takes my eyes a few moments to adjust before I can make out the ground beneath my feet.

The new moon is just a sliver of light over the mountains, and heavy clouds obscure the stars. I hold on lightly to Jasper's elbow, and then he takes my hand and presses it firmly beneath the warmth of his arm.

Jasper owns a small gray house nestled in the foothills. There's a trailhead not far from the end of his street, but we stay on the sidewalks, following the row of cottonwood trees. It is already April, but still we pass the occasional tree wound up in unlit holiday lights. The air smells of chimney smoke. For several blocks, neither of us speaks. I watch the fog of our breath and listen to our work boots on the pavement, the soft swishing of our nylon coats. In the distance we hear the high-pitched howls and yips of coyotes. I consider telling Jasper about the art grant I applied for. It's small, only a few thousand dollars, but it would take the pressure off a few months' rent. Introducing my money stress, though, would only kill the moment. It's so peaceful, everyone else in these houses asleep in their beds. I slide my hand from beneath his arm, link my fingers through his. He gives a gentle squeeze, and I know he is right there with me. I am wide awake.

We stay away from downtown and gallery row and instead make slow laps around his neighborhood. We pass an elementary school and stop next to a chain-link fence. Just behind it sits a rusted swing set that looks like it belongs on the set of a movie, one where two impossibly fetching actors come on a night like this one to confess their love for each other. Jasper drops my hand and leans against the fence. "Thanks for the walk," he says, his voice soft.

I look at him and try to picture the knotted thoughts that keep him up at night unfurling now, hopefully dissipating in the cold air. I try to do the same with my own worries about money. About work. About Jasper and whether this feeling between us can last.

"It's beautiful out," I say and focus only on the sky, which looks like rain. He smiles and lifts my chin, kissing me gently.

"This is my new favorite night," he announces, and now I smile too. *What a good idea to take him for a walk,* I think. *Am I some kind of goddamn healer?* Maybe.

"Heads or tails?"

"Sorry?"

Jasper holds a coin in his palm. It is slightly thicker than a quarter. I take it from his hand and laugh. "Of course."

"What?"

"Of course you don't carry a regular quarter in your pocket."

He looks wounded. "It's an Eisenhower dollar," he says, his face grave. "My grandfather gave it to me just before he died."

"Oh, I'm sorry—"

"I'm kidding." He nudges my shoulder. "The lady at the 7-Eleven gave it to me with my change. I think it's actually an arcade token."

He flips the coin. "Heads," I call. He looks up at me and shakes his head, sorry. "You're going over first." I laugh and step my foot into his cupped hands. He hoists me over the fence, then gracefully hops over after me.

Jasper sits on one of the three swings and motions for me to join him. I take the swing next to him and we sway back and forth. The night is quiet and so are we. Coyotes yip again in the distance and a tease of that sinking sensation returns. A feeling that Jasper and I won't last. Despite what feels thrilling when we're together, something picks at me around the edges and won't leave, like someone offstage whispering a forgotten line, telling me all truly good things are ephemeral.

I need to know that we are not doomed. I stand and move to his swing and he pulls me onto his lap. I lean my head back so that we're cheek to cheek. Breathing the same air. Then I shift so I can see his profile, his dark lashes, the outline of his full pouty lips. It's impossible to be concerned about anything else besides how soon we can have sex.

There is no one else out. The playground is empty. We've kicked off our boots and the sand is cold on our feet.

"I miss you," I tell him.

"I miss you too."

"Do you know my favorite movie?" I ask.

"Mmm. Something . . . Italian?"

I smile. "That narrows it down."

"Japanese?"

I push against the sand to give us a little swing.

"*Die Hard Three,*" he says with a grin.

"Nope." I shake my head. "It was a trick question. I don't have one."

"Why are you tricking me?"

"Why don't you know my favorite movie?"

"Because you don't have one." Jasper kisses me. The warmth of his lips on mine pulls me out of my spiral. He does know me. Better than anyone ever has. I look up at the sky, eager to drink in this expansive feeling. Jasper kisses my throat with small, sweet kisses, pulling down my T-shirt so he can suck on my breast. I hate that sex can fix anything with us. It has too much power. It can make any moment extraordinary. *Just enjoy it,* I tell myself but a part of me still believes I am postponing the inevitable.

Jasper takes my nipple in between his teeth and bites it with just enough pressure. I close my eyes as his mouth moves back up my neck, the kisses becoming more intense. The first raindrops fall, wispy and wet against the sand at our feet. Headlights wash over us then disappear as Jasper sucks hard on the side of my neck. I think of the bruise he'll leave. We are past the point of it leaving a mark. Fuck it. I'll wear turtlenecks all summer if I have to. He pulls his mouth from my neck and whispers in my ear, "I want to fuck you now. Is that okay?" The rain falls harder, in steadier, fatter drops. A warm sensation spreads through my groin and I feel Jasper growing hard beneath me. I lift my hips and, never leaving his lap, slide my pants down my thighs. He pulls my underwear aside and I take him in my hand, caressing the head of his penis up and down the wettest part of me. I tease him as I guide him closer to my vagina, but pull him up so he's rubbing against my clit instead.

"Is this okay?" he asks again, breathier this time. I don't answer. I give him what he's waiting for and press the full weight of my hips into him, grinding into his pelvis so he can be as deep inside me as possible. He shudders inside me. "Jesus, Diana. You feel too good."

The swing starts to sway as I lift myself up and down. It's a new sensation entirely. The rain soaks into us both, our skin slippery. Jasper wraps his fingers in my wet hair, holding on tight. He twitches inside me, fighting the pleasure so he can last longer.

I squeeze my legs around him and he stays deep and warm inside me as I slowly circle my pelvis into his. My movements are exaggerated, like a slow turning clock. We have all night, I think. Each circle I turn, Jasper moans in my ear and I'm overcome with the sensation of wanting him everywhere. Deeper. Closer. More of him.

Jasper pulls my head back and slips his tongue inside my mouth, kissing me hungrily. I lift my hips again and the cold hits us both as he slips out of me, glistening wet and even harder than before. We are soaked and swollen and pulsing.

Then with agonizing slowness, he presses himself back inside me. The pressure is more intense, so intense I feel like I might break. "Diana," he whispers into the falling rain. "Hold still," he pleads. I hadn't noticed that I was unconsciously moving my hips in those same small circles. I try not to move as he pulses inside me, about to burst. "I want more," I beg. He enters me millimeters at a time, pulling himself out most of the way, then slowly back in. The moment he reenters me feels better than anything ever has and I grasp his knees for support to make sure I stay open. Over and over. "Just like that," I moan, again and again, loud enough to wake the neighbors but I don't care. We are so connected. So in love. So warm. I feel myself contract around him as he continues to gently thrust inside me. "Touch me," I tell him, grabbing for his hand. He spreads my legs apart and glides his fingers around me, sometimes deep inside me, sometimes circling with more and more pressure. "I'm going to come," I gasp as the orgasm overtakes us both, rippling through my entire body. We press our bodies together for balance, the rain falling harder.

Both of us dripping in ecstasy, Jasper takes me by the hand and we run through the driving rain to the school's overhang. He pulls me to the ground and we lie together, still barefoot, fighting to catch our breath, sheltered from the heavy drops.

Jasper wraps his arms around me and I burrow my face into his chest. His heartbeat is loud and his breath grows steady—so steady that after a few minutes I think he's fallen asleep. But then he kisses the top of my head and says again, "Thanks for the walk."

For the next several weeks, we get up every night at nearly the same time and take long quiet walks around the neighborhood. When we get home, we have sex on the couch or in the shower or against the kitchen counter, never displacing Pippi from the bed. Our desire for each other is constant, bottomless. Some nights Jasper cooks for us, pancakes with honey, omelets and thick buttered toast, strong coffee. We stay up eating and talking and then both drift to our work. Jasper in the darkroom and me at the kitchen table. Partly because Justine liked it, and partly because I've been turned down for the art grant, I've gone back to the painting of Clea and tried to improve it.

One night while I'm working, Jasper comes and sits beside me, lining up my most recent sketches in a row. He touches the edges of each one and says they remind him of sexy recipes somehow, the way the text and image are combined. After that, I can't stop thinking of laying them out like a book, rather than hanging them on a wall. Being with Jasper has inspired something more unrestrained in my work. My sketches come more quickly, like my hand can't move fast enough to keep up with the pencil. Maybe it's spending so much time, so uninhibited, around another person. But there's something else too—it's being with Jasper up close and watching him work. His energy is infectious and easy to get drunk on. Sitting at the table, I ask if he'll photograph the sketches for me, in sharper focus and better light. He smiles and says, "Happily." I spend the next few weeks assembling the photos into a book proposal and mailing copies to publishers for consideration.

"Is that orange ochre? Shit! That's not orange ochre. That's *yellow* ochre." Justine's standing over Melodie's shoulder. "Stop! Stop what you are doing!"

Melodie drops her needle as if it had burst into flame. She's been working on this section for a solid three hours. Justine's been here for at least two of those hours and is only now noticing. "I . . . you said . . ."

"No, no, no. This is all wrong. Diana—tell her." She grabs the fabric panel from Melodie. Increasingly, every time Justine decides something is wrong, I'm the only one she lets fix it. I hate it. Melodie will start to resent me, if she doesn't already.

"Diana." Justine holds the fabric panel up to the window. Melodie's work is precise, and Justine's piece as a whole is abstract fields of liquid color, so if this patch was meant to be orange ochre as opposed to yellow ochre, well . . . "Look," Justine says, jabbing at Melodie's work. "Look at that."

In the sunlight, I recognize how yellow it is, but I also see the familiar strain on Justine's face. This is not just about the color. It's the familiar way Justine metabolizes stress around a deadline.

"I see what you mean," I say, treading carefully. "But I still think it's beautiful. The way the yellow vibrates against the black."

Justine sighs, as if I've let her down too. "Start again." She pushes the piece into my chest, picks up her bag, and leaves.

If hands could weep, my hands and Melodie's hands would be weeping. I massage my palms. I could argue with Justine. I could run after her and tell her there isn't time, we'll never finish. But there's no point. Justine knows we'll get the work done. We always do. I set the panel on the windowsill and squint my eyes. I turn the fabric in every direction hoping to see something other than the truth: Justine's right, the color is all wrong.

In the early morning, Alicia comes over to listen to me complain about the art grant rejection, about not hearing from a single publisher yet, and then about Justine. "She's vibrating. Like stress-vibrating at a high level, even for Justine."

It's my day off, and I'm still in bed. Alicia brought two cups of coffee and my favorite donut holes. And because my apartment is always drafty in the morning, we're eating under the blankets. Alicia scoots closer to me and lets me warm my ice-cold feet under her legs.

"Maybe she's just trying to keep you all captive so she doesn't have to hang out with Boring Mark alone. What do you think he's like in bed? I bet he's a premature ejaculator."

Alicia usually picks on Mark with a little more gusto, but there's a noticeable lack of enthusiasm behind her joke. And no one likes to sleep in more than Alicia. It's not like her to come over so early.

"What's wrong?" I ask.

She pulls the covers up over her head.

"Alicia!" I try to pull them back but she doesn't budge. "Now you're scaring me. What is it?"

"I got into grad school."

My stomach lurches. "You applied?"

She nods.

"Where? Are you moving?"

She nods again.

"You said grad school was a waste of money. That everybody comes out of film school making the same kind of movies."

"I know. But I need structure. Deadlines. I think it'll be easier for me there."

When she throws back the blankets, her face is shiny with sweat. "I'm tired, Diana. I thought when I moved here, big things were going to happen. I don't expect to be famous or crazy successful, but after all these jobs and hustling, I don't even have a foot in the door."

"I don't—" I start to argue that I don't either. "Where?"

"NYU."

Behind us, the radiator clanks, and above us, my neighbors' radio spits ads. Alicia turns on her side and I do the same, so we're lying face-to-face.

"How long have you known?"

"I found out three weeks ago."

"Oh."

"But it took me a minute to make up my mind. It's not happening for me here, Diana."

"We haven't been trying for that long."

"I still haven't finished a short or worked on a professional film. There's no real film scene here. I'm just working longer hours at jobs I don't like and making less stuff. My dad says he'll pay for school and that as long as I'm enrolled, he'll help me out."

In high school, I used to sit on the floor of the bookstore and read self-help books without buying them. I remember reading that "envy" meant wanting what the other person has but not wanting to take it from them, whereas "jealousy" meant wanting what the other person has and not wanting them to have it either. I feel ribbons of heat run through my entire body, envy and jealousy coursing through my veins, up to my head. She has a net to catch her. A soft place to land. She has a plan and somewhere safe to be.

I swallow to quiet the thrum of blood in my ears. *This is good for her. She's leaving without me. This is good for her. She's leaving.* "It'll be weird here without you."

Alicia brightens. "You could come too?"

"To New York?"

"Why not? I can float you until you find a job. There are a *ton* of catering jobs there." She sees me wince. "I'm not saying you'll cater forever. You'll keep painting—it'll just be until we get our big breaks."

I cling onto her optimism, like I have for years, but I also want to shake it right out of her. "I can't leave Justine right now. She has three big shows in the fall." Alicia knows I don't want to leave Jasper, either, but can't bring myself to say it yet.

"Justine doesn't give a shit about you, Diana. Don't stay for her. She'll be *fine*."

Despite her optimism, I can see that she's afraid too. "*You'll* be fine without me," I tell her. "It's going to be life-changing."

She narrows her eyes, studies me closely, then smiles. "You'll change your mind."

I laugh. "Probably." Then with a deep exhale, "Barry's going to be fucking crushed."

"He'll replace me."

"Barry loves you." We both know that by "Barry" I really mean "me."

She nods. "I love him too. But I need something good to happen, Diana. Something that makes me feel like I'm not crazy for wanting what I want."

"You're not crazy. It's a smart move."

We sit up and sip our coffee in silence.

Three nights later, I wake in a cold sweat. I dreamed the most obvious dreams of rejection. Manila envelopes full of my work being opened then thrown in the trash. Even asleep and inside the dream, it all felt too long and too boring, but still the sting of rejection felt real.

I pick up Jasper's heavy silver watch from the nightstand. Three twenty-seven. I shut my eyes tight in hopes that I'll fall back to sleep. I try to focus on the sound of the rain hitting the roof. It's no use. My body is tense and wide awake. I kick off Jasper's quilt and pad quietly into the living room. The door to Jasper's darkroom is shut tight, so I knock to be sure it's safe to enter. Immediately the handle clicks in response and Jasper ushers me inside.

"What are you working on?"

"I thought I'd develop the Las Cruces roll. I had an idea that I might do a river series next."

He stirs the paper in the developing tray, and I watch the Rio Grande appear, snaking through a canyon, its surface glistening like wet tar.

"Wow," I say. The image is breathtaking. I rest my elbows on the counter and watch him work.

His latest roll isn't just his usual landscapes but portraits too. A closeup of weathered vaqueros; a group of Mormon teenagers sitting on haystacks. His subjects trust him. They allow him glimpses of who they are. They give and he takes, and they're fine to walk away from one another afterward. Nobody worries that anyone will leave too soon.

"Do you like it?" Jasper asks, shaking chemicals from the image of a rodeo cowboy lying on the ground, his hat covering his face.

"I do." It's my favorite yet.

"Diana?"

"Yeah?"

He studies my expression. "You're sexy when you're worried."

I smile. I'm sexy when I'm laughing. I'm sexy when I'm painting or driving or drinking a glass of water. I've never been with someone who found me so endlessly sexy. These past couple days, I've been down—the combination of not getting the grant, the stress of money, and my sadness over Alicia leaving has had me in a kind of freeze when it comes to making anything. But inside Jasper's darkroom, the outside world is far away. He lifts my chin so I can't avoid his brown eyes. My body melts almost immediately. "I'm really, *really* worried," I whisper. He kisses me gently until I can't help but smile.

"I have something for you." From the developing tray behind him, he pulls out another photo, this one of my unfinished Clea piece.

"I didn't know you took this."

He hangs it to dry and we both stand back, letting our eyes focus in the dim light and bring the painting into sharper focus. "I thought maybe seeing it like this, with a kind of distance, might help you figure out how to finish." He's right. Even in the dim light, I can see the roses are too much the focus, and the man's expression is too stiff.

"Thank you." I wrap my arms around his waist and nuzzle into his warm chest.

I love and hate that my body is so constantly ready for him. The immediate sensation between my legs. Sometimes a throbbing. It's become an expected physiological reaction, like shivering in the snow.

Jasper lifts my chin and gives me an easy smile. "Are you tired?"

When I tell him, "not at all," he replies, "I don't think I've ever made love in here."

The darkness makes me think of outer space. I show my eagerness by pulling him tighter against me. Then I move my hands to the front of his pants, unzipping them slowly and slipping my hands inside. He groans, soft and low, in my ear. Then in one quick move he lifts me up and holds my legs around his waist. He turns us in a circle and sets me down on the counter. His turn to undress me. He pulls down my pajama shorts, slowly. For a second I feel embarrassed, wishing I'd worn prettier underwear, something with lace as opposed to faded cotton. But now he's moving his hands so slowly, so deliberately, that I almost grab the underwear and pull them off for him. But he leaves them on. I feel myself get wet. I want him inside me.

But he makes me wait, as if we have all the time in the world. He fingers the edges of my T-shirt. He slips it off and kisses my breasts. Then his lips move down my bare stomach, slowly, all the way toward my hips. He presses his hands against the fabric of my underwear. I grab his hand, I need him to touch me. I lead his fingers toward my wetness and he smiles, aroused by my desire. He stands and undresses me completely. Then he hitches my hips farther back on the counter.

He kneels in front of me. I inhale in anticipation. He dips his head between my legs. He kisses my inner thighs, lightly, and I run my fingers through his hair, careful not to grip too tightly. His tongue makes slow circles inside me. He sucks on me and the pleasure is so intense I think I might break open right here in his darkroom. A wave of desire runs through me and he lifts his head. He kisses my stomach again as he slips his fingers inside me, moving with more urgency. I take my hands from his hair, afraid I really will pull too hard. Instead I hold the edge of the counter. And when his mouth is on me again, sucking, I'm gone. I'm not here, I'm not in the room. I throw my head back and moan as I come. Jasper lifts his head and kisses me again, this time all the way up to my neck as I try to catch my breath.

Chapter 13

The weeks of nonstop rain have finally ended. Outside Jasper's bedroom window the July sky is cloudless, clear and black. Jasper has been up for hours. I hear him in the kitchen making tea, with the *tip-tip-tap* of Pippi's nails on the hardwood floor as she follows Jasper's every move. Then I hear the sliding glass door to the backyard open and shut.

Earlier tonight, we celebrated. An editor from a tiny art press outside of Dallas called to say she likes the story my paintings tell and, with a little more work, could see them as a book. She's offered to publish them. Jasper bought us pink champagne and we toasted. He looked at me so steadily and raised his glass. "Good work, you."

I stretch and pull on one of Jasper's T-shirts and a pair of socks. It's still dark out, and Jasper is in the backyard with a flashlight, trying to teach Pippi to fetch. I put on the work boots he keeps by the door and join them on the grass.

"Go on! Get the stick!" He throws it. She follows it with her gaze, then sits resolutely at his feet. Without turning he asks, "Do you think it's because she's lazy or stubborn or both?"

I consider Pippi. "Maybe she doesn't get the rules of the game?" The summer air is thick and warm, but I still pull my socks up as high as they'll go, to just below my knees.

Jasper throws another stick then shines the flashlight to show Pippi where it landed. She follows the movement of the light with her whole head, then rolls over on her back. "You're totally useless," he tells her, scratching her belly.

Then he stands and gazes at me. "I wish I didn't have to go away tomorrow." Jasper has a shoot outside of Phoenix, this one for a travel magazine. "I've gotten so used to having you with me every night."

"It's only a week."

"A week! How will I sleep?"

"You can take Pippi, can't you?"

"Of course, but it's really not the same." He stands behind me and kisses my neck, then pulls me close. He places his palms against my stomach. "Diana, I think we need a change of scenery."

"Okay, but I definitely need to put on pants," I say. "Want to walk down to the creek?"

"No, not a walk." Jasper paces the yard. He stretches his arms high above his head and his T-shirt lifts with them, showing just a hint of smooth skin. "We need to get out of town."

I think of our time away at the Airstream in Marfa. "I can get time off, just not until after Justine's show. After that, I'm in."

Jasper takes a seat at the wooden outdoor table, lost in thought, and uses Pippi's stick to scrape off some of the peeling paint. There's a chair next to him, but I fold myself onto his lap. He traces a finger along the inside of my wrist. "We're artists, Diana," he says. And I can't help it—I like hearing him say it. After the editor's phone call, I'm starting to let myself believe it.

"I'm thinking that we should get out of here for a while, not just a vacation. A friend of mine has a place in Taos. He's never there and he's been telling me I should go and stay as long as I want. So let's both go. We can focus on our work. When Taos gets stale we'll think about where we want to go next. Maybe Europe. Berlin? You'd love Berlin."

I'm listening to him and trying to digest what he's saying. I'm excited and surprised and frightened all at once. I don't know how to answer.

"What do you think?"

"You want to just leave Santa Fe? I'd have to quit my jobs."

"So? You don't care about them. Not really."

He's right, I don't care about the jobs, but I do care about earning enough money to get by, and I do care about Barry. Ever since Alicia announced she was moving, Barry and I have been spending more time together outside of work. It's like we're preparing ourselves for her departure. Some days, he comes over to my apartment to see what I'm working on and to talk about it. His responses are always honest and kind. He makes me want to keep going.

But maybe Barry will be in my life whether I work for him or not. Maybe it's time to give the next newcomer to Santa Fe a chance at having the world's greatest boss.

My feelings about Justine are more complicated. I sometimes have soap operatic daydreams about quitting—me storming out, her scarf coiled around my neck, the box of her favorite green tea tucked under my arm. But *The Map* is so close to being finished, and I want to see it completed. It's beautiful, and we've all spent so many hours making it.

"The book money isn't much," I say. This is putting it mildly. It'll be just enough to pay off my credit card and two months' rent.

"Diana, watching you put this book together, all your excitement, it's like a reminder of why I like doing any of this. And we should in-spire each other. If we don't keep moving forward . . ."

What? We die. If we sit still too long, we'll disappear? Is that why he never sleeps?

"I don't want a slow death," he says, as if reading my mind.

I settle against the warmth of his chest. The lease on my apart-ment is already month-to-month, and the truth is, Santa Fe has begun to feel small lately. What once felt like an expanse of anonymity and never-ending possibility feels more like a sticky web of networking that's grown stale.

"Let's do it," I say. "Let's go to Taos." As if sensing she might be left behind, Pippi jumps up so we share Jasper's lap. "Who knows, maybe the mountain air will be good for Pippi's skin."

He takes my face in his hands and looks into my eyes and then kisses me deeply.

I lead him inside to the bed and by the time I've slipped off the work boots and slid in next to him, Jasper is already asleep. Even when Pippi jumps up and snuggles into him, he doesn't stir. I watch the gen-tle rising and falling of his chest and think this is the most peaceful I've seen him in weeks. Maybe Taos is what we need. Maybe we can't leave soon enough.

Pale fingers of sunlight are poking through the blinds when Jasper wakes me to say goodbye. He kisses my forehead. "See you in a few days. There's coffee in the pot." I roll over and drift happily back to sleep. I'm not due at Justine's until the afternoon.

It's nearly lunchtime when I finally get up. I find a pan to heat the coffee in and help myself to some thick crusty bread and raspberry jam. Then I rinse and dry the dishes and wipe down the counter, care-fully brushing the crumbs into the trash.

I dread going to Justine's. If I ever become successful enough at anything to have my own employees, I'll never make them feel guilty for quitting. I'll send them off with a smile. I find myself envying Jasper for being his own boss, no jobs to quit before we leave town or people to disappoint.

When I arrive at the studio, Melodie and a sweet-voiced woman named Hannah, who was hired to help us finish *The Map* in time, are already working. Justine isn't in yet. Hannah gives a wave and continues her story, pausing to catch me up. She and her roommate are fighting, something about whether or not he really found a four-leaf clover. She pauses a couple times to say, "The point is, he's a *liar*. It's not about the *clover*." Melodie nods along supportively.

When Jasper calls a few hours later, just the sound of his voice through the phone, and the fact I won't see him tonight, lays me flat with longing.

Justine doesn't turn up until the early evening. I hear her before I see her. The tinkling of her gold bangles, the sound of her kicking off her shoes before she pads over to examine our work. "Mm-hmm. Good, Diana. Really nice." Melodie stiffens, waiting, while Hannah takes a break and stretches. Justine looks over Melodie's sections. She sighs. "Honestly, Melodie, it's fine but haven't you been in the same place for quite a while now? Hannah's just started and look how far along she is." She gestures to the panel Hannah has been working on, tall stalks of brick-colored yarn flecked with bright yellows. "Diana, come and look, tell me how we can help Melodie's patches over here. Maybe we mix in another blue?" Hannah blushes and turns away. Melodie's chin is quivering.

I stand up. This isn't going to get any easier by waiting, and I don't want her to accuse me of not giving enough notice. "Justine. Do you have a minute?" I make her a cup of tea without her even asking for it. Then I pour out a handful of almonds into a little dish in front of her.

"Please don't ask me for another day off," she says. "Those days you took off for impromptu vacation nearly killed me."

"No, not another day off . . . I . . . well, I'm moving." The next part comes out sounding rehearsed. "It was a last-minute opportunity and I couldn't say no."

"What do you mean?"

"Jasper and I, we're moving to Taos."

Justine scans my face, to see if I'm joking. When I don't smile, she asks, "When?"

"We haven't set a date, but, well, as soon as we can wrap things up here. We have a place to stay in Taos already." I figure I can trash most of my stuff. All I need are my clothes and Jasper's photograph of the running girl and my tape recorder and paints. Everything else is from the Goodwill anyway.

"Leave," Justine says.

"Now?"

"Now. Go. I can't have this negative energy around me so close to a show." She puts her teacup in the sink. "If you're not committed to the work, then I don't want you here."

"But I can help you for a few more weeks. I can make sure we finish *The Map* in time," I offer.

"Leave." She waves her arm as if shooing a cat. "I expected more from you, Diana. I never thought you'd get waylaid by a man. Melodie, maybe. But not you."

My mind races. Not from her confusing relationship advice, I'm used to that. But because I want to say something about the gratitude I really do feel for her. "I'm sorry, Justine. I thought you would understand. You told me to prioritize my own projects . . ."

"Stop. Stop. I don't want to hear it." She turns her back to me, rinsing her cup in the sink, so I go. Hannah looks as confused as I feel as I hand her my set of the studio keys and remind her to feed Henri. Melodie gives me a hug and whispers, "Good luck."

"Thanks," I whisper back. I need it. Because the unscrambled part of my brain is beginning to drown in regret.

Chapter 14

I cross the parking lot in a daze, trying to calculate how badly I may have just fucked up. But when I shut the car door and close out everything around me, I'm ravenous. I drive to my favorite taco truck and order a burrito with everything they can fit in it. I eat behind the steering wheel, watching a steady stream of customers come and go. By the time I'm halfway through the burrito, it's like a flip switches—I feel free. The next week stretches out in front of me with no commitments. I drive slowly through downtown, thinking I might stop in one of the galleries, or at the bookstore, but then I see the revival movie house is showing *Stage Door* and I buy myself an enormous bucket of popcorn and sit in the back. When I get home, I fall onto my bed feeling sick and excited and completely exhausted.

Two days later, I drive Alicia to the airport, speeding all the way so she doesn't miss her flight.

At the curb, I hug her tight. She's been my warm place for six years and I don't want to say goodbye. "Who's going to make me laugh like you?" I whisper into her hair.

"I guess you should just come." She squeezes me back.

When we pull away, we're both crying. I wipe salty tears from her cheeks. "You have to run. You'll miss your plane."

She waves away my concern and digs for something in her bottomless purse. A crumpled piece of notebook paper. "Hold on to this."

I smooth it open and printed in Alicia's small, careful handwriting is a list of coordinates.

38° 27' 51"N and 90° 51' 25"W

I look up at her grinning face, confused.

"It's *exactly* halfway," she announces. "Between Manhattan and Santa Fe. We can meet there, okay?" She kisses me quickly on the cheek. "And get this, the town is called *The Diamonds*. The Diamonds, Missouri." At the airport's revolving doors she calls over her shoulder, "Perfect for a couple of sparkling broads like us!" then disappears inside.

I spend the next morning scrounging boxes from two different liquor stores in town. I pack up my dishes, books, and all the bits of ephemera that I've collected since moving to Santa Fe. I tape up my paintings, a shoebox full of minicassettes I've recorded, and a stack of half-finished sketches.

By Friday, all that is left to do is to load everything else into my car and drive it to the Goodwill. Driving home I feel light enough to float away; only my seatbelt is holding me in place. When Jasper calls, I tell him I have a surprise for him and ask him to come straight to my place when he gets back to town.

Jasper arrives around ten o'clock Saturday evening. "Wow," he says, looking around my empty apartment. "Going minimal?"

"You're looking at a woman with no earthly possessions." I'm sitting on the floor with a beer and a box of crackers I'm calling dinner. Pippi curls up in my lap and waits for her ears to be scratched.

I expect something like a round of applause or at least an admiring whistle. But Jasper looks serious. "What do you mean?"

"I donated it all. I gave my landlord notice. He made me pay for this month, but it's okay."

Jasper folds his hands and rests them on top of his head. "You didn't tell Justine, did you?"

I refuse to acknowledge the look of total panic in Jasper's eyes.

"Of course I told Justine. I can't just disappear on her."

"Oh, Diana." He says this like I'd left the door open and Pippi has just run out into traffic.

A dead-weighted fear creeps into my belly, the terrible sense that he's switched channels on me. "I had to tell Justine. We're moving to Taos, remember?"

"I do remember. It's just . . ."

No.

"We didn't solidify anything . . ."

No.

"I had no idea you would act this quickly."

Don't do this. Please don't do this.

"Did you quit the catering job too?"

I shut down in that moment. My face goes pale, I can feel it. My world is suddenly underwater. "There was no Taos . . ."

"No, of course there was. Is. No, I'd love to go to Taos with you. Someday."

"So, let's go—"

Jasper sits on the floor beside me. "My manager called. He got an offer for me, from the Hayworth in London. They want to show my work . . . You know he always said my stuff wouldn't travel. And now they're calling. I can't say no."

"You're going to London?"

Jasper follows me into my empty kitchen where I dump the rest of my beer down the sink. I have never hated living in a studio more. I'm desperate for another room to walk into, a door to close and a place to be alone. My skin flushes, hot and cold at the same time. I think about my conversation with Justine. *Waylaid.*

"You can get your job back. Justine loves you. She knows she can't live without you. And Barry will weep with joy. Right?"

I take a deep breath. On the exhale, I force the question I'm scared to ask. "Why did you ask me to move with you to Taos if you didn't mean it?"

"I *did* mean it—when I said it. But I was fantasizing. You know. You're a romantic, like me—that's how we think, right? Thinking about what we could do someday. Together. I didn't expect you to start packing." He paces around the empty apartment like a trial attorney entering into evidence how crazy this all is.

The flush to my skin is humiliation. The sight of my packed duffel bag, sitting in the empty corner of my apartment, fills me with shame. I clear my throat and lift my chin. "That's not how I remember the conversation," I say quietly.

Pippi paws at Jasper's leg until he picks her up. "My sister is happy to take care of Pippi while I'm in London. Her kids have been begging for a dog. And I just thought, with all your jobs, and now this book you're putting together . . ." He looks at his feet. Our little family is dissolving before my eyes.

When I don't say anything, he adds, "Would you like to stay with me tonight, since, you know, you don't have any stuff?" I see the room through his eyes, bare and more than a little desperate. The strange sensation I've had for the past few months, like I'm running on a hamster wheel, trying to figure him out, melts away. It's replaced by something achingly sad. He will never love me. The clarity of it settles into my bones.

He's rocking back and forth on his heels, and I know he's ready to go. I walk to the door and open it for him.

"Diana." He hesitates. "Someday we'll go to Taos, okay? I promise."

I hug him, mostly so he won't see my tears. Then I slip from his arms and close the door between us.

I'm waiting on the doorstep of Justine's loft when Melodie shows up early the next morning. My heart is an exposed organ beating outside my chest, on display for the world to see. I can only imagine what I look like when Melodie sighs and says, "Oh, Diana."

"Change of plans," I tell her.

"Fuck."

Melodie lets us in and goes immediately to the kitchen. She pours half her thermos of coffee into a mug for me and tears her chocolate croissant down the middle. One look at my face, and she can tell I don't want to talk about it. We switch on the lights and sit down before Justine's unfinished piece, both of us regarding it, and the hours of work stretched out before us. She taps her thermos against my mug in a gentle toast. "To getting this fucker done by Sunday?"

It gives us a week. A little over a week until Justine's show and still so much work in front of us. I smile and take a sip. While Melodie picks out a Dolly Parton album from Justine's collection, I shake some food into Henri's tank and pray Justine will take pity on me.

Two hours into our work, we hear the door open. I hold my breath as Justine sweeps in. I hear her slip off her jacket and boots.

"You're back." Her voice is icy.

"The move was called off."

"You mean Jasper called off the move." She stands over me.

"I'm sorry I left you in the lurch."

"We're way behind now, Diana. We'll never catch up." But I can hear a softness creep into her voice.

"Justine, I'm so sorry. My work with you has been really meaningful to me." I lay it on thick. "Really an honor. I'll work all night if I have to. I'll make up for the lost time, I promise."

Her gaze lingers on my hands, then my face, before she sighs and turns on her heels. "Let's see how you do today."

I don't stop working for the rest of the day. Justine leaves around four. Melodie leaves an hour later. "Sorry, Diana, I'm babysitting my niece tonight." Then it's nighttime and I'm alone and I know there's no way I can do all the work that needs to be done with just my two hands. Maybe Justine is just setting me up. She knows I can't finish this much embroidering by tomorrow and that will give her an excuse to fire me for good. She'll think of it as my punishment for having quit. I fight the urge to just lie on the velvety couch and close my eyes. I want to finish this task, and I also want to avoid thinking about Jasper. How easy it would be to leave and drive to his house and take the small pieces of him on offer.

I sit up straighter and get back to work for another solid hour. Then I stand and stretch my legs, my back, and my fingers. I linger by Henri and watch him swim. My eyes get heavy and so I hop up and down on my toes to try and wake up.

I hear someone at the door, and think possibly Hannah has come to help.

Then I look through the peephole and see Jasper's familiar outline. He's holding two large cups of coffee. "Hey," he says when I open the door. "Can I come in?"

"Okay." After that, I don't know what to say. I'm too afraid that if I speak, I'll cry, and I do not want to cry anymore, so I turn my back to him and get to work. The whole time I feel his eyes on me. He sets the coffee down and pulls up a stool, close. He watches me thread the needle and then watches as I stitch even lines of sapphire blue across one of the panels. Jasper didn't ask me to go with him to London. It doesn't need to be discussed. I wonder when he's leaving, but I don't want to ask. When I sneak a peek at him out of the corner of my eye, I hate how my body responds. I fight the urge to reach for him, to pull us closer and remind him how good we make each other feel. I can feel his eyes on me and I wonder about all the things he's thinking but not saying. I focus on the work.

Without saying anything, Jasper walks to the other side of the stretching rack and sits down in Melodie's place.

"Where should I start?" he asks.

I look at him, confused, until I realize that he's come here to help me finish the piece. He hadn't been silently searching for the right thing to say, he'd been watching me work. Studying the motions and figuring out where to jump in.

Tears pool in my eyes. I can't help it. I'm tired from sleeping on my bare apartment floor or maybe it's from the exhaustion of his push and pull—just when I want to hate him, I love him; and when I want to love him, he's not there to be loved. "You can start with that corner." Jasper nods and gets started. He moves slowly but deliberately and handles the embroidering with no trouble. I put on a Neil Young album and we fall into the rhythm of *Harvest Moon* on repeat.

We work for hours, steadily making progress, until the sun splashes across the floor and we've finished all my section and Melodie's. When our bodies are wrecked with exhaustion, Jasper walks over to where I am sitting on the floor. He kneels down, touching his lips to my forehead and kisses me softly, then whispers the words I had been longing to hear for the past several months, "I love you."

After Jasper leaves, I look at *The Map*, now nearly finished, and I know in my heart my time in Santa Fe has come to an end. Everyone is gone and I am utterly spent.

At a red light, I cry so hard that I think the woman in the car next to me might get out to check on me. I give her a little wave and mouth *I'm okay* and the whole thing is so ridiculous that I'm laughing at myself by the time the light turns green.

He picks up on the third ring.

"Did I wake you?" I ask.

"I'm up," Barry lies. "Or I should be. Too much karaoke last night. Oh my god, you were right, I invited Rod and he said yes and guess who has the voice of an angel?"

I laugh for what feels like the first time in days. "I'm sorry to call so early. I didn't want to leave without saying goodbye."

"Where are you?" he asks.

"Outside your house."

"Easy there, stalker."

I laugh again.

"Don't go anywhere, I'm coming down."

When Barry comes outside, I'm standing on his front lawn. He pulls a baseball cap down low over his bedhead curls, then adjusts his hoodie like he's on the staff of an English estate and the lord of the manor has just pulled up. He's wearing his signature white platform sneakers, unlaced. His face falls when he sees my red, swollen eyes. He doesn't need to ask, he just opens his arms and I fall into them.

"What a dick," he says, shaking his head in disbelief. "What a total, complete idiot."

"He's not that bad," I say. Sniffling. "We tried?"

Barry looks somewhere over my left shoulder, like he wants to say more, but stops short. "What's next?" he asks hopefully.

"I hear Dallas is all the rage." I keep my voice light.

"Don't let Jasper ruin Santa Fe for you."

"It's not just him. I'm done with Santa Fe." Barry flinches. "I mean, I think Santa Fe is actually done with *me*." I laugh.

Barry shoves his hands into the pocket of his sweatshirt. He doesn't say anything for a long minute and instead makes a lap around my car. He peers through the open window at the odometer.

"How are your tires?"

When I don't answer right away, he says, "Follow me." He jumps in his van and I follow behind him in my car. He pulls in to a Shell station, and I pull in after him.

"Dallas is a long day's drive," Barry says. He tests the air in each of my tires and refills the water in my cooling tank, and when he thinks I'm not looking, stuffs two twenties in the glovebox.

"Barry." I can't pretend I didn't see.

"Have one decent meal on the road. You'll pay me back."

"Thank you." Before I hug him, I search the car for something to give him in return. I pull a box of my favorite charcoal pencils from a bag.

"What are these?"

"You can use them. To make stuff."

Barry shakes his head. "I'm not an artist."

"Just a muse?" I tease.

"Exactly." His eyes light up. "Like Camille Claudel."

"Okay, but she was a muse and an artist."

Barry rolls his eyes. But with an arm around his shoulder, I point our bodies toward his catering van. "You make stuff every day."

His eyes get glassy, like he might cry. Instead he holds up a finger "Wait! One more thing!" Barry rushes to the cooler in his van and comes back with a bag of cocktail weenies. "Don't eat them cold."

"Only Alicia would do such a thing."

He hugs me tight. It would be nice to stay right here. "Don't stop making stuff, okay?" he whispers into my hair.

"Never." I kiss his cheek and get into the car. I know he's watching as I drive away, but I don't look in my rearview mirror until Santa Fe is miles behind me.

Santa Fe, New Mexico

NOW

Chapter 15

After I hang up with Alicia, I can't sleep. I book a flight from Dallas to Albuquerque for early the next morning, pack my suitcase, then sit at the kitchen table and watch the sun coming up.

The plane is mostly empty, and without having to hold extra snacks for Emmy or Oliver's neck pillow, my bag fits easily under the seat. I lean my head against the window and doze most of the way, thinking about New Mexico and what I might be going back to. I haven't let myself think about Jasper or my Santa Fe life in so long.

As soon as the plane touches down, I text Oliver.

Landed.

K. Good luck.

We've barely spoken since he told me his secret. I saw him briefly this morning and left for the airport moments later.

I text Alicia.

LANDED!!

And she responds

!!!!!

On the curb outside the airport, she screams, "Dirty Diana!" and pulls me into her. "I've missed you like *crazy*." She hugs me like she never learned that you're supposed to hold back. And I realize I've missed her like crazy too.

As we're driving the hour to Alicia's house in Santa Fe, memories come flooding back. We pass dozens of places where we catered events with Barry. We pass the Cross Gallery where I first met Jasper, and I can't help staring. It has a fresh coat of paint and new plantings out front but otherwise looks the same. At a red light, Alicia taps her fingers against the steering wheel, her wedding band making a faint tapping sound in time with the music. I glance at her profile—she's only gotten more beautiful, any hard angles filled in and softened. She seems so at home in Santa Fe. As soon as grad school was over, Alicia moved back here and started teaching film classes at the university and she never left again. What if Oliver and Emmy and I did the same? What if we picked up and moved here now? Would I feel more at ease too?

We pass the turnoff for Jasper's old house and I wonder where he is right now. All this time, I've resisted the urge to look him up, even though it would be so easy to do.

The rest of downtown speeds past us until Alicia pulls in to the driveway of a small adobe home. When she opens the front door, her three-year-old, Elvis, comes running across the polished wood floor. "Mama!" Elvis throws his arms around Alicia's legs and she swings him up and he wraps his legs around her waist.

She kisses Elvis on his cheek and announces, "Auntie D is here!"

"Hi." Elvis places a chubby hand on each of my cheeks and presses them together until my lips purse.

"Sorry. It's his favorite greeting." Alicia's husband, Nico, appears and plucks Elvis up and throws him, giggling, over his shoulder.

"Oh, Elvis." I sigh and look at his upside-down face. "I am *so* happy to see you."

Nico gives me a warm hug, nearly as tight as Alicia's. His eyes are a deep green and he has the same rosy red lips and wide smile as Alicia, only a little less mischievous than hers. Nico asks me to remind him how I take my coffee then takes my bag to the guest room while Alicia shows me around the house.

In her sun-drenched backyard, we sit on a bench and watch Elvis sway on his stomach on a wooden swing hung from their elm tree. My sunglasses are somewhere inside; the bright light burns my naked eyes, and I have the most disorienting feeling of having traveled from one world to another. Wherever I am now feels both familiar and alien.

"I'm really glad you came." Alicia squeezes my knee.

"Me too. I should have come sooner."

"It all happened so fast. Barry didn't really tell anyone how sick he was, except his sister. And me, because I made him."

I shake my head. "He loved you so much. He used to let you get away with murder."

Alicia laughs and sighs all in one breath. "We have an hour before the service. You must be hungry?"

"Starving."

Alicia turns toward the house and calls, "Nico! Waffles!" Then to me, "Don't worry, he orders me around too. We're into it."

As soon as I got settled in Dallas all those years ago, I sent Barry a check for the money he lent me, and he never cashed it. So a few months later,

I sent him a goofy card with a hand-drawn picture of bananas yelling "Thanks a bunch!" and cash inside. He emailed me back a photo of himself in front of the catering van with all new shiny, metallic purple rims and a note that said, "Money put to good use."

A year later, when my book came out, the publisher offered to send me to an art book fair in New York. Alicia was still in grad school at NYU so I had a free place to stay and Barry flew out to join us. While Alicia was in class, Barry came with me to the book fair. The organizers sat me at a tiny table near the back with a pile of Sharpies. Barry and I had planned that I'd be signing books for an hour or so while he browsed the convention floor and found us some good books to take home. But when it grew clear to us that no one was coming by my table to get my book signed, Barry pretended his feet hurt and asked if he could sit with me. He kept us distracted by asking me to read from the book. Twice he interrupted me to say, "You made this, Diana," and he held up the book, admiring the cover. "Can you believe where we are?" We sat back in our folding chairs and looked around the fair. Barry shook his head and made it feel like it didn't matter that no one had come by because we were already in the most exciting place on the planet. To repay his kindness, I researched the city's hottest culinary spots. With Alicia, we waited in long, snaking lines for dim sum and knocked on unmarked doors for cheeseburgers, then sang karaoke until all three of us were hoarse. We stayed up for what felt like forty-eight hours straight.

Soon after I got back to Dallas, I met Oliver, and Barry got busier than ever with work. Over the next few years, his catering business doubled and then tripled in size. He had a new kitchen space built and hired a team of chefs and more reliable cater waiters. Our correspondence became less frequent and more focused on the big occasions—phone calls on birthdays and holidays, then a lot of missed calls and voicemails and text messages. Occasionally, one of us would write the other a long meandering email but usually our check-ins were brief. He wrote asking about Oliver and apologized for not making it to our wedding, and I apologized right back for scheduling it the same weekend as his sister's, and we both promised to visit as soon as things were "less hectic." He always asked for more pictures of Emmy and reminded me to share what I was working on. And the less time I spent writing and drawing, the less I wrote to him, as if him knowing how little I was working would make it all suddenly true.

Then Alicia called to tell me Barry had stage four pancreatic cancer. I called him and told him I was way overdue for a visit and to clear his dance card. He made me promise to wait until he was done with chemo because he wanted to feel "electric" for karaoke. I laughed and told him he had a deal. I sent him playlists with all his favorite songs and gave them titles like *Slow Jamzzz for Fast People*.

Now I rest my head on Alicia's shoulder. "I'm sorry."

"Honestly, Diana, it all went so fast. Mostly he just held my hand and made me promise to not let his sister serve any food at the funeral except for the stuff he'd already put in the deep freezer."

Nico sets the table and we eat breakfast in the sunshine of Alicia's yard.

"How's Oliver?"

"Really good." I hope I sound convincing. "He wanted to come, but we'd have had to pull Emmy out of school. . . . It's a whole thing."

"Are you painting much?"

"Here and there."

"I wish you could stay longer," Alicia says, cutting into the small talk.

"Me too." I mean it. It's so calming in her backyard, with stalks of purple and pink flowers and a bright yellow slide. Nico brings us coffee and sits beside us.

I want to tell them all about the cassette tapes I found in my closet and my overly strong reaction to losing them. And about what Oliver said to me before I left, and how disconnected we've become. About how little I desire him, how sometimes it seems like there's not much about my life in Texas I desire at all. But I don't know how or where to begin.

The service is packed. Barry's sister, Nancy, sits in the front row with Barry's mom, who is tiny and frail, and his three aunts. It's as if anyone Barry ever catered a party for is here—at least every gallerist, events coordinator, and party planner in Santa Fe. I see a few of the clients from our regular jobs, but most of the faces are new. Halfway through the service, a tall, lanky guy with a close-cut beard slips into the pew opposite mine. I recognize his face, but I can't place him. I try to catch his eye, but he only looks straight ahead.

After the service, we go back to Barry's house and Nancy pulls Alicia and me into a double embrace in the kitchen. "Oh, you girls. You're so good to come. Barry would be so happy."

"We wouldn't miss it," Alicia says and takes another tray of baby quiches out of the oven.

Nancy busies herself counting flatware so she won't cry. "I want you girls to each pick out something from Barry's room. A keepsake." She can't be more than five years older than us but she calls us "girls" in the most maternal way. She squeezes my hand. "He'd want you to have something." Her lip trembles, and she wipes her eye with the back of her other hand. "It's upstairs. Last door on the left. Don't leave without taking something."

Barry's room is exceptionally tidy. There's a bookcase full of cookbooks organized by rainbow color, and beside it, an impressive shrine to Julia Child. Alicia scans the space. "I'm not sure what to take."

"Me neither." Just beside the window is a set of floating shelves lined with tiny clay figurines. There must be nearly fifty of them, each one three or four inches tall and a bit misshapen, with crudely painted faces and ornate hats, mostly shaped like giant flowers. "Did Barry make these?"

"Oh." Alicia stands next to me. "I remember these . . ."

I pick up the one with a mushroom for a hat.

"Is that the Mario Cart guy?" Alicia asks.

"I think . . ." I squint harder. "I think it's Barry?"

She leans in to get a better look and sees the teeny white platform sneakers. "Oh. I loooove him!"

I cup him in my palm and make a lap around the room. I've never felt so relieved by the weight of something, the figurine heavy in my hand. I think of Barry checking in on my work and reminding me to always be making something, no matter what it is. When he said this, I'd think, *just like you,* and I'd picture him cooking, the artist in his kitchen. But the figurines have a different kind of permanence. I wonder if he had always made them or only started after getting sick. Did he know we'd all be desperate for a piece of him to carry with us?

On Barry's dresser, I find a few framed photographs. One is of him and Nancy and their parents; there's another of Barry with his three aunts, at what looks like his culinary school graduation. And beside the frames, there's a weathered copy of the book I made so many years ago. When I open it, a Polaroid falls out—the three of us, me, Barry, and Alicia, posing in our aprons in front of Barry's van.

My eyes fill with tears, blurring our photographed faces, and I feel Alicia's hand on my shoulder.

"I have an idea," she says.

"What's that?"

"Let's get really stoned."

We lie on Barry's bed side by side, the windows wide open to air out the smoke. Nico is downstairs with Elvis. He'd shooed us away after we set out the buffet. "Have fun."

"You're the best," Alicia told him. I watched as she kissed him. I tried to remember the last time I kissed Oliver that way.

Now I'm stoned and my defenses are depleted. I bite my lip and turn my face up to the ceiling fan. "Alicia, can I tell you something?"

"I already know what you're going to say." She props herself up on an elbow and peers down at me. "You're getting a divorce."

"What? No! Why would you even say that?"

"I don't know, you just seem . . . secretive? Like you're hiding something. And you're not talking about Oliver. At all."

"Okay, well, maybe, but that's not why. I've been wanting to make something new, but I don't know what it is. And I'm scared. I've let so much time pass since I've really made anything. But now I feel disconnected, and just, off. Like I've lost something, but maybe it was never really mine?" I drape my arm across my face, hiding in its crook. "And then I found these old tapes and I keep thinking, what if I talk to women, the way I used to, about love and sex, but maybe different this time." The weed has made my mouth dry and my head fuzzy. "Like I've started wondering, maybe if I could live in someone else's place for a while, in their desire, I could find my own. Does that make sense? I don't know. I can't figure it out, exactly. What it could be."

Alicia is so quiet I worry that perhaps, in combination, the weed and I have put her to sleep.

But then she says, "Oh thank god."

"What?"

"You always do your best work when you have no idea what you're making. Remember when you tried to make those creepy nightmare dioramas? Those were wild."

"That was so so long ago."

"Who cares what this thing will become? Maybe that's not for you to know yet. Love and sex and desire . . ." She lets it roll over in her mind. "You've always been fascinated by how squeamish we all are about sex. That was the whole idea of our point system."

"That was *your* idea," I say.

"No." She shakes her head. "No, I told you the story about the frat boys who were bragging about it, but it was *your* idea for us to do it."

Suddenly I know she's right—I hadn't remembered it that way at all, but she's right. "Okay, but you were better at it than I was. Bolder—"

"No, I was having *more* sex than you, maybe. In more interesting places, probably. And with hotter people . . ."

I roll my eyes and Alicia smiles.

"I just thought, the more sex I have, the more chance I'll get to what feels right. I liked to try things out. I still do. Oh my god—" She bolts up in bed. "Ask Nico about how we bought him a cock ring to try out. It said 'one-size-fits all' but it didn't fit his balls!"

"What?" I say, laughing.

"Nico?" When he doesn't answer, she goes out to the hallway and whisper-shouts from the top of the stairs. "Nico!"

She lies back down on the bed and I smack her with a pillow. "When he comes in, ask him to tell you."

"I'm *not* asking him."

Nico appears in the doorway in his short-sleeved shirt and tie. He doesn't look even the tiniest bit annoyed that he's been summoned by his stoned wife and her friend.

"Tell Diana about how your saggy balls wouldn't fit in the cock ring we bought."

Nico looks at me like he's about to describe the weather. "Diana, it didn't make any sense. I mean, it fit on my"—he briefly glances over his shoulder, then back at me—"my *shaft* . . ."

Nico's expression is so earnest that it makes us laugh harder. He shakes his head, recalling his bewilderment. "I don't get it. Whose balls fit in that thing?" Then he leans over and kisses his wife on the forehead. "I gotta get back downstairs. Barry's sister is feeding Elvis insane amounts of chocolate babka."

When he leaves, Alicia flips through the worn-out book of my old paintings. She traces her fingers along the cover, then places it on the nightstand. She smiles. "Never stop making stuff, whatever it is— that's what he'd say, right?"

Thinking of Barry opens an ache in my chest. I stare up at his ceiling fan and hold the mushroom-headed figurine high above me. I close one eye, and then the other, so that Mini Barry does a kind of jig, suspended in midair.

"Silent Rod!" I sit up, excited. Alicia furrows her brow and I quickly explain. "That tall, quiet guy who walked in late to the services. *Rod*, the botanist-bartender. He was there today! Remember he studied flowers and . . ." I wave my arm. "It doesn't matter." Just knowing he was here today makes me happy. I look at Barry's shelf of flower-hatted figurines and smile, feeling suddenly closer to him and to what he was making and thinking. And then, annoyingly, I start to cry. Maybe it's because I'm stoned, but I'm smiling and weeping and I don't want to be. Alicia grabs my hand, which only makes me cry harder. I feel like a kid, suddenly alone and turned around at an amusement park, her family evaporated into a sea of strangers. My shoulders shake and I sob.

Alicia wraps a steady arm around me until I catch my breath. When I do, she hands me a tissue. I blow my nose then roll my eyes at myself. "Alicia, am I having a nervous breakdown in Barry's room?"

My best friend squeezes my hand and shrugs. "Seems like a healthy place to do it?" She grabs another tissue and gently wipes the mascara from my face. Then she stands and pulls off my shoes.

"Alicia—"

"No one will care. Get under."

She kicks off her own shoes and crawls beneath Barry's quilt with me, pulling it over both our heads. We turn our bodies toward each other, our faces so close they nearly touch.

The closed-in space feels like a confessional and in the quiet I say, "I'm really lost."

"I know."

My marriage is at sea. My desire for my husband has vanished. I want to make art, to produce something beautiful that helps people connect to one another, maybe. But instead I work in an office, helping people move their wealth around in an endless loop. I was on a path, I thought, and then it, too, disappeared. I don't need to say any of this out loud. Beside me, Alicia stays still, keeping her eyes open so that I can close mine.

When Alicia comes back to wake me, the sun has already set. Barry's house has nearly emptied of guests; only a few stragglers remain, saying goodbye on the front porch. Alicia, Nico, and I put away the food and finish up the dishes while Elvis naps on Nancy's chest. When the house is tidy, we hug Nancy goodbye. Back at Alicia's, Elvis shows us how he swims in the bath and washes his own hair. The grown-ups applaud, and Alicia beams with pride. I never thought that I'd feel unsettled in comparison with Alicia and her restlessness. But that's how I feel right now, like I'm champing at a bit that she doesn't even feel in her mouth.

While Alicia and Nico tuck Elvis in, I wonder if I'll be able to sleep after such a long nap, but as soon as I lie down, I drift into a deep, dreamless sleep.

On the way to the airport the next morning, I double-check I have everything—wallet, phone, tiny mushroom-hatted Barry figurine. At the curb, I hug Alicia hard, like I don't know you're supposed to hold back.

I feel lighter at thirty-five thousand feet. My flight is nearly empty and in the hum of white noise, I begin to form a plan. I'll keep making stuff, even if I'm not sure yet what it is. And in the making, I'll find what's been lost. When I close my eyes, I can almost see lines of text and new paintings, like scrying stones for my own desire. I begin to imagine recording new interviews, each one a little like Barry's figurines, with its own story to tell. I'll try harder with Oliver and fight for what I know is there. If it's sinking, I'll pull it to the surface.

Dallas, Texas

NOW

Chapter 16

"I took it all off and I'm *so* glad I did."

At the baggage claim, I eavesdrop on two conversations at once: a couple fighting over spilled lemonade in a carry-on; and two young women discussing bikini wax options. The full monty seemed to win in their opinions. "It hurts a little. But *so* worth it."

Before the cabdriver turns into my neighborhood, I have him drop me at the Wax Pot. I don't give myself time to second-guess. Instead I imagine Oliver's face, so surprised and delighted by the effort that I've put in that he'll agree that what we need is a reset. We can fix things.

"Just the sides?" the waxer asks as I lie flat on her table.

"No." The exam paper crinkles and shifts beneath me. "The whole thing."

She frowns and pulls on her reading glasses. "I hope you're not in a rush."

Emmy greets me with a huge smile when I get home. I'm lighter and stickier, but the women at baggage claim would be proud. After I put Emmy to bed and my bag is unpacked, I pour a glass of wine for me and Oliver and find him on the couch.

"Trip okay? How was the service?"

I tell him how well attended it was and how Barry would have been happy that everyone ate the food. I hesitate and then add, "You know when you go home or to a place that feels like home and you remember things about yourself that you actually liked? That were fun?" I keep my voice light and sunny.

"Like sports you used to play?"

"No. Not really. More like how I lived. I was so curious. And sensual. And I felt really young."

"You were so young when you lived there."

Why does this conversation feel combative? I expect my wine to be sour on the next sip. "I was just reminded that there are things I miss about myself. And I want to share them with you. I want to include you in them."

"Like what?

This is the moment. I stand in front of him and unzip my skirt. I let it fall to my ankles and slowly strip off my underwear. I freeze when I see Oliver's face contort in an odd way.

"Oh shit. What happened?"

"What do you mean?"

"What did you do . . . what's wrong with your vagina?" he whispers.

"I waxed it. I thought it might be fun. Something different for us."

Oliver leans closer to get a better look but not in a good way. "Is it supposed to be so red?"

"Well. I just had it done."

"I'll get you some ice. It looks . . . kind of angry."

Oliver hurries to the fridge and I want to sink into the couch and pull up my underwear forever.

"Try this." He hands me a Ziploc bag of ice cubes, scooping up his car keys with his free hand.

"Where are you going?"

"Poker. I texted you in Santa Fe."

"Oh, right." I don't think he did, but I don't want to argue.

"Maybe we can come back to it later?" he offers.

It. He can't even say the word.

"Sure."

"Nice to have you back." His kiss is quick and he's out the door.

As soon as I hear Oliver's car pull out of the driveway, I snuggle deeper into the couch cushions and apply the ice. It feels surprisingly good. I imagine how ridiculous I look and my cheeks burn with humiliation. Did I really expect it to be so easy? I remember the resolve I felt on the plane: *I'll keep making stuff, even if I don't yet know what it is.* I find my laptop and take it to bed. Then, like a serial killer returning to the scene of a crime, I book a room at the Rosevale for next week. I book a single night, though I'll only need it for the day. A hotel in the middle of the day? It feels unnecessarily clandestine, but where else can I go that's quiet and private?

When I arrive at the Rosevale, I'm relieved to see the suite flooded with sunlight. It has a huge living room with soft colors, every wall padded in fabric, velvet chairs, the couch perfectly erect and the carpet just vacuumed. I open the glass doors onto a small veranda overlooking the pool. It's hot enough for a swim but the pool is deserted except for an older couple reading the newspaper in their chaise lounges.

I set out several bottles of water and wait for the first knock on the door. I've spent the last several days arranging three interviews, one after another, all with women I've never met. When I asked Alicia's advice on who I should talk to, she suggested I cast a wide net—I hung flyers outside my painting class and even placed an ad on Craigslist. One respondent has already flaked over text, but that leaves two others.

I check myself in the full-length mirror beside the door. I'm wearing a cream silk blouse and camel trousers. Pearl studs in my ears. If I put on a lab coat, I'd look like a well-dressed gynecologist.

There's a knock and I open the door. The woman standing on the other side is drop-dead gorgeous, like a supermodel from the eighties, tall and statuesque, with thick, lustrous hair, and an actual mole to the right of her wide smile.

"Diana?" she asks.

"Yes, come on in!" I move to let her pass, but she stops to kiss my cheeks. "Sandra," she says, "with a long A." Then she sweeps by me in a cloud of ylang-ylang perfume and leather, a Louis Vuitton handbag and Gucci heels.

"This hotel is gorgeous. I love coming here."

"You've stayed here before?" I ask.

"All the time. The calamari from room service is amazing."

"We can order some?"

"Maybe later." She smiles warmly.

She flops her bag on the couch and slips off her shoes. "I never answer Craigslist ads—I was helping my brother-in-law post about a job when I saw it—but I read it and thought, hey, this one looks interesting."

"Right?" I laugh. "I bought a futon off there once . . ." Sandra's gaze has an unnerving effect on me. "Thanks for coming today." I pull out my phone and set it on the table. "It's okay if I record us?"

Sandra shrugs. "Sure."

She sits on the sofa and pulls her long legs beneath her. "What do you want to know?"

"A long time ago, I did a series of paintings—a book actually—all about women and sex and how they feel right after. Only now, I'm more interested in bodies and how they feel during, or even before sex. I'm interested in desire. Is there a moment for you, something that comes to mind when you think about feeling most inside your body?"

"Work related or nonwork related?"

I flash on Oliver and me when we first dated, how we used to sneak away and make out in the office stairwell. My urges took me places, led me on adventures. "Depends. What do you do?"

"You're funny." She crinkles her nose at me. "Let's see." She folds her arms behind her head and leans back. "I'll tell you about a client who flew me to Paris. Does that sound interesting? But why don't we settle up before I dive in?"

One might think that while sitting in a hotel room across from a woman who answered an ad I placed on Craigslist, I would have put it all together—what she does for a living—a little quicker. But it only clicks now. A million questions flood my brain.

"You can pay cash, right?" Sandra asks.

"Of course," I say, still trying to recover. I hand her a hundred-dollar bill across the table.

She looks at the money. "I'm two grand an hour, Diana."

"Right, right," I stammer. I wish I had enough cash to talk to her for a couple of hours, but I have nothing close. After apologizing profusely for wasting her time, I walk Sandra to the door.

After she leaves, I sit on the couch, stunned. I'm even surprised by my own surprise. I try to gather my thoughts. Did I think this would be simple? I pour myself a Jack Daniel's from the minibar and sip it slowly. I think about canceling the next appointment. There was no name in the woman's email to me, just "The Sexagenarian" and a phone number. When I called, she answered the phone on the second ring with no hello, only, "I've been expecting you!" Then she very warmly accepted my invitation to meet.

Just when I pull out my phone, there's a knock at the door. She's early. I smile with relief when I open the door to find a woman with naturally graying hair wearing an oversize wrap made of some organic-looking undyed fiber. She smells like maple syrup and patchouli.

"I'm Diana," I say. "And you're . . ." I wait for her real name.

"The Sexagenarian." She sits on the couch next to her enormous canvas tote. "I'm a menopause facilitator. Women come to me seeking spiritual guidance as they make their crone transition."

"That's so interesting." I'm not sure what a crone transition is, but I'm excited by any woman in Dallas who owns her age. The Sexagenarian smiles at me, and her eyes are a bright, sparkling blue.

I give her my rehearsed pitch about what I'm interested in, and what I hope to talk to women about, and she asks, "So you're looking for me to share a fantasy?"

"It could be. Or a story from real life."

"Mmm." She opens a bottle of water and takes a long sip. "What I have in mind is neither. It's a sexual journey. And"—she points a finger at me—"you must loosen your sphincter muscle to open yourself up to its pleasures. Do you struggle with constipation?"

"Sometimes?" I clear my throat. "I'll try and relax."

"Your sphincter."

"Yes. That." This is not off to a great start.

"Are you recording?" she asks.

I nod and she leans forward so she's speaking directly into my phone. "My inspiration is diverse and my techniques are quite sophisticated. I don't usually share them out of the boudoir."

"I see."

"Do you like surprises?" Her blue eyes get bigger. "Do you like to be pampered with exceptional experiences?"

"I think so," I reply quietly, feeling like I'm cracking open a door that should remain closed.

"My journey is a unique blend of sensual massage filled with otherworldly pleasure. High-class meetings proven and practiced over hundreds of years."

The order of her words confuses me, like someone's thrown random darts at a Learning Annex course guide and this is where they landed.

"Make sure you're recording this part," she warns me. "Have you ever had an orgasm that begins in your nostrils and ends in your parfem?"

I want to ask what a "parfem" is, but I stop myself.

"Dionne." She looks at me straight on and I don't dare correct her. "I'm ready to share." Then she sits up very straight and holds out her arms. "Time travel with me, okay? I need you to come with me. To a time when winged creatures performed cunnilingus on unexpecting fairies. Are you with me? I want you to attend high-class meetings with Merlin and his enormous staff." She leans forward again, and the words tumble out, rapid-fire. "Let me paint a sophisticated picture for you. A Minotaur, alone and lost in the enchanted forest. I approach cautiously, but he can smell my intimate pleasure. I float toward him, like the Angel of Touch, and lift his supple horse tail so I can penetrate his—"

I'm up out of my chair. "You know what? I think I should stop you right there. Thank you so much for coming."

When the Sexagenarian leaves, I take out my phone and google "parfem."

There's an aggressive rap on the door, and my heart does a jump in my chest. If she's coming back to tell me more, then I don't want to answer the door. I freeze. If I stay still, maybe she'll go away.

There's another, louder knock on the door. "Ms. Wood, this is Leonard, the hotel manager. Would you open the door, please?"

Sweat beads along my hairline.

I set down my phone and open the door. I paste a polite smile on my face while Leonard looks over my shoulder, scanning the room.

"Is everything all right?"

"We've noticed a few . . . outside guests to the hotel. Should we be expecting more?"

I wish for a massive claw to descend from the sky and pluck me from the planet. "No," I say. "As a matter of fact, I was just leaving."

"I suppose that would be best," he says.

I don't think the day can get any worse, but then I'm forced to ride the elevator eleven floors down with Leonard. Although I shouldn't care what he thinks of me, I can't help myself. "I was conducting research."

Chapter 17

In front of the school, the snaking carpool line grinds to a halt and we all patiently wait for the school doors to open for morning dropoff. I turn up the *Star Wars* soundtrack for Emmy.

I peek at a text from Alicia, who wants to know more about yesterday's adventures at the Rosevale, especially Sandra.

I think my dad brought home a call girl for Thanksgiving last year.

As I'm about to respond, the car door opens and Raleigh offers Emmy a hand. "Good morning!"

Raleigh is in a bright orange volunteer vest, her hair damp and cheeks flushed, helping direct kids safely across the parking lot and into school. A wave of guilt washes over me for everything L'Wren, Jenna, and I gossiped about on the drive to Roundtop—Raleigh's affair, her lips, her divorce.

I should just smile and keep driving. But seeing her standing alone, holding a stop sign and directing traffic, I can't just pull away. "Hi. Raleigh!" I say it a little too loudly. "Thanks for volunteering."

"Of course, yeah. I signed up a while ago. . . ." She looks exhausted.

"Raleigh, if you ever need anything—"

"Please don't be nice." She looks up at the bright blue sky. "If you're nice to me, I'll cry, and I still have six minutes until the bell rings and I can take off this vest." She smiles and tears gather in the corners of her eyes.

"I'm so sorry, Raleigh. But really if you ever need anything, or the kids need anything . . ." The car behind me honks.

"You're sweet, thank you." She wipes her eyes with the sleeve of her sweater.

Raleigh and I have been on dozens of school-mom text threads but have never actually spoken on the phone. At every school function or L'Wren-hosted party, she's someone I've genuinely enjoyed making small talk with, but that's been the extent of it. We've never had a solo playdate for our kids or gone out for lunch or drinks, just the two of us. She strikes me as someone who spends hours putting herself together. Her dirty blond hair curls gently to her shoulders, her teeth are dazzlingly white and perfectly straight. Today she's wearing a pale pink tank dress with a thin cashmere cardigan over the top and turquoise-studded boots. And to Jenna's point, she does have perfect lips.

"Call if you need anything," I say, more just to say it. I know we'll likely never talk about anything personal again. But just as I'm about to pull away, she leans down again, sniffling. "Diana. I could really use a place to stay," she admits in a near whisper.

"Of course. Sure, sure. I'll just wait for you in the faculty lot," I respond, a little taken aback.

I sit in my car, parked under the shade of a willow tree, and wait for the first bell to ring. I watch Raleigh in my rearview window—she pulls off her volunteer vest, neatly folds it into a square and tucks it into the pocket of her cardigan. When she reaches my car, she asks, "Should I follow you?"

"Sure." I think about what Oliver will say. Maybe that I've picked up a stray like one of L'Wren's many cats.

At the house, I give her a quick tour before hurrying to the office.

When I get home that evening, Raleigh is organizing her things in my guest room. I'm still surprised she took me up on my offer. But here she is, soaking her delicates in my guest bathroom sink as I make room in the closet for her boxes of shoes and collection of cowboy hats. "Do you have anything to cover these windows? I'm a light sleeper and the light from these streetlamps is going to drive me insane. I just know it." She has brought three wheeled suitcases and is actively sorting through them all. "I know what you're thinking—I'm not staying till Christmas, promise. I see that look on your face." She's right. Oliver and I had exchanged nervous glances when we saw her SUV was packed to the brim. "I just can't find anything so I had to bring everything inside. Divorce is so much fun!" she trills as she rinses out another lace thong in my sink. "You are so sweet to do this. Really. Where do you hang your lingerie?"

"I don't," I say. I don't own any lingerie that's "hang" worthy, I suppose. Or maybe I'm too lazy.

"I'll find a place." She dangles her damp, brightly colored underwear on the bedposts, on the knobs of the dresser, even from the corners of my bluebonnets painting above the bed, until my guest room looks like a fireworks display of undergarments.

I'm confused about what role to play with Raleigh. I hardly know her—does she want someone to talk to? Or maybe she just wants to be left alone, to make phone calls and piece her life back together? I'm about to ask if she wants some hot tea when she holds up a bright pink vibrator. "Do you have a charger for this? I think they're all the same.

Vibrator chargers, I mean. Sorry. Are we allowed to talk about vibrators? I forget what's off-limits."

"No, of course. But I don't have a charger."

"Hmm. Maybe I'll get you one as a thank-you present. A vibrator, not a charger." She winks. "They can do what no human can."

"Yes to tea?"

"Or maybe some cocktails?"

A few tequila and sodas later, Raleigh is wearing three of her cowboy hats stacked one on top of the other. "This is my favorite." She holds up a gray felt cowboy hat with a long pink feather in the brim. "I added the feather." She knocks the other hats off and replaces the stack with this one. She wears a baggy T-shirt with black underwear. After another sip, she drunkenly sorts through the painted canvases and old art supplies in the closet. "Okay. So, what are these?" She's found the pile of my old drawings. "Please don't tell me they're pictures of all the women you and Oliver murdered in your guest room?" We're both three drinks in and feeling very punchy. Maybe it's just the booze, but I'm impressed and maybe a little relieved that she's able to be so light.

"I wanted sex all the time," she tells me over our next round of drinks. "I know, hard to believe because Dustin is such a troll. Let's be honest. But he was my troll, and I could go every day! Twice a day, even. Whereas he was fine sleeping in separate beds. Do you know what it feels like to be rejected by your own husband? Over and over again?"

"I'm so sorry."

"We were great roommates. But who wants that? I'm not dead yet. And now that it's over he suddenly has all this *passion*! Passion for taking me down."

"What does he want?"

"Everything. The kids. The house. Everything I care about. I'm not lying—Dustin could have given two shits about taking care of the kids when we were together, and now he's making their lunches and braiding Izzy's hair and posting about it on Instagram like he's father of the fucking year. And he *hates* that house. He was always moaning about how much work a lawn is and how we should just move to one of those condo communities. And now he's planting lemon trees and putting in a new fucking pool. He wants it because he knows I want it. It's too fucked up."

Raleigh refills her glass for the fourth time and licks the tequila from her lips. "You didn't answer my question from before, Diana." She picks up the drawings in front of us. "What are these drawings?"

A warmth spreads through my chest when I think of Santa Fe. *Potential*, I want to tell her. They're the moments before you kiss on a first date. They're happy confusion.

I can see Raleigh squint to read my signature in the corner. She raises her brows as she reads, "Dirty Diana?"

"That's me." I laugh. "I used to draw a lot. At one point I had a project where I interviewed women about love and sex and then made paintings—it was a long time ago. A hundred years ago."

"Fascinating."

"I think so. I tried it again recently. Or some kind of version of it. But it didn't go well."

"You interviewed people?"

"One woman, really, in the end. The Sexagenarian."

"What the fuck, Diana? Who is the Sexagenarian? I need every single detail right now."

I've already said too much, but so has Raleigh. Emmy is fast asleep and Oliver is working downstairs so I pull out my phone.

"Is this just a woman off the street?"

"Sort of?"

"Who am I with right now? I'm sorry, Diana, but I always thought you had a stick up your ass." Raleigh grabs the phone and hits play. I hear my own voice, so clearly trying to sound authoritative as the Goddess launches into her rambling monologue. Less than a minute into the recording Raleigh laughs so hard she rolls off the bed. "Ouch!" she calls from the floor. "My parfem!"

This only makes us both laugh harder.

"Who the heck is the Angel of Touch?" Raleigh asks.

"I think you have to attend a high-class meeting to find out?"

"Oh Jesus." Neither one of us can sit up, we're laughing too hard. "Ohmigod, Diana." Raleigh catches her breath. "You need to erase that. Or keep it forever. I'm not sure."

There's a knock on the door and we both jump. Oliver peeks his head in. "Is everything okay? I heard a crash."

Raleigh sits up straighter and adjusts the cowboy hat on her head. "I'm so sorry, Oliver. We are not talking about an enchanted sexual forest, I promise."

"Sorry," I say. "We're just catching up."

Raleigh giggles and I smile at Oliver, shooting him an *I'm in over my head* look as soon as she turns away—it's unfair, I know. But for some reason I feel the need to pretend to be miserable with Raleigh for Oliver's sake.

"I'm off to poker. Have fun."

He shuts the door and Raleigh grins. "All the moms have crushes on Oliver. You know that, right?"

"Really?" I'm not surprised. Oliver is good-looking, and he knows how to make people feel special. And he genuinely likes other people's children, not just his own. Some of the dads at our school look panicked when a kid other than their own tries to talk to them, but Oliver can listen to someone else's daughter describe the entire plot of the *Wizard of Oz* in painful detail. He sees the good in people, no matter how big or small.

"Oh yeah, honey. They all think he's *cute*-cute, not just *dad*-cute. You know those suburban sixties parties where everyone throws their car keys into a bowl and you go home with whoever's keys you pull out? Listen, if anybody brought back that key party theme, you know they'd all pray for his."

"Thanks. I think?" It's like taking pride in a Participation Medal.

"So where is he really going tonight?"

"What?"

"Poker is never really poker, is it?" She sees my face fall and walks it back. "I mean, out drinking with the boys, being dumb, you know." She slaps me gently on the thigh. "Unless it is! Play me another interview!"

"It's all I have. And I'm going to erase it. It was good for a laugh, though."

"No! Don't erase it. Yes, if word got out you were recording porn stories and talking about screwing, okay, yes, maybe Emmy would have a few less playdates in Rockgate. But fuck that. We're so trained to color in the lines. I'm sick of apologizing. I'd let you interview me about sex. I've been dying to talk about what happened anyway. About my *affair*." She puts air quotes around it, like the whole thing is untrue. "Turns out the ladies I know don't really want to hear about it. They want to talk about what they heard, with each other, but nobody wants to hear about it from me. I'm not asking anyone to take my side. But if you're going to hate me, don't you want to know exactly why?"

"No one hates you."

Her smile is small and sad.

"I want to hear about it."

"Yeah? I'll tell you right now."

She looks down at my phone on the bed. I open my voice memos and hit record.

"Where should I start?"

"How did you meet him?"

Raleigh leans over my phone, addressing it directly. "Well, first off, you should know that my husband never went down on me. Dustin said if he did, then I got too wet and sex didn't feel as good. Not enough friction."

"Did you want him to go down on you?"

"I wanted *him* to want to. I don't particularly enjoy having *his* dick in *my* mouth, but I did it because it made him feel good. Honestly, I don't know how he could have been satisfied with our sex life. I think his standards are lower. He eats the same turkey sandwich for lunch every day. Zero variation. Mayo, mustard, tomato. I get it—I've spent enough time in my own therapy trying to figure him out. The predictability comforts him. He grew up in chaos." Raleigh shakes her head. "But I got sick of that. It didn't comfort me, I wanted something exciting." She pulls her T-shirt over her knees and hugs her legs close to her chest.

"Where did you find it?"

"On a plane! On a fucking plane, Diana! I swear to god. I mean, thank god I had shaved my legs because that doesn't happen on the regular anymore." She leans back against the bed. "I was flying home to see my mom who was really sick. Dustin had booked me a first-class seat for the trip, which was nice of him. He said he didn't want me crying in coach. And as I was boarding the plane, I saw this man in a firefighter's uniform."

Raleigh sees a flicker of disbelief cross my face.

"I know it sounds ridiculous, but I swear to you, there he was; well, not in full about-to-knock-down-a-burning-door gear, but he was wearing his navy polo shirt, with the fire department insignia, and these matching navy trousers. He was broad and muscular, of course, and I overhear him talking to the agent at the gate. He's flying to Florida to see his mom because she is feeling poorly and he's on standby. He's in a panic, but the agent finds him a seat and hands him a boarding pass. As he passes me, heading back to his coach seat, I offer him mine in first class. I couldn't imagine this big guy, this hero, squeezing himself into a coach seat, while I'm sitting up in first class. And he's so sweet and grateful. I tell him I'd heard why he was flying, and that my mother is sick too. It's this nice little moment of connection, like for a minute we're not strangers. It feels . . . intimate. And then I go back to his seat in coach. I sit down and I feel warm just thinking about him, and a little less alone and sad. And I guess he thinks about me, too, because as soon as the seatbelt light goes off, the flight attendant brings me a Crown and Coke, compliments of my firefighter. It's not my drink, but let me tell you, it goes down easily. So then I send *him* a drink. And then he sends me three at once!"

She crosses her legs and settles into the pillows.

"So I think, is he flirting with me? Maybe he's just being polite? But you know what finally makes me realize there's something going on? The flight attendant. She's so *judgmental*. When she comes back with the drinks, there's this look of distaste on her face. 'This isn't a nightclub. I can't keep doing this,' she says to me. Of course I'm mortified, and I assure her there won't be another time. Then I drink each drink. I start to feel like I'm floating. You know when you smile and you don't even realize you're smiling? So, I decide, *Fuck her, I'm going to pay my firefighter a visit in first class.* I get up and peek my head through the curtain and there he is, looking right back at me. Strong jaw, broad shoulders.

"I mouth the words *thank you* to him. I have this overwhelming urge to comfort him. I want to kneel down next to his seat and hold his hand. I'm not even thinking about sex. I'm thinking maybe I could give him a hug or let him talk to me about his mother. And then he unbuckles his seatbelt."

She looks at me, and then at a spot over my head. I hear the garage door creak shut as Oliver's car drives away. Raleigh looks like she's trying to decide what to leave out.

"He gets up and walks to the bathroom, and I follow him. Slip in right behind him. He's slightly confused at first. Then he kisses me. And we keep kissing, and it's that kind of kissing you do when you're a teenager. Kissing that could last hours. There's nothing but us, and our mouths. We're connected, me and this stranger. But he keeps his hands at his sides. He doesn't touch me anywhere. I get a feeling like he's waiting for me to take the next step—if there's going to be one. So I take one of his hands and lead it to my blouse. Together we unbutton the top buttons so I can slip his hand inside my shirt and he can feel my naked breasts, my nipples getting erect. He studies my face and smiles. He's like me, he wants to keep going. So I lift up my skirt to let him know I want more too. He watches me pull my skirt up around my waist, standing in front of him in my lace underwear, ready to be touched, and I can hear his breath catch. Now it's his turn. He unzips his pants and they fall to his ankles. His legs are massive, all muscle, and when he pulls down his boxers I swear I can see his erection throbbing. I slip out of my underwear and let him know I'm ready. His arms are solid and strong and he scoops me off the ground and I wrap my legs around him and suddenly he's inside me, pushing deep into me, and we're fucking. He's so *strong,* and no one has ever made me feel so tiny and safe.

"I have this strange, primal urge to inhale as much of him as I can. All of this, his smell, his skin—the feeling of him inside me—his strength. I just give myself over to him completely. I think we're both so desperate to feel anything other than our sadness. It feels like something we have to do. I *had* to follow that grieving man into an airplane bathroom and have the most exciting sex of my life."

Raleigh stops. She studies my expression.

"Did you ever see him again?"

She shakes her head. "I cried after we both came. It was like something inside me broke and hit me like a tsunami. He held me after and I cried into his chest until someone knocked on the bathroom door. I apologized. Then we got dressed and went back to our seats. I tried to diminish the experience just so I could survive it. I told myself he couldn't be as magical as I wanted him to be. Back in my seat, I forced myself to imagine him turning me off, like driving away from the airport in a neon monster truck, drinking one of those tallboy energy drinks and belching. But I'd only start laughing. It didn't work. He was still magical. And as if to prove my point, just as the pilot announced we would be landing soon, the flight attendant walked over to my seat and said, 'This is from 3D.' Then she plopped down a plastic bag from duty free. Two Toblerones, a carton of cigarettes, and a whole bottle of Crown. I laughed again, even though she was scowling at me."

Emmy wakes me up in the morning by jumping on my bed, and I immediately regret drinking so much. My head feels like it's stuffed with wool. Oliver must have come home when I was fast asleep and is already up and out of bed. I pull on my robe, reminding Emmy to be quiet when we pass Raleigh's room so she can sleep in.

But Raleigh's already up, too, sitting with Oliver at the kitchen table, both of them red-faced and sweaty. "You didn't tell me Oliver was a runner."

"I'm just starting again. Please. I could barely keep up." Oliver refills her water.

"Well, I was grateful for the company. Thank you." She gets up and pours me a cup of coffee. When she hands it to me, she pulls me into a hug. "But you're the revelation," she whispers in my ear. *"Dirty Diana."*

I give her a squeeze, and when she pulls away, there are happy tears in her eyes. "I'm going to pack up and stay with my sister. She just kicked out her loser boyfriend, thank god, so it's perfect timing. She's a little kooky, if you can believe it—" Raleigh smiles, giving Oliver and me permission to laugh politely. "But at least we can wallow in heartache together."

Chapter 18

Most mornings, arriving at work is like walking onto the set of a cozy sitcom. Every setup is the same, every scene routine and consistent. When the elevator doors open on my floor, I'm greeted by familiar sounds: morning pleasantries, assistants typing, and somewhere, a printer jamming. Endless phone-ringing. The reception area smells like it always does, like lilies and lemon furniture polish. And still, despite how always-the-same it is, I feel a tiny flicker of shock every day that I've worked here for more than a decade.

This morning, I dropped off Emmy, and then on a whim stopped by Oliver's favorite café. The one with the espresso he likes and that always has a line down the block. They take a painstaking amount of time making each drink and no amount of people waiting makes them move any faster.

When we were dating, I would've waited in a line three times as long to buy Oliver coffee and a warm scone. Standing there, I think of all the little things neither of us do for each other anymore. Somewhere along the line, after Emmy was born, it was as if we made a silent pact—like we'd looked into each other's overwhelmed faces, over the head of a newborn baby or maybe it was a tantrummy toddler, and quietly made a deal not to expect the small gestures. Like we said, *Hey, I know you're just hanging on, let's do our best.* Or maybe we never made that deal. Maybe Oliver has been quietly calculating the debt that my lack of small gestures is racking up, steadily building resentment. But where have his small gestures been? Have they not been there or have I just not noticed them? Has he betrayed me or have we both been playing by a completely different set of self-invented rules? When the barista hands over the coffee, I remind myself that I want to be the kind of woman who waits in long lines to make her husband smile.

I find Oliver's assistant, Cara, at the copier. I feel terrible that one of the two coffees in my hand isn't for her.

"Have you seen Oliver?"

Cara cuts her eyes in the direction of Allen's glass-walled office, and when I turn the corner I see Oliver in there. He's getting chewed out by his father while people in the cubicles out front try not to stare. Allen stands and strides over to Oliver, towering over him, still yelling. Oliver's shoulders collapse. He does a lot of nodding but I can tell he's somewhere else. I should have predicted this. I've noticed him absent from meetings and slow to respond on email, not returning clients' calls. His head is clearly somewhere else, one of the only things we currently have in common.

When Allen finally sits back down behind his desk, Oliver rises and shuffles toward the door.

I follow him into his office. "What happened?"

"I fell behind," Oliver answers quietly.

"How behind?" Our clients are wealthy and spoiled. Keeping any of them waiting never goes well.

"Very."

"I can help." I hand him a lukewarm latte.

"This isn't your fault. I can do it."

"The Aldon estate?"

"Yeah."

"Okay, good, I know the account. Let me help. What's our deadline?"

"Yesterday."

Shit. "No problem. We'll get it done."

"Diana, there's weeks' worth of work. I fucked up."

"My day is light. We'll fix it."

We work in silence for a few hours, wordlessly passing receipts, letters, forms, and invoices between us. In the quiet, I think about distracting Oliver with a funny story about Emmy or even telling him that I'm dreaming up a new project. But the idea feels too new.

After sorting through a stack of receipts, I have to ask. "How did you fall so far behind?"

"I don't know. The work feels harder to do these days. I don't know why."

I do. The work is tedious. And Oliver's heart has never been in it. "Do you ever think about quitting this job? Finding something else?"

He looks up at me. "Every day." It feels like the most honest thing he has said to me in months. "But I'm in so deep. I even brought you in."

I laugh. "It's not prison—"

"I don't know what else I'd do. I've waited too long. I'm sorry I pulled you in."

"It's okay. I don't mind it as much as you do."

"Of course you do. Who would like doing this shit? This place. It just feels like . . ."

"Your father."

"Exactly," he whispers.

We order a pizza for lunch and eat on the floor. We make a real dent in the work, and Oliver is calmer. By seven, the office has cleared out.

"You should take a break," I say. "We can easily finish in the morning."

Oliver looks at me as if slowly recognizing someone he thought was a complete stranger. His face softens and he smiles.

"I don't have to play cards tonight. Maybe we could grab a drink. We have a sitter anyway. It might be nice."

My heart all but leaps. It would be nice. But I haven't let up on finding other women to interview. Alicia found me a woman named Jada, a friend of a friend from her NYU days, who she swears I'll think is fascinating. I've asked her to come to the office at eight, figuring everyone would be long gone.

"I would love to, but I can't. I have work of my own to catch up on. You go to your card game, and I'll see you at home later."

Oliver looks dejected, but he knows he can't be upset after I helped him all day. He sighs and grabs his keys. "Okay," he says. "If that's what you want."

"Do I just start talking?" Jada sinks into my office love seat wearing a bright green sundress. I can tell by the way she settles in that there's no need for me to try and make her comfortable.

She tells me about her new job at a tech start-up. "Our offices look like a millennial blogger threw up. I'm not kidding. There's a tire swing and a free cereal bar, the whole deal." She looks around my office. "I like that this place is like, fuck it, we're old and crusty, so get on board. Or don't. You know?"

Jada is easy to talk to and when I tell her about what I'm trying to do with gathering other women's stories, she smiles brightly. "Okay. Cool." She runs her fingers through her shiny black hair. "I love it when it's all about me. This is very on brand." She has a hint of a non-rhotic accent, like a New Yorker who drops her Rs and occasionally sticks them back in, in a different place. "Let's start."

On the drive home, I have a familiar, electric feeling. I replay pieces of Jada's interview in my mind and thrill at how willing she had been to share. We talked about longing and sex and I asked her about the last time she felt the most in her body. Jada thought for a long time, and then like the sun breaking over a field, her face lit up.

When my girlfriend and I lived in New York, we had this tiny fourth-floor walk-up apartment. I could never live there now, I've gotten so lazy. I drive a block to the grocery store these days. You know?

But once, I got really sick with strep, and I was basically bedridden for a week. Bored out of my mind but too sick to read or really focus on anything. So I'd spend hours just lying there and watching my neighbors in the building next door, waiting for something interesting to happen. The street between the apartment buildings was so narrow that I might have been in the same room with them. There was a banker who had endless coke parties and ordered dim sum every night. There was a sweet old lady whose face would light up every time the phone rang. And directly across from my apartment was a woman with long dark hair and short bangs. I decided she was French and I named her Celine. She must have worked from home. She was always on her laptop. But she would leave once a day with her yoga mat and return with coffee from the shop on the corner that I thought was too expensive. She had a dancer's body. Tall and lean with small, perfect breasts. She lived with her girlfriend and they'd have sex right there by the window, the drapes open.

When I get home, Oliver is still out. I pay the sitter while she tells me about the new game Emmy made up, where the two of them played Disney princesses lost in a dinosaur jungle with only Capri-Sun and a guide to eating insects to survive. "We legit played for over an hour. Then she fell asleep, fast."

Once she leaves, I find my drawing pad and pencils and sit at the kitchen table with my headphones on. I hit play, and my voice fills the empty room.

Does that turn you on? Watching them?

No! Jada answers me. *No, the sex was so boring. Always the same. Even with the drapes open there wasn't much to see. She was on her back, the sheets pulled up over both of them. The good part was always when they finished. After her girlfriend fell asleep, Celine would masturbate on her own. With no sheet. She'd turn away from her partner, toward the window, and it was like she was looking right at me. She'd lay on her side, and stretch out her legs, pointing her toes like a dancer, like maybe she was showing off for me. Then she lifted an arm over her head and sighed. Like she had all the time in the world and she wasn't going to rush. She would exhale and let her arm fall slowly and gently to her neck. I think about that a lot, the way she caressed her neck. Her fingers kind of lingered, eventually finding their way to her chest. That's where she started, caressing one of her breasts, then the other. Then her hips started to move, like they were waking up to the greatest sensation you could feel and they shifted, writhing just slightly beneath her. Her body was ready to be touched, everywhere, aching the same way I was aching to touch her. Then she teased herself. She traced her fingers up and down her stomach then back to her mouth where she'd suck on them, looking at me the entire time. My face was so close to the window, watching, waiting. And finally, she moved her hand between her legs and turned onto her back. She spread her legs wide and shifted her gaze so that her eyes were locked on mine. Then she slipped her fingers inside, moving them in and out. Slowly at first, and then much faster when the feeling started to grow. Then she pulled her hand away, teasing us both. But her body wouldn't let her get away—her hips rose up and her fingers found her again, moving in circles, faster and with more pressure, her hips moving in circles, too, until her body clenched, holding* in the sensation. She turned away from me then, her eyes closed, she didn't need me. She was on another plane. And that only made me want her more. I could see her face when she climaxed, flushed and pleased.

I can't get the slope of Jada's neck right. I pause the recording and pour myself a glass of water. For several minutes, I wander the house, quiet and still. I take my sketch pad and pencils to bed and make a desk on my lap with pillows. I press play. Jada continues:

I have this fantasy I think about sometimes. I think about walking over to her apartment, once her girlfriend leaves for work. She lets me in, like she's been waiting for me to arrive. Then she leads me to her bed and slowly undresses and puts my hand between her legs so I can feel her soft wetness. And the minute she does this, I can feel my orgasm building. It's immediate. Nothing like when I'm with my girlfriend and it feels so far in the distance, and I'm concentrating hard—any rogue movement can throw it off, any miscalculated dirty talk can destroy it. But this, it's right there for me. I'm the one trying to stop it for once. It must be what men feel like all the time.

I draw Jada at the window, her back to us, and through the window, Celine in her bed.

Then what happens?

I lay her down on the bed and suck on her breasts, and kiss between her legs and slide my fingers into her. Seeing my fingers disappear inside her, she holds me even closer. She kisses me deeply, breathes into my ear. I know how good I'm making her feel. Better than her girlfriend ever could.

It's such a feeling of power, you know? Pleasing a stranger. And I'm determined to make her come. I can't leave her unsatisfied the way her girlfriend does. But she wants me to come, too, so she starts kissing me, all the way down my stomach. And it feels like, this is the moment, the only moment I've ever really wanted, and now it's here and I don't ever want it to stop.

My pencil hovers over the paper, not moving, and I just listen.

It's 12:30 in the morning. Oliver still isn't home, which makes me imagine all the places he could be and all of them make me worry. I picture everything from a car accident to an illicit affair with Connie Britton, the last woman Oliver told me he found attractive. I find an old Xanax from my nervous flying days and pray that it still works. It kicks in ten minutes later, and I feel more relaxed than I have in months. As I lie in bed, I stop thinking about Oliver and focus on Jada. Her desire is right there on the surface. Waiting for her.

Do you come?

Like a freight train. As soon as her tongue slips inside me, I can't stop. I come harder than I ever have. And then she lies back on the bed and I tease her with the vibrator she hands me, bringing her so close to climax, and then pulling away. And she kisses me with desperation, with want, and she's kissing me so deeply and her breasts are pressed against mine and she feels so soft that I want to fucking melt inside her. When I touch her, she's so ready that it takes less than a minute. She laughs when she comes and there's something incredibly gratifying about it, like putting the last piece in a thousand-piece puzzle.

But then we hear the front door open. Her girlfriend is home early and I have to climb out on the fire escape, and we're both laughing uncontrollably, like teenagers. She makes me promise to find her again the next day. It all feels so real. That attraction. It's so powerful.

Do you go back? The next day?

Do I go back? . . . Wouldn't you?

Suddenly, I'm not thinking about Jada. Or Oliver. I'm in a parking lot and it's cold and snowing, and someone is there, but I only feel his body, I don't see his face. He's strong and slim and I'm pushing him against my car. Our hands everywhere, searching.

Alone in my bed, a throbbing sensation builds. My body is begging to be touched. I slide my fingers between my legs just as my phone vibrates on the bedside table.

I don't want to answer but I know I should.

"Hello?" I say brightly, trying to not sound like a woman who has been interrupted while masturbating.

No answer on the other end, only music.

"Hello? Oliver?" I check the screen again to make sure and Oliver's name is as clear as day.

"Oliver? Can you hear me?" The music is loud, a deep thrumming bass.

Then, a woman's voice. Slow and kittenish. "Is this how you like it?"

Then a voice that is unmistakably Oliver's. "Yes. That's how I like it."

I feel pinpricks of shock on my face, across my back and belly. "Oliver. I can hear you. *Oliver.* Pick up!" I yell into my phone.

Then the woman's voice again. "You're so fucking hot."

Oliver moans in response. "Amanda."

"Yes, baby."

"Oliver?" I say again, quieter this time.

I sit up in bed. I disconnect the call. My own desire drains out of me as my mind races trying to understand what I just overheard. I draw myself a bath and run through every scenario of how to act when Oliver comes home. Some versions play like the soap operas I'd spent an entire summer watching when I was nine. I picture myself demanding answers and throwing something, narrowly missing Oliver's head.

I slip under the bubbles into the warm water. Beneath the surface, I think maybe I should just forget it ever happened, swallow it down with another Xanax and fall asleep. Maybe it will feel different in the morning, farther away and less important.

Or maybe he will find me here—sitting in the bath and totally confused.

Eventually the water turns cold. Oliver still isn't home. I shiver and climb out of the bath, dressing myself in warm pajamas and crawling into bed.

Close to three A.M., I hear the rattle of keys in the door, then footsteps on the stairs. In the bedroom, Oliver drops his wallet on the bedside table and shuffles toward the bathroom, peeling off his clothes as he goes.

"How was poker?"

Oliver jumps. "Holy shit. Diana. I thought you'd be asleep."

"I can't sleep."

He sits on the very edge of the bed. "Is everything okay? How's Emmy?" I smell beer and perfume. He's flowery and sweaty.

I turn on the lamp and Oliver blinks and squints in response. He looks rumpled. I ask him again. "How was poker?"

"What?" he asks, pretending again that he didn't hear.

"Poker. How was it?" Now I just want him to tell me the truth. If he does, maybe I'll feel closer to him, like we can still tell each other things.

He studies my face to see what I know—and that's when I know he's going to lie to me.

"Good," he says, without flinching. "I won forty bucks."

Chapter 19

I *wasn't going to tell you the truth.*

I sit in my office, letting Mia's voice play through my headphones. My seventh interview in two weeks. It's been two weeks since I interviewed Jada. Two weeks since Oliver lied to me about poker. So far, I've coped with his lying by no longer asking him where he's going when he tells me he's "off to poker." At night, I watch him walk to his car and I can hear the music in my head, the loud thrumming bass of whatever club he was calling me from, the snippets of a lap-dance conversation and heavy breathing. But I don't say anything. I don't want to give him the chance to lie to me again. I've almost confronted him so many times, but then what? I avoid him more than ever, making up excuses to stay late at the office on the nights he's home, then lining up interviews, which have steadily trickled in, one after the other, by word of mouth alone.

Mia is a friend of Jada's, and as soon as she sat down, Mia let me know she was not interested in talking about her real life.

The truth is, I haven't had sex in a year and all my friends are getting married and I'm meeting assholes with bad breath online. But I do feel it all—I feel it in my body all the time. Just not in real life. Jada said she told you about one of her fantasies?

I told Mia she could talk about anything she wants, so she does.

In my fantasy, I'm a coat-check girl at one of the snottiest bars in Dallas. I actually did that job in real life for years. I'm a terrible waitress and I'm nosy as fuck so it works out well.

I love looking in people's coats and purses after they've left them with me. I've never stolen anything. I'm just curious what their lives are like. The bottom of my purse is like the bottom of a trash can at the beach. Crumbs from an old granola bar, a tampon that's lost its wrapper, old receipts that I don't even know why I took in the first place.

But these Dallas women—their purses are meticulous. They smell like a fragrance counter. Everything is clean and new. A fancy tin of mints. A monogrammed wallet with crisp bills. A lipstick the shade of rubies. And in my fantasy, well, I do steal one thing—a card. This SoulCycle mom—perfectly manicured in every way—tosses her Stella McCartney car coat at me without even making eye contact. I can smell her perfume as she walks away and so I rub my wrists on the inside of the jacket, you know, to steal some of her scent. In her coat pocket is a thick black business card, like a black American Express, expensive and heavy, like something dumb that Tesla would make. And it's blank, except for a phone number, hand engraved in gold type. I know instantly it's for sex. These wealthy women are all bored and underfucked.

I call the number on the card and a man answers. His voice is low and gravelly. He asks me for my address. I race home and clean my disgusting apartment and wax everything that needs to be waxed. I smoke a joint and drink a glass of wine. I've never done anything like this before.

So this guy knocks on my door and I answer. I don't know what I imagined. This guy looks like nothing, really. Reddish-brown hair, nondescript eyes. He's just a guy you would pass and never even remember. Totally anonymous. But he walks around my apartment with a confidence that makes me horny, like he owns the place. Like nothing is off-limits to him.

He tells me to show him the bedroom and he follows me in there. Then he tells me to sit down on the bed. So I do. I'm used to taking control in the bedroom. That's the way it's always been. I've never had someone order me around. But I want him to. I'm hanging on his next command and it's turning me on. "Take off your pants," he says. I keep trying to read him—he's direct, but his eyes are soft and curious.

I do exactly what he says. Sort of. I take off my pants but I leave my underwear on, which annoys him. He comes closer, so he's standing over me, looking down at me on the bed. "You know what I meant," he says. His voice is commanding but gentle. He is showing me how to play the game. "Do you want me to leave?" he asks. "No," I say. "Please." I pull my shirt off and lie back on the bed. "Don't move," he says. But it's hard to stay still when he touches me, slipping my underwear down my legs and spreading them open.

He sucks on his fingers and immediately pushes one inside me, then two. It's surprising and powerful. His fingers reach a place most guys miss. Then he tells me to turn over. For a moment, my body freezes. Maybe I've taken this too far. Maybe lying on my stomach would feel too vulnerable, not being able to see what's coming next. But part of me wants exactly that. The thrill of not knowing what's coming, or what he is going to do to me next. I feel as if he can see my mind turning, or maybe my legs starting to quiver, thinking about how it would feel to have him fuck me from behind, when he repeats, "Turn over."

I do what I'm told, flipping onto my stomach. At first, nothing happens. He doesn't move and neither do I. In the stillness, I imagine him admiring my body, lingering on my legs, my body glowing. Then I hear him shift. He leans over my body, resting one hand on the bed next to me. With the other hand he grips the back of my thigh, pulling my legs farther apart. I moan, my hips lifting up toward him. He slips a finger inside me and moves it in a circle, then pulls it out again. "You're ready," he says. He found what he was looking for.

"Where's the money?" he asks me. I tell him I don't have the whole amount, I can't afford what he charges. I bury my head in my hands, terrified now that he's going to walk out of the room. Because I want him to keep touching me so badly. When I don't hear him move, I turn over my shoulder and find him staring at me. He walks away from the bed and I think he's going to tell me he's leaving. But then he comes back, takes my hands, and ties them behind my back. I keep my head turned so I can see and he likes that. He stands at the side of the bed close to my face. He unzips his pants and pulls out his dick. And it's big. Thick and heavy. Then he kneels on the bed and pulls me to my knees. From behind, he holds my hips in place and slides inside of me. I've never been with a guy this big, so I gasp. He fills me up. Moving in and out, and in and out, over and over. And he's so deep he's hitting a spot that no one has touched. He moves in a steady rhythm, pushing inside me while resting one hand lightly around my throat. It's a soft pressure. Like a hint of his power. My legs are spread and I'm sweating and open so deeply to him because I've let go of the control. Suddenly it feels like I'm going to come. I try to slow it down but he says, "No, let go. You're so close." And then he whispers in my ear that I feel so good to him and that's it. I let go. And I have this crazy once-in-a-fucking-lifetime orgasm. And then he pulls out, gets dressed, looks at me, and says goodbye.

I listen to Mia, alone in my office. My mind wanders to the sound of Oliver's voice against the loud thrum of the strip club, until that is all I can hear. Distracted, I shut off the recording. I think about catching up on some work, since I had told Oliver I'd be at the office late, and Emmy is at her grandparents' for the weekend anyway.

Instead I open a folder on my laptop with the audio files I've recorded. Lately what this project might be has shifted for me. I'm no longer just sketching the women who are sharing their stories with me. I've begun to feel they don't need my interpretation of their words. Their desire. Their fantasies are perfect as they are: raw, unvarnished, and true. With permission, I've been sharing links to audio files of the interviews with Alicia. I told her how the stories have taken on a life of their own. "I'm thinking about giving them a place to live where other women can listen."

She agrees. "My friends keep asking when the next one is coming."

"You sent them around?"

"Only to a few people I trust. They're good, Diana."

Sitting at my desk, I think about what a website could look like and how I would design it. I search for a domain name and find exactly what I was hoping for. *Dirty Diana* is available.

When I get home, Oliver is falling asleep to a *Seinfeld* rerun. Everything is normal.

Quiet.

Safe.

And I can't fight the urge to blow it all up.

"Who is Amanda?"

Oliver squints at the TV as if the plotline has just gone wildly off script.

"What?"

"Oliver. I know. You called me. Or Amanda's ass called me as she was dancing on your lap."

Oliver stammers. "Sorry, what?"

"Do you ever go to poker?"

My voice is steady. I want to show him that I'm not angry. Not really. I just want the truth. Oliver looks at me then down at his hands.

"I hate cards."

"So. Who is she?

"Why? Why does it matter?"

"It matters because you're spending time with another woman. What do you like about her?"

"If you're going to get mad, then just get mad. You have every right."

"I'm not mad."

"You're not?"

"No. I don't think so."

"You either are or you aren't."

"Is Amanda pretty?"

"Yes." He says it carefully.

"Okay. And what else?"

"Nothing else."

"You've been lying for months."

"I'm not always there. Sometimes I just drive. I know you don't believe me—"

"I believe you."

"Some nights I pull over and fall asleep in my car. But yes, some nights it's a strip club." He sighs. "She thinks I'm sexy."

"You *pay* her to think you're sexy."

"Diana, if you're going to turn this into a fight, let's just fight. I'll never go again. Okay?"

"How do you know she thinks you're sexy? Does she tell you?"

Oliver stares up at the ceiling. "I can feel her get excited."

At the thought of Oliver with another woman, I feel a quiver, part jealousy, part something else. "You're allowed to touch her?" Oliver looks different in the flicker of the TV's light, the outlines of his face sharper.

"I don't know the rules. Maybe not. But she lets me."

"I want to meet her."

"What? No." Oliver laughs nervously.

"Why not? What don't you want me to see?" I grab my purse by the door, strangely excited. "Let's go."

"Seriously?" His voice is high and pinched. He clears his throat. "Now?"

The summer raindrops are fat, falling heavy against the windshield. Oliver is silent in the passenger seat except for offering the occasional driving direction. "This is a terrible idea," he says.

I feel like screaming *I'm just trying to fix us!* over the sound of the pounding rain, over all his doubt, over the slow disease that is spreading through our marriage. But I stay silent and focused on the road. The buzz of arousal still tingles in my veins, giving me a sort of hope that I feel compelled to chase.

As I pull in to the parking lot of the strip club, Oliver's knee bounces up and down. "We didn't bring an umbrella." We stare out into the dark rainy night together. "We don't have to do this. Now you've seen the place."

"Let's go." I open the car door and make a break for it, not turning around to make sure he is following.

Inside, it smells like sharp perfume and stale beer. I squint in the dim, pulsing light. I can't make out the faces of any of the men. They seem to merge into the walls, the booths, the barstools. But my eyes travel to each of the women in the room, each seeming lit up by their very own spotlight. The sparkle of their makeup makes them flicker. "Which one is she?"

"We should sit down, not just stand here."

We stop at the bar to order drinks and we take them to a velvet-covered half-circle booth with a sticky cocktail table in the center. The chill of the air-conditioning gives me goosebumps; my clothes and hair are damp from the rain outside, sticking to me. I shift in my wet jeans. I see one woman who looks different from the others, a little older and rounder, with less makeup on. Long blond hair. She wears short black shorts that hang low on her hips and a paper-thin tank top.

Oliver sees her too. "That's her."

"Invite her over."

"Diana." Oliver sounds petulant, like I'm asking him to get up and close the window even though I'm the one who is cold. "You invite her if you want to meet her so badly." But even as he says it, he waves his hand in the air like he is ordering a drink. Amanda flashes a wide smile when she sees him.

"She's pretty," I say.

Oliver refuses to respond.

"Hey, you." Amanda leans in so close to Oliver that she might be about to kiss him. But then she stops, just inches away.

"Amanda," Oliver says, sounding so formal that Amanda might laugh if she wasn't so frozen and confused, "this is my wife, Diana."

"Oh," she says, seeming to notice me for the first time. "Hi." The light goes out of her eyes.

"It was her idea to come here."

"Ooooh," Amanda replies. "I love that."

I can see through the performance. Amanda doesn't love anything about this. "Please," I tell her. "I'm not here to judge. Go ahead and do whatever you would normally do."

"This is not . . ." Oliver looks at me and whispers, "Please don't do this."

"He wants a lap dance," I say, avoiding Oliver's pleading eyes and looking at Amanda. If I meet his gaze, I'll lose my nerve. And I don't want to chicken out. I want to know what he likes about this place. I want to know him again.

"Are you sure?" Amanda directs the question to Oliver. "How about we start slow? Like last time."

She sits in his lap, focused on Oliver, looking like she wants him every bit as much as Oliver had said. She grazes Oliver's shirt with her nipples, and I watch them as if outside my body, hovering in some space above their heads. I can see Oliver become aroused despite himself, and I reach out to feel his excitement, to touch him. I can't help it. When I move my hand across his warm, hard erection, I feel a warmth of my own. It turns me on to see him so aroused, to be experiencing something entirely new with him. I slowly start to massage him, feeling him grow. He clutches onto the top of my hand tightly, as if warning me, but not pulling away. A soft moan escapes his mouth as he leans his head back into the leather booth. Amanda smiles. "I have a better idea."

"We don't have to do this," Oliver says. But we are already moving, pulled by an invisible string down a hallway bathed in blue light.

The private room looks, disappointingly, exactly how I had always imagined or at least seen in movies. Mirrored walls. Leather banquette seats that sag in the middle. A shiny pole in the center of the room. But when Amanda closes the door behind her, I'm relieved that the noise of the other room is muffled.

Oliver and I sit in the corner of the L-shaped banquette. My left knee touches his right. Amanda climbs immediately into Oliver's lap. "Do you want to show Diana what I like?" She places his hand on her breast. Oliver pulls away as if he'd burned himself. "Relax . . . it's me . . . You like this?"

"Yes," he says quietly.

This time, I feel weighted down by my body, not like I'm floating above. It's as if someone has pinioned me to the leather. I should get up, but I can't. I should want to get up, but I don't. I want to keep watching. I stare straight ahead, into the mirror, at the image of all three of us.

"Your wife is beautiful," Amanda says loud enough for me to hear. Then, into his ear, "You know I like to be touched . . ."

"I can't."

"But you're so hard." This is their routine. He touches her when he gets hard. And she lets him. I study Oliver's confidence as he caresses her breasts softly.

The heaviness in my body turns to a prickly heat—a flush that starts in my legs and moves up through my body.

"We should stop . . ." Oliver turns to face me. More like a question this time.

I reach out and grab his hand. "No. Keep going. Please." I want this new feeling I'm experiencing to last. I recognize it now—a cocktail of desire and greed—I want to remain jealous. I shift my body so I'm watching them not in the mirror but right next to me.

"I make your dick so hard, don't I?" The strap of Amanda's top falls down her shoulder, exposing her naked breast.

"Yes."

"How hard do I make you?"

"So fucking hard." I've never heard Oliver speak that way. I want him all to myself. *I* want to make him hard. Not her.

But Oliver is no longer thinking of me. He had been so aware of me until now, so worried, constantly looking over at me. Now his hands are all over Amanda, grabbing her hips, her legs, her ass. I lean into him so that I'm partially sharing his lap with Amanda. I put my lips close to his. "Kiss me . . ."

"*I'll* kiss you . . ." Amanda tries to intercept me.

"No," I say. "Oliver." It's *my husband* I want and it feels so unbelievably good to finally feel that.

"What?" he whispers.

"Kiss me," I tell him.

Oliver's eyes widen and his lips meet mine and I feel a rush of desire for him. We keep kissing and the dulled throb of the music from the bar fades and Amanda fades and it is just us. I breathe in his scent, and it is good, it is the scent I'd always loved, of cedar and soap. Safe and warm, but not just that—there is something else, too, the way Oliver's tongue strokes my lips, the way our bodies move together, like a dance that is sexier for having been practiced. Oliver feels more confident in his own skin. Our lips part and he says, "God, I've missed you."

The moment we stop kissing, the club returns and the music grates and there is Amanda again, leaning over Oliver, wearing her pretend smile. "What about me, love?" she says. "Can I kiss her too?"

Oliver looks between the two of us, and Amanda once again grazes his chest with her breasts, leaning across him toward me. At this point I will do whatever Oliver wants me to. If he wants me to kiss Amanda, I will. Oliver nods yes and reaches between my legs while Amanda leans in.

When Amanda's lips are just inches from mine, she pauses, her mouth curling into a smile. "You're just a horny little bitch, aren't you?"

Oliver flinches and we all feel it. The needle scratch.

"Diana." He looks at me, as if for help. I must be looking at him the same way, a mirror image—two stricken faces—we're both feeling it—the strangest sensation of looking at yourself and at a total stranger all at once.

"I need some air," Oliver stands up, grabbing for his drink and finishing it in one big swallow.

I call for him but he strides out through the club and into the rain. *Don't leave, Oliver. Not now. We can save this.*

"Oliver!" I catch up to him. "You can't leave like this. Let's go back in."

"What are we doing here, Diana? This was a horrible fucking idea." He finds his keys, finally, and unlocks the car.

"Don't run away. Not now. That was the closest I've felt to you in so long. We can salvage this. I *know* we can," I plead.

Oliver shakes his head, pulls my hands off his shoulders. I'd been gripping him so hard. "Stay. Please." I plead. "I don't want us to go home."

"That isn't me. That isn't . . . us," Oliver says and he gets in the car, waiting for me to follow. "I can't go back in," he says and I see there is no changing his mind.

Once I'm in the car, we buckle our seatbelts and I pull out of the parking lot. Not a word is said. Another night ends in us both soaking wet, this time drenched in rain and a prickly kind of shame. We sit in it the entire way home.

Chapter 20

"Not every marriage that ends is a failure," Miriam says softly. She reaches for another sip of her tea and Oliver nods solemnly in agreement as if he'd come up with this little nugget himself.

"Well, but it is though, right?" I ask. "I mean, a failed marriage *is* exactly that, a marriage that ends." Why is Oliver looking at me like I'm speaking in a foreign tongue?

"Of course, Diana. But I'm not saying your marriage is at its end. The notion I'd like to introduce—that I think is important in our work together—is to understand the successes you've achieved together." I'm so confused. Are we succeeding or failing? She's been doing this the whole hour, talking in tightly knit circles that confound me. "Diana, you look panicked."

All eyes on me again. "I just feel like, maybe last time there was progress?"

There wasn't any progress. Last week, I'd tried to incorporate an exotic dancer into our relationship and now whenever Oliver looks at me it's like he's genuinely frightened of what I'll suggest next. And now we're here, to lay all the pieces in front of Miriam. And worse, now that we're here, I can't follow what she's saying and Oliver seems to speak her language and not mine, and my head is starting to pound, just behind my right temple. I'd honestly thought I'd be better at therapy.

"Would you like to share what you feel has been progress? How did you feel after we met last?"

"Good." I jump in too quickly.

Oliver looks at me curiously. "Which part felt good?"

I can't think of a single thing in the moment. My mind goes blank as I grope for a positive detail from this week. "We had Emmy's game. We were a real unit, it felt like, cheering her on."

"Were we going to root for separate teams? At our own daughter's soccer game?"

"These days, I don't know." If he is going to get shitty, I can too. But I want to demonstrate for Miriam that I'm in control. "Oliver's a great dad. We love our daughter. And we've always been on the same page. So many of our friends argue over parenting—how to discipline, how much screen time, et cetera. I think it's a big deal that we've never fought about any of it. We're really good friends, who love each other."

"Is that enough for you?" Oliver asks. "I'm not trying to be an asshole, I'm really asking."

I pause. Friends isn't enough for me. I know it's not. "I don't know," I say quietly. I look down at my hands. I rub my thumb into the opposite palm and try to think of something else to say. What's the magic sentence with just enough information to appear like sharing but without divulging anything I might later regret? Until I stop thinking of therapy as a game, we won't get anywhere, I know, but I can't seem to stop.

Oliver clears his throat. "We should tell her."

Jesus. Why does therapy have to mean being honest about everything?

"Do you want to or should I?" he asks.

"I don't think it needs all this buildup and fanfare, does it?"

Oliver looks down and mumbles what feels like a confession. "I've been going to strip clubs and Diana thought it would be a good idea to have a threesome with one of the dancers."

"I didn't ask for a threesome!"

"Well then, what was that?"

"It was an attempt. An attempt to . . . try something different. Just like you were trying to do."

We both look to Miriam, but her expression is blank. She jots a note in her book.

"It didn't go well," Oliver adds.

"Which part?" I interrupt. "You going to a strip club or me trying to go with you?"

"Where is all this even coming from? You go from avoiding sex with me to Girls Gone Wild."

"That's so unfair. You're the one lying about going to strip clubs!"

"I'm not cheating on you. It's just an escape. And you're so far away. I feel like I don't even know you anymore."

"Can you articulate how Diana feels different?" Miriam chimes in like we're discussing flavors of ice cream.

"The old Diana would never have done that. Tried to kiss someone in front of me." I suddenly feel like I'm in therapy with Oliver's father. "Can't we just go back to the way things were?"

It's the only question today that I know the answer to. "No," I say. There's no going back to the way things were. Because there are no "old Diana" or "old Oliver" versions of either of us. They don't exist. There are only ever our perceptions of each other. And Oliver's image of me has shifted. Maybe the lenses we see each other through got cloudier or sharper, I'm not sure which. Maybe a slant of light has changed and that's enough.

The room is quiet and still, and when I turn to Oliver, he does something that I don't expect. Tears well in his eyes and his voice begins to tremble. "I just . . . don't know how to make her happy anymore. Like we're in quicksand. And we keep sinking and we're trying all these ideas to keep above it and none of them are working. They just make us sink farther. And faster."

This is the first thing to come up in therapy that we've actually agreed on. But what else can we do but try to keep our heads above the sand? What's the other option? Divorce? We love each other. I could never do that to Emmy. Maybe the story of our marriage that we tell ourselves isn't true anymore, but couldn't it be revised? What if there's a way to shed our old story and let a new one emerge. An even better one. I didn't do all this, live here and work this job and pay for this house, and fit into this life, so that we would just let it burn.

"So what do you suggest we try?" I'm asking the room, hoping someone has a better idea.

"Maybe we don't try. Maybe we acknowledge we're in quicksand. And there's no getting out of it."

Chapter 21

Do not cry on the sidelines of your daughter's soccer
game. Do not cry donotcry.

It's almost noon and the day is bright and hot. The opposite of
crying weather. *Do not cry.* All around me, parents chat happily to one
another and cheer on their kids. Oliver and I have barely spoken since
yesterday's therapy session, silently passing each other in the halls of
our house, afraid we will say something we'll regret. Something *else*
we'll regret. Whatever this new path we're on is, it's scary and unset-
tling, nothing like the warm safety of mediocrity. I miss it, suddenly.
Feeling nothing.

In front of me, a woman slides her hand into the back pocket of
her husband's Levi's, easy. In my head, I hear Jenna's voice from
months ago, telling me about how unnerving it was to see Raleigh,

post-breakup, crying on the soccer game sidelines. "Maybe she just shouldn't come?" Jenna had suggested. I look around today, and Raleigh isn't here. The sun beats down on the back of my neck so I angle my body toward Oliver's. As I do, he turns away. He offers everyone near us a drink from our cooler.

Everything is fine, I tell myself. The game is only an hour long.

But everything is not fine. And now here I am, standing on the sidelines, biting my bottom lip in an attempt not to cry.

"Emmy!" Oliver claps his hands. "Look alive!" Oliver laughs as Emmy turns a crooked cartwheel then picks a wedgie.

Her coach shouts at her to pay attention—"The ball, Emmy, the ball!"—but now Emmy is kneeling in the grass, distracted by a roly-poly. Usually in moments like these, I would look over at Oliver and we would laugh together. Our horrible little soccer player, surrounded by a sea of kids and parents who are seriously out to win. I reach for his hand and he buries it deep in his pocket.

I lower my big black sunglasses as the tears start falling. I turn on my heels and head straight for the car. Safer to cry there.

I keep walking. I notice Oliver doesn't call out to me. Just feet from the car, I drop my key fob on the ground. "Shit."

"Diana?" Liam stands behind L'Wren's Range Rover, unloading canvas L.L.Bean bags full of halftime snacks. "Are you okay?"

That's all it takes. I think of Raleigh again—this time in that orange volunteer vest, begging me not to be nice to her or the dam will break. In the glow of Liam's genuine concern, the tears fall faster.

"Oh, shit, Diana. Here . . ." He opens L'Wren's passenger door. "Get inside before the soccer moms smell weakness."

"I'm so sorry. I don't even know why I'm crying like this. I'm fine." I try to laugh but it comes out more like a strangled hiccup.

When I look up, his eyes are full of sympathy. There's not a hint of panic at the sight of a sad woman crying in his car. He leans over me to the glove box and hands me a tissue.

"It's okay to not be fine, Diana. What happened?"

"Ugh. Just a bad day. I don't even know why I'm crying."

"Yeah, you said that."

"Things with Oliver suck." I wipe my nose. "He's been lying to me about playing poker when he's really going to a strip club."

"Shit. That does suck. Which one?"

"Yellow Rose. I think that's what it's called."

Liam hands me another tissue. "That one's better than most. Not like it's gonna make you feel better, but at least he has decent taste."

I blow my nose again. "I don't know what I'm doing with my life, Liam, you know?" I can't really believe I'm confessing all this to a twentysomething, to my friend's stepson. But now that I've started talking it's like I can't stop. "I keep 'making a plan' but what does that even mean? Most of the day, I feel numb. Like I'm watching my life unravel from the sidelines and there is nothing I can do about it. And the only pleasure I get is from interviewing other women talking about their sex lives." I laugh-cry. "Meanwhile my own sex life is a fucking disaster."

Liam looks out the front windshield and exhales. I am stunned with what I've just told him—and he seems stunned to have heard it. But I also feel better, lighter somehow. Liam turns toward me, "Uh, let's pause on this interview thing. What's all that about?" I chuckle, letting my ragged breathing kill the quiet.

"No? Okay. Wanna hit?" Liam offers up a joint from the pocket of his T-shirt.

Just as I'm shaking my head no, I say, "Sure."

He lights it, and I take a long drag. A warm sensation washes through me, familiar and nostalgic. I sink back into the passenger seat.

"Does L'Wren have another way home?" I ask.

"Kevin's here with his car, so yeah."

"Good. Do you mind getting us out of here?"

"I'd love to."

It feels incredible to speed away. I roll down my window and hold my arm out into the breeze. I lean into the warmth of my buzz. I have no idea where we're going.

"So. Interviews?"

I can't help giggling, like I've blown Liam's world right open.

"Can it stay between us? For now?"

"Naturally."

I tell him about the site I'm figuring out how to build. "I thought the interviews would be more like they'd been before, like backgrounds for more paintings," I explain. "But what I'm realizing is how they stand completely on their own, full of longing."

"Like auditory erotica."

I like the sound of that. I had never put it that way before. "I guess the thing is, I'm realizing that I don't feel whole unless I'm making something. It doesn't really matter what it is."

"Yeah. I get it." Liam is quiet for a while, his eyes on the road, before turning down the music and asking, "Can I take you somewhere?"

We pull up to L'Wren's empty house and Liam walks me inside. I've been to L'Wren's house hundreds of times over the years—for baby music classes and playdates, book clubs and so many holiday dinners, but in all those times I've never once seen the basement where Liam lives. The door to his stairs is always closed and there's no reason for me to go down. And as he walks me down the steep staircase, the first thought that crosses my stoned brain is *a serial killer must live here.*

The room is dimly lit, and L'Wren's foster cats are sleeping on every available surface. More alarming, two of the cats are playing tug-of-war with what looks like a bloody wound on discarded skin. On the desk, beside Liam's computer, there's a bust of something like a bashed-in head and three spare limbs in a pile.

"Welcome to my sanctuary." Liam holds out his arms and does a slow spin. Despite all the cats, all I smell is acrylic paint.

"Liam? What is all this?" I pick up a silicon wound, one of five lined up on the cookie sheet on top of his neatly made bed. It's the size of my thumb and an orangey kind of flesh color with a blood-red gash down the middle.

"Yeah. I made all this."

"You made these?"

"I sell them for Halloween costumes, murder-mystery parties, and to a few people in the industry." His chest puffs a little when he says *industry,* just a little. "I have my own website. And a pretty cool Etsy shop. And not to brag or anything, but I just sold three bullet holes to the NCIS makeup team."

"Liam! That's great! Does L'Wren know all this? That you make these?" I hold up an impressively deep and real-looking wound the size of a small plate.

"Yeah, that one's a throat slit. It took me almost three hours to get it right. It still needs some work."

He holds up the bashed-in head. "Thank you, Wonderland murders. Barbara Richardson's head was so messed up the top of her skull was flat. It's on YouTube if you want to see it."

"Oh. Maybe later," I deflect. "L'Wren told me you've been painting. Does she know you're making all this great stuff? Or your dad?"

"Painting? Is that really what she says? Or is it more like, 'he stays in that dungeon all day doing lord knows what!'" His impression is so spot-on we both laugh. "She and Dad know a bit. I asked if I could practice on them, but they turned me down. I need more guinea pigs."

"I like this one," I say, touching a thin, deep wound.

"Yeah, me too. It's a kitchen-knife gash. Three inches deep. Serrated knife. I have more tentative wounds, but I like the confidence of this one."

Liam talking about his work with such love and affection is the best thing I've heard all day. "Wanna try it on?"

"Sure."

Liam nudges a sleeping cat off his La-Z-Boy recliner and places a pillow over the seat, which the cats have clawed to shreds. I sit and he explains that he designed this wound to fall across the abdomen. His ears go pink as he realizes I'll have to at least partially lift my shirt. I roll up my T-shirt to just below my bra then lean back into the massive chair. I close my eyes.

I flinch when the first stroke of some kind of cold gel touches my skin. "Sorry," he apologizes under his breath. He is deep in concentration, his brushstrokes slow and delicate. I'm reminded of the seaweed wraps my mother-in-law takes us for at the spa. I'm almost drifting off to sleep when Liam asks, "So are you going to divorce Oliver?"

"No. We're in a weird place, for sure, but we wouldn't get divorced." I suddenly wish Liam were my therapist and not Miriam. He's so much easier to talk to. Or maybe it's the weed. Maybe edibles before couples therapy is the answer.

"Diana." I open my eyes and his face is inches from mine, a small makeup brush in his hands. His eyes are red and glassy and earnest. "I'm about to drop some real knowledge on you."

I laugh, but he doesn't break his gaze. "Okay."

"Love the thing that loves you back."

I smile. "Deep."

"Thanks. I heard it on a podcast L'Wren and I listen to while we bathe the cats."

"There is *so much* to unpack in that sentence."

"I know. Right?" He stands to stretch his legs and study his work. "But I kind of agree. People are paying me to make this stuff—it's loving me back and I'm loving it, you know? So can I give you some advice?"

"More?"

"I've seen a lot of Rockgate divorces. And it never goes well for the women."

Again I think of Raleigh and feel a heaviness in my chest. "Yeah, so I've heard."

"A few years later, the men are already remarried and living in even bigger houses and the women are left holding a big shit-bag of resentment. And they're pissed because they put all that energy into something that wasn't working."

"But what if it's their fault it wasn't working?"

"Is that what you think? That it's one person's fault? It never works that way."

"Jesus, Liam. You need your own podcast," I say, then worry it came out too sarcastic. "I mean it. You're really smart."

"I just don't want that to happen to you. Unless that's what you want." He dips his makeup brush in two different shades of red, then paints around my knife wound. "I guess what I'm saying is, whether you and Oliver stay together or you split, have the thing that's just yours."

He fans his hands over the wound to help the paint dry.

"Do you want some strangulation marks? Around your neck?"

"Why not?"

As Liam brushes on some purple and blue bruising around my neck, I look around his tiny, dark space, covered in makeup and rubber and sleeping cats. I can feel his pure desire to make something that he can call his own. I know this desire.

"Take a look." He holds up a mirror. "Now you finally look how you feel."

Chapter 22

A few days later, I sit at my computer and upload a new interview to the Dirty Diana site. The page is simple and clean. Each story gets its own link, with just a first name beneath a loose sketch I've drawn, a silhouette of the woman being interviewed. This one is Carrie, one of my favorites.

I have a few fantasies. I'm not sure which one to share.

Tell me about your favorite one.

My favorite . . . I'm actually my age in my favorite. Usually I'm younger in my fantasies.

How old are you?

Sixty-one.

And where are you?

I'm at a brothel. I know. So old-fashioned. Maybe I've been watching too many movies. It's only my fantasy in my dreams. When I'm awake—well, it's different.

What happens in the brothel?

Usual things. Lots of corsets and velvet and loud men drinking at a bar downstairs. There's no one playing the piano or anything. But it still feels like something you would see in the movies. . . . Should we have another drink?

Sure.

Anyway, in my fantasy, I'm the only woman there. No one else is working that night. My boss tells me there are some sailors coming in that night. They haven't seen a woman in months.

Does that excite you?

Not at first, no. I'm worried they'll be disappointed. I'm the oldest woman there. I'm afraid that when they see me, they'll ask for another girl—or won't be aroused. All those destructive little voices. But they're supposed to walk through the doors any second, so I force my insecurities aside and I put on some lingerie and a silk robe, and I wait for one of them to come in. I look in the mirror a thousand times and lie on the bed in a hundred different positions, trying to find my best angle. There's a tentative knock on my door. And then he walks in. And he's so young. Like one of those old black-and-white photos your grandmother would have carried. Classically handsome in a tragic sort of way. And he's even more nervous than I am. I can practically see him shaking. So I stop thinking about how disappointed he must be and I start trying to make him less nervous.

I peel off his clothes until he's naked. He's already hard. A kind of hard I forgot about. Like he's about to burst through his skin. And so I put him in my mouth. I feel him grow even more inside me. And I know he's not disappointed because he moans in pleasure and looks at me in astonishment. I know how to please a man. And it feels so good to please him.

I work my hand around his erection and slowly at first then faster as I take all of him in my mouth and I hear him gasp in disbelief. I know that no one has ever made him feel this way. I love it, he tells me. You're so good. I meet his eyes for a few seconds, tracing my wet lips with the head of his erection. I watch as he gives me permission, leaning in, then silently begging. I can *feel him pulsing in my mouth, and he tells me he's close, so I slow down and draw it out as long as I can, moving him in and out of my mouth until he finally comes. And as I get up to leave he pulls me into him, pinning me against the bed with his lips, kissing me with such passion. But I have to pull away, I have another client in the next room.*

I wrap my robe around me and walk next door. The man waiting there isn't disappointed. He takes me in his arms and tells me how beautiful I am. How happy he is to see me. He opens my robe and tosses it on the floor. I push him onto the bed and climb on top of him. His mouth is open, searching for anything to suck so I let him find my nipples. I push into him, inviting just the tip of him inside me. He slides in and out of me, gasping in pleasure. I've never felt so desired. So wanted. And I get bolder and bolder. I stand up, leaving him writhing on the bed. I walk into the next room completely naked. I can please any man. I know it in my skin.

What about you? Who pleases you?

The last room I enter.

Who's in the last room?

All of them.

I shut my computer and check the time. I spend extra effort on my hair in preparation for seeing my mother-in-law, then wait for Oliver to finish getting dressed.

When he comes down the stairs, I almost lose my breath. He's wearing a gray flannel suit perfectly tailored to his body. I've always been a little unnerved by the fact that his mom still buys him clothes, but she does have impeccable taste.

"You look nice," I say.

"Thanks. I'm running every day now."

"Wow," is all I can think to say. Raleigh's words echo in my head, "If I were at a key party, I'd pray for his." Oliver usually shaves before we see his mother, but he's left a three-day-old shadow. A subtle fuck you or laziness? Whatever the reason, it suits him. Of course other moms have crushes on him. "You really look great."

"Shall we?" he replies flatly.

Oliver is quiet on the drive to the gala. That's how we are in each other's company lately, like we're waiting to take the other person's temperature. But mostly we just wait.

The first time I attended Vivian's annual fundraising gala, Oliver and I were an hour late because I couldn't leave his bathroom. Oliver had tried to coax me out from the other side of the closed door. "I could run out and get some Pepto?"

"I think I'm done. I'm so sorry. I didn't expect to be so nervous."

"My mom is going to love you." Oliver sounded so confident I almost believed him. But when I looked down at my Steve Madden pumps that were chipping at the front I wasn't so sure. "Do you have a Sharpie?" I spit onto my finger and tried to rub the scuff marks away.

"A Sharpie? Not on me, no."

Three flushes later, I finally felt confident enough to stand up and look at myself in the mirror. The pearl-colored silk slip dress I spent an entire paycheck on was creased at the crotch because I'd been sitting on the toilet for so long. "Don't suppose you have a steamer?" I called out nervously to Oliver. The night was already a disaster, and it hadn't even started.

Oliver knocked softly on the door. "Can I come in?"

"Fine. Just hold your nose."

Oliver walked in and immediately turned around and walked out. "Probably better if I don't come in."

"Oh my god. Just tell her I'm sick. Please. I don't think I can pull it together and we're already so late."

"Nothing has changed, Diana. I love you and so will she. It literally smells like death in there and my eyes are watering, but if you told me you wanted to have sex right now I'd take you on the toilet. You look stunning."

Oliver's parents lived on the other side of town, in one of the oldest and wealthiest sections of Dallas. I tried to steady my breath as we drove north on Oak Lawn Avenue and the houses got older and grander. Oliver had told me stories about his childhood, about the neighborhood kids daring each other to TP the multimillion-dollar estate where the owner of the Dallas Cowboys lived, and how it wasn't uncommon to spot Laura Bush power walking on the next street over.

As I tried to smooth my dress, he drove around a circular, hedge-lined driveway, past a valet station, and pulled up next to a Rolls-Royce and a vintage Jaguar. His parents' home was a stately English Tudor flanked by live oaks on a lot that seemed to go on forever. It was glowing from within, perhaps from the sheer amount of diamond carats inside. Before we got out of the car, I sprayed my bare arms and legs with mosquito repellent, knowing I would get eaten alive. Oliver put a hand out to stop me. "You don't need to worry about mosquitos. My parents have a guy for that."

"Really?"

He smiled. "He's a mosquito bouncer."

"Very funny." But his joking helped put me at ease.

Vivian swept down the stairs to meet us in the foyer. "Oliver, I swore I gave you the right time. What on earth happened?"

"It was my fault actually. I wasn't feeling well. I'm so sorry."

Vivian looked at me and plastered on a smile. "No matter. Let's get you upstairs and get you dressed!"

"Mom . . ." Oliver said, a warning tone in his voice, but Vivian pressed on, feigning innocence. "You should have told me Diana didn't have anything to wear. I would have sent something over."

I crossed my arms self-consciously over the slip dress Cindy Crawford had worn so well. Of course it wasn't appropriate for a Dallas gala. What was I thinking?

"And what size are you, Diana? You're absolutely petite."

"A medium?" I said, my face turning bright red.

"I meant the shoes, sweetheart."

"Oh. Right. I'm a seven." The shoes hadn't passed inspection either.

"Perfect. I'm a seven too!"

We settled on a two-piece Chanel suit that made me feel about eighty years old. Closed-toe shoes because I hadn't had a pedicure, and also that was all Vivian had to loan me. "Sandals are for the desperate," she muttered. *Like me,* I thought, as I wedged my foot into a Burberry pump.

When Oliver saw me, he couldn't help laughing. "That's what you chose?"

"The outfit chose *her,* Oliver. Doesn't she look darling?"

"She looks like one of your sorority sisters."

"I love it," I lied. I didn't want to be the source of Oliver and his mother arguing. "It's beautiful, Vivian. Thank you."

"I better go downstairs. Everyone must be wondering what emergency had pulled the hostess away from her own party for so long!"

When she left, I buried my face into Oliver's chest. He rested his chin on my head. "Would it make you feel better if you knew she bought my entire outfit? She likes to dress people. That's all."

I spent the entire party wishing I was somewhere else. Two of Oliver's ex-girlfriends were there, both dressed in lovely, age-appropriate Diane von Furstenberg wrap dresses. Every single person he introduced me to looked at a spot over my head when they talked to me, craning for the next person to talk to. I had never felt so insignificant. I was the Golden Boy's plus-one, and clearly someone they'd assumed they would never see again.

Tonight, we pull in to the same circular drive, past the valet station once again. The house looks unchanged, all the many windows glittering against the dark night. Vivian greets us in the foyer, this time wearing a tightly fitted dress with a long skirt of blue chiffon.

"Fashionably late, per usual. Oliver, why didn't you shave? You look unhoused."

"It's nice to see you too." Oliver kisses her cheek.

"Oh, please. Don't be dramatic. Your father is by the bar. I hear some more groveling is in order." Oliver nods obediently and leaves me alone with Vivian.

"Remember the first time you attended one of my galas?" She brings this up every year. "And you were wearing one of those—what are they called? Those undergarments?"

"It was a dress. Not a slip."

"Yes, exactly. A slip. But look at you now. Quick learner. Does Oliver seem unhappy to you?" She switches gears abruptly. "He's lost that spark, hasn't he?"

A waiter walks by with a tray of champagne flutes and I grab two of them, looking for anyone to give one to and save me from this conversation.

"I don't know. I don't think so," I lie.

"But isn't that your job? To know when your husband is unhappy?"

Vivian doesn't wait for a response. Already bored by me, she flits away on her own. She has always held me at an arm's length, unable to make a final verdict on whether I'm good enough for her son. I thought for sure the ice would melt after Emmy was born. Sometimes I still catch her looking at me from across the table, squinting toward me as if to ask, *Who are you, really? And where did you actually come from?* The subtext of nearly everything she says to me sounds like *I'm on to you.* Just as I turn into the hallway to find a bathroom to hide in, I bump into Oliver.

"I'm officially sixteen again, getting scolded by my father in public," Oliver says.

"I'm sorry. How long do we have to stay to not be rude?"

"At least an hour."

"And how do we survive that?"

"Two words," Oliver says. "Shrimp. Cocktail."

I give him a confused look and he laughs. "I'm kidding. Open. Bar."

Hearing him laugh puts my whole body at ease. Like I've been summoned to the principal's office only to have her say, *Relax. We know you didn't do it.* That's how I feel around Oliver lately, like a kid always on the verge of being in trouble. Miriam would have a field day with this.

Over our first glass of champagne, the frost between Oliver and me continues to melt. "You really do look good," I say to him. "Really fit."

"I've lost six pounds from running." I imagine you can't grow up with Vivian as your mom and not feel proud every time you lose a pound.

"You look so nice."

"You do too," he says. "I should have told you that earlier."

"Thanks," I say. "Why didn't you?"

Oliver doesn't answer. He orders us two more champagne cocktails and hands one to me. "I don't know."

Please don't. Please stay present. Please let's look at each other like we used to. I didn't know how badly I needed that until it was gone.

"I get it," I say. "We seem to have lost the plot, haven't we?"

"It happens. It's not like anyone here is on their first marriage." He gestures around the room of tightly pulled faces and obscene privilege.

Beside us, a toothy woman is discussing the benefits of redshirting her six-year-old, which she hopes will give him an advantage on the lacrosse field. And behind us, a crowd of familiar real estate scions debate which plane to charter for a hunting trip to Wyoming.

"I don't want a second husband," I blurt.

Oliver sighs. "Same. I don't think I have the energy." It's not the exact affirmation I'm looking for, but I lean in anyway. I take a deep breath and exhale. "Want to look at the art?"

Oliver almost spits out his drink.

Years ago, when we would visit Oliver's parents, before Emmy was born, I would ask Oliver if he wanted to look at the art, which was code for *Do you want to have sex in your old bedroom?*

"Look at the art now?"

"Sure. Why not?"

His expression is impossible to read. "With everyone here?"

"Let's go look at the art," I say again.

After a moment of silent torture, Oliver nods. "Let's look at the art."

We slip from the crowd and up the back stairs to Oliver's childhood room, holding hands the entire way. Oliver closes the door behind him and smiles. His room has not been touched since he left for college, except to be cleaned, Vivian making sure his rugby trophies are polished regularly. "Shhhh," he tells me as I start laughing, while kicking off my heels. "We should make it quick," he adds, still seeming unsure we should do it at all.

"What if I don't want it to be quick?" I ask. I hate how I sound. I'm trying so hard to seduce him that it feels like a charade. Isn't seduction always a charade? Why does this time feel so flat-footed?

I carry on and unbutton Oliver's shirt. I kiss his naked chest, then stand on my tiptoes and start on his neck. But when I look up, he's not smiling. A dark cloud passes behind his eyes and his jaw clenches. Where I usually see tenderness, there's only anger. Instead of kissing me back, he grabs me by the shoulder and turns me around so I'm facing the wall. Then he presses his hands on the wall on either side of my body. He moves close to me.

"Why now? Why tonight, Diana?" His voice is almost shaking, as if he's fighting the urge to be here. "What are you doing?" He doesn't want to want me.

I lift my dress, inviting him to make love to me. I hear him exhale. I let him tug my underwear to the side but I'm still taken aback by how agitated he's become. This isn't how we have sex. He doesn't fuck me against walls. I gasp when he wedges his knee in between my thighs to open my legs.

"Oh, Oliver," I moan, but Oliver covers my mouth with his hand. I turn my head to see his face; I need to know what his expression is. I want to look in his eyes, but he keeps his gaze down, watching himself enter me from behind.

It's surprising being fucked by your husband who is nothing like your husband. He is potent and passionate. There is nothing tentative about him. He tugs at my bra until my breasts fall out and then he pinches my nipple tightly, rolling it between his forefinger and thumb. I turn my head to the side so he can see me moan. But he's upset. He doesn't want me to moan in pleasure. He lifts my leg and forces himself even deeper inside me so I can feel his power. His wet lips on my neck, the smell of champagne on his breath as he exhales into me. And then a sharp pain on my earlobe where his teeth meet my skin. I waver for a moment, unsure if the pain is too much. But I'm wet. So wet I can hear the slapping of his erection thrusting in and out of me. "Fuck," Oliver almost yells. "Fuck."

"It's okay," I tell him. "Keep going. Fuck me." He uses his entire body weight and presses me flush against the wall, my breasts pressed hard against his plaid wallpaper. I stick my hips out even farther as he speeds up, until it feels like a pounding and I'm riding a fine line between pleasure and pain. Then, in a flash, Oliver changes positions. He pulls himself out of me, takes me to the bed so that I'm kneeling. From behind, he pulls my underwear down to my ankles and enters me again. "Harder," I whisper. "Even harder," I tell him. Oliver does as he's told, clutching the headboard for extra resistance. "Now?" he asks. Before I can answer I feel him pulsing inside me as he comes harder than he ever has.

When he pulls out, I turn to him, finally looking him in the eye. I'm speechless and not because of the pleasure. I don't know what to say to this man who fucked me from behind and avoided eye contact. Oliver quickly zips up his pants and buttons his shirt. "We should go back to the party," he says, his voice cold. It's the strangest response to the strangest experience. So I follow suit. "Sure." I slide back into my dress. "Let's go."

On our way downstairs, Oliver is grabbed by a pair of investment bankers. I go in search of a quiet place where I can process what just happened. I lock myself in a guest bathroom. It's neat and clean and decorated with seascapes and family mottos. *We may not have it all together, but together we have it all!*

My breath is impossible to steady. Even now, surrounded by Vivian's bath towels that match the bath mat that brings out the pale yellow in the floral wallpaper, it's hard to believe that someone who lived here could ever struggle.

I wonder if Oliver is looking for me in the crowd. But I don't actually want to know. In my heart, I know he's not.

I finally let myself out of the bathroom and spend another hour making small talk at the party. Then Oliver and I find each other and agree it's time to head home.

We return to a quiet house. I fight my instinct to ask what he's thinking. To reach out to him and spin what happened in his childhood bedroom as something positive. I want to believe it was a step forward, not back.

Oliver drives the sitter home, then lies down in bed beside me.

In the dark, I ask, "You know what you said to me—a few weeks ago?" I can't help myself. I need to know where we stand. "About us being in quicksand. Do you still feel—"

"Diana." He doesn't let me finish. "Aren't you tired? Let's just lie here for a while." He turns on his back. "I still haven't figured out where we are."

My heart is pounding in my chest. "But we need to."

"Not tonight." He gets up and grabs a blanket from the bed, which means he plans to sleep on the couch.

"Maybe we should take a break," I say in a desperate bid for his attention. I regret the words as soon as they leave my lips.

"You want to take a *break*?" He looks at me. "We're not going steady, Diana. We're married."

It works. I have his attention. And now I don't know what to do with it. I hold it briefly in my hands and immediately want to set it down, somewhere, anywhere. "Something needs to change. Maybe we need to shake it up. We could take a break for a few weeks to figure out how we feel?" Even as I speak, I'm thinking less about the words tumbling out of me and more about how I want Oliver to respond. He'll snap out of his iciness and come to his senses. He'll pull me close and wrap his arms around me. We'll apologize to each other at the same time.

But he doesn't do any of that. "Okay."

"Okay?" I echo into the dark room.

"Yeah." He gropes on the floor for his pants. "Let's take a break. This is all too much."

I turn on the bedside lamp and we both squint into the light. This has all gotten so out of hand. "What should I tell Emmy?"

"Is Emmy the only reason you're even in this anymore? Emmy, and this." Oliver waves his arms around, taking in the room, the house. "If the house disappeared tomorrow, if we hadn't had Emmy, would you even still want to be with me?"

Oliver's words hang in the air for a second too long. I reel at the thought of making a choice like that—of having that choice to make. "I'd never wish away our life."

"That's exactly my point. You would never wish away our *life*. You'd just wish away *me*."

"Oliver." My head spins. "No. You're twisting things—"

"Diana. You're right. We need some space. Because I'm out of ideas." He's grown suddenly calmer, as if a task that's been plaguing him has finally been crossed off his to-do list.

"Where are you going?"

"I don't know." He finds his running shoes and laces them, sitting at the edge of the bed. "A hotel. I think it's a good idea. Let's take a few weeks, a month. See what happens."

My mouth goes completely dry. I try again. "But Emmy . . ."

"I agree with you—I don't think this version of us is healthy for her. I'll still pick her up from school and bring her home."

"And the weekends?" What are the right questions to be asking? What's the question that will break the spell—the one that will make us both see this is silly—this isn't us, we aren't here, not yet.

"I don't know, Diana. We'll figure it out."

"Wait . . ."

"What?" It isn't coldness in his voice now, it's sorrow.

"You're just going to leave?"

"That's what a break is. You leave."

"What about . . ."

Neither of us speaks.

I fill the silence with words that say nothing. "I don't know. Okay . . ." The doorway where he stands feels so far it might as well be the moon.

"See you later."

"What hotel are you going to?"

He shrugs, then a sad smile. "Anywhere but the Rosevale." He grabs his sweatshirt, which I'd hung yesterday on the hook on the back of our door. He doesn't pause at the threshold, doesn't turn around, just closes the door. I listen to the sound of his feet on the stairs, his car door opening, him pulling away.

To the back of the door I ask, "So that's it?"

Chapter 23

Eric shimmies up to the table carrying a fresh round of drinks. He sings a Billy Idol song from at least a decade before he was born. "In the midnight hour, she cried more, more, more!" Then he adds his own sparkle, "More Ladies' Night!" With a flourish, he places a glass of rosé in front of L'Wren and a martini in front of me, vodka splashing from the glass. "What are we eating tonight, ladies, the usual?"

"Actually, hon, we need another minute." The first couple times Eric danced up to our table, L'Wren gave him a kittenish grin, but his shtick has grown tired and her tone is more bored than coquettish. "This is a serious question," she says, as he walks away. "Do you think that routine gets him laid?"

I smile for the first time since we sat down. I'm grateful to be here with L'Wren, for finally coming to my senses and opening up to her. And here we are at P.F. Chang's, looking like a pair of eHarmony hopefuls, drinking away my marriage sorrows.

L'Wren swirls the wine in her glass. "So . . . strippers? That's his thing, huh?"

I shrug and take a long drink. I'm drinking too fast. My head swims with the din of restaurant noise and Eric's singing from another table. I tell L'Wren how Oliver came home from the strip club that one night smelling like a Yankee candle.

"And the jerk didn't even bother to take a shower first? After being in a place like that?"

"No."

"Oh. My. God. Fucking, Oliver. He's the *nice one!*"

"Turns out . . ." I know I should come all the way clean. About me going to the club with Oliver, about every terrible thing we've said to each other. I'm so pathetically desperate to have L'Wren fully on my side that I can't be totally honest. I still want to be the person L'Wren thinks I am—a grounded, good person who wants all the same things in life that she does. But of course I'm naive for assuming I know what anyone really wants.

I'm about to tell her about the Dirty Diana site, to see what she thinks, when she shakes her head. "Everyone has secrets. No one really knows the real anybody." L'Wren chews delicately, seemingly lost in thought.

A week after Oliver moved into a hotel, we clumsily explained things to Emmy. I called in sick to work all week, partly because I was too sad to get dressed and partly because I couldn't face everyone at the office yet.

At the end of the first week, when it was clear Oliver wasn't coming home for the weekend, he and I sat Emmy down on the sofa. We told her we were seeing a counselor to help us "work out our differences."

"Daddy is going to take a break," I said.

Oliver shot me a look. "*We're* taking a break. It just means differ-ent arrangements and that you'll be loved under two roofs."

Oliver must have googled that line.

"A break?" Emmy looked from me to Oliver and back to me.

I turned to Oliver with the same question in my eyes. The break I had suggested was supposed to have been met with vehement protest and quickly forgotten about, but the longer it lasts, the scarier it feels.

"It means," Oliver said, "that your mother and I both love you very much, and no matter what happens between the two of us, we'll always be your parents and you are always the most important person in the world to us."

Again, Emmy looked at us both. After a quiet moment she said, "I don't want to watch your explosion."

Then she tented her fingers together—I guess like the sides of a volcano—and made the sound of an eruption as her hands broke apart.

"We're not . . ." Oliver started.

"We won't explode," I finish.

"Can I go play upstairs?"

I've spent the past couple weeks scouring her artwork, looking for her distress hidden in her rainbows and caterpillars, but if there is pain there, I can't find it. I went back to work and she hummed around the house and didn't seem to notice whether Oliver joined us for dinner or not. In the early evenings, I take Emmy on long walks around the neighborhood. One night, after dinner, I watched her play alone in the backyard catching fireflies. "Don't forget to let them go!" I called through the screen door.

"So what's the game plan here?" L'Wren waves Eric down and orders some chicken lettuce wraps. "If you want a divorce, I'll get you the best woman in Dallas, she's a beast. Or if you want Oliver back, I'll literally drug him and lock him out on my catio with a litter of hungry kittens until he comes to his senses."

What do I want? I stare at the drink in front of me. It goes blurry through my tears. But even through watery eyes, my thoughts crystallize and I know one thing to be true: I have only ever known what I want in opposition to what I never had. I built something safe and steady. I chose Oliver and this town and our house and my job as a way to erect the most impenetrable foundation I could. No moving from one crappy apartment to the next, outrunning angry landlords and bill collectors. Emmy would never have to hold her breath when she flicked a light switch, hoping for power, or dance around a parent's capricious moods.

"I don't want a divorce," I say. "I want my life back."

"Okay. Okay." L'Wren processes this, as if running it through some kind of plan-hatching filter. "You need to go to him. It needs to come from you and you need to put yourself out there. You need to swallow your pride and go to his apartment and tell him you want him back. You need him back. Use the word 'need' a few times because men get total boners for it."

I'm stuck on the word *apartment*. Oliver's been living in a hotel. Day-to-day. Temporarily. "What apartment?"

"Oh shit. Oh shit, shit. I'm such an idiot. I'm so sorry, Diana. I assumed you knew about the apartment?"

"What apartment?" I ask again.

"Kev and Oliver went out for a drink. He said Oliver rented a loft downtown because the hotel was costing a fortune. I can't believe he didn't tell you!"

Breathe, I tell myself.

"I'm sure it's one of those sad divorced-dad apartments that'll make him miss y'all even more. So, show up to his shitty, midlife crisis apartment with a trench coat on and nothing else. He won't know what hit him and he'll be back home in no time. If that's what you want, of course."

I watch as L'Wren texts Kevin for Oliver's new address, pretending she wants to drop off a housewarming plant. The truth is I don't know what I want. The only thing I know for certain is that this middle place we are in is horrible. I keep thinking of ghosts trapped in the middle—not allowed into heaven or hell because of unfinished business on Earth. Maybe this is my unfinished business. I need to know that I have tried everything to save my marriage before I can accept that it's gone.

I tell L'Wren I want to go there now, to tell Oliver how I feel tonight. She offers to give me a ride and on the way there, I realize just how drunk I am. I'm grateful to L'Wren for the lift. My body feels fuzzy with too much vodka and not enough food. To calm my nerves, I imagine this all playing out the right way: Oliver's initial confusion at seeing me will give way to excitement. I won't even need to speak. He'll see me standing on his threshold and he'll take me in his arms. He'll slip my shirt off and let it fall to the floor. The fact that I'm wearing no bra will seem planned and not the reality of a depressed person who barely got dressed to go out.

I imagine Oliver undressing himself quickly so we can stand naked in front of each other, lovingly drinking the other in. Then after we have sex, I'll tell him how sorry I am that I pushed him away and ever suggested the break in the first place. And he'll tell me he's ready to come home, that he never meant to leave like this. We can fix this.

Can't we?

When we pull up, I immediately sense the flaws in my vision. Even his apartment isn't what I imagined. I pictured his building would have some kind of brick facade, maybe with units overlooking a neglected swimming pool that residents, mainly divorced men, would try to coax their kids to swim in every other weekend.

This building looks brand-new. It has five stories that rise up at all different angles to showcase each apartment's enormous teak deck. Even at night I can see how beautiful the surrounding gardens are, bursting with flowers manicured to look just wild enough without being messy. The outside is lit with fairy lights that illuminate a stone path that leads to the glassed-in lobby.

"Let's go home," I tell L'Wren. "This is a horrible idea." *I'd rather land in hell,* I think to myself.

L'Wren takes in every detail of the building. "Who the heck does Oliver think he is? Don Draper? Mr. Cool McCool guy? We're not giving up now. You're going in."

A young couple is exiting the building, and L'Wren shoves me out the door so I can slip into the lobby without having to be buzzed in. L'Wren shouts at me as the door closes. "You got this! Call me tomorrow, postcoital!"

I take the elevator to the sixth floor and knock on Oliver's door. I wait for what feels like a long time. I knock again. It's only nine-thirty, but maybe he's already asleep. Then I hear footsteps. Oliver opens the door wearing a slim-fitting T-shirt and dark jeans, neither of which I recognize.

I smile up at him. I'd glossed my lips in the car and run my fingers through my hair, hoping to look tousled, in a sexy way, instead of spun out.

Oliver squints as if I'm backlit by the sun. "Diana? What are you doing here? Where's Emmy?"

"At L'Wren's. Kevin took the girls to the movies."

"Oh. I . . ." Oliver glances over his shoulder.

"Can I come in?" I slide past him, purposely grazing his biceps with my chest.

"I didn't know you were coming over. Did I give you this address?"

"I need to talk. I hope that's okay?" The door opens up to the living room, with a kitchen off to the right. The place is small but tidy, with blond wood floors and beamed ceilings. I'd been hoping for more of a Top Ramen and mattress on the floor vibe. "This is nice," I say brightly. "Much better than a hotel," I add, so he'll know he's off the hook for not telling me.

"I like it." Oliver stands in the foyer, seeming uncertain what to do next. Behind him, I hear water running from what must be the shower. Through the living room, the sliding glass doors are open onto the deck, with a small café table and two chairs.

And two empty wineglasses.

When I turn to him with the obvious question on my face, he's ready with the answer. "That was a friend. We were just having a glass of wine. Which I gather you have too? Maybe you need some food. Why don't we go to Delmonico's?"

"Oliver. It's late."

"Of course. Right. What about Sam's? They're open late?"

"I'm happy here." *Keep things light,* I tell myself. I can't ruin it right off the bat by seeming wounded—I need to be fun and playful. Of course I want to know who the friend was, but I won't ask. "Go ahead and shower; I hear it running. We can talk when you're done." I almost offer to join him, but something about seeing those wineglasses has sobered me.

"Right. Just give me five minutes."

While I wait, I lap the living room. On the side table, I see a framed picture of Emmy from when she was four years old, all arms and legs and big front teeth. "Where did you find this? I haven't seen it in forever!" I remember it was taken on a father-daughter camping trip. They'd come home covered with mosquito bites and Emmy beaming that she'd jumped off the highest rock into the river. I remember the way Oliver stood behind Emmy and shook his head, mouthing, *Not that high,* just so I wouldn't have to imagine Emmy in danger. I walk toward the bathroom holding the picture. "Oliver, I love this picture. Where did you even find it?"

And that's when I see it. A felt cowboy hat with a big pink feather, sitting on the arm of the couch. The cowboy hat Raleigh made herself.

My legs stop working and I lean against the wall for support. Was Raleigh the one drinking wine with Oliver? Is this why Oliver is trying to rush me out of his house? Is she in the shower? *Go! Go now,* I tell myself. *Leave before you have to see her.* I rush toward the door, hugging the picture of Emmy to my chest, my heart beating hard against it, but I'm not quick enough.

"Diana?" Behind me, Raleigh's voice is soft.

This is so far from the plan that I dreamed up I feel as if I've stumbled into someone else's plan. Someone with a cruel sense of humor.

"Hey," Raleigh moves closer, but I can only shake my head as I try to unlock Oliver's front door. There seem to be about four extra bolts and none of them are opening.

"It's the top one, Diana," she says gently. "Just pull it."

"Please don't talk to me. Please." My hands are shaking so hard the picture frame slips from my grasp and hits the floor.

"How did you even know I was here?" Oliver has appeared again and picks up the frame.

"Fuck you, Oliver. We're *married.*" My plan to be fun, easy-on-Oliver Diana has flown fully south.

Oliver's T-shirt is stuck to him and I can't tell if it's from the shower steam or his own flop sweat, but either way the body beneath is unfamiliar, muscular and hard.

"I'm not doing anything wrong," he says, his voice rising with defensiveness. "You agreed to this."

"It's been about thirty seconds, Oliver, and no, I never agreed to you fucking my friend."

"Let's talk about this in therapy. I'm not doing this with just you." I swear I see him look back at Raleigh, as if to a coach on the sideline. "It's too toxic."

"Toxic? Oh god." I roll my eyes and keep them on the ceiling, praying for godly hands to reach down and extract me. Or at least unlock the fucking door.

"Diana, please. Why don't you stay and we can talk this through," Raleigh says.

The room spins, but I manage to grab the photo from Oliver and get out the door. I take the stairs this time, running down every flight and out into the night. I hear Oliver's footsteps racing behind me. *Now he'll take me in his arms. Now he'll realize his mistake.*

"Diana. Diana, stop. You showed up here." In the parking lot, he catches me by the shoulder. *"You left me."*

"I know. It was a mistake to suggest the break. But I was flailing. I never thought you would agree."

Oliver studies my face, but I don't know what he's looking for. I couldn't rearrange it the way he wants if I tried. "That's not what I'm talking about, Diana. I mean you left me *months* ago. I've wanted nothing more than to be close to you. I would have done *anything* for you, Diana. Anything."

My shoulders drop. The fight drains out of me. "So ask her to leave and let's talk. Just you and me."

Oliver lets go of my arm. He looks at his hands, then up to the sky. He seems to consider the stars, their light cutting through the thick, humid night. "I can't do that right now."

I take an involuntary step backward, like I've been pushed. Oliver looks as innocent and sweet as he ever has, but he isn't the man I think I know. "Then go back upstairs," I say. "But don't you *dare* think you're the good guy in all this. Because you're not."

"Diana . . ."

"What." My skin is on fire. I think I might burst into flames.

I spin on my heels and march deeper into the parking lot, which is pointless, because I have no car here, but Oliver doesn't know that. I wait for him to come after me again, for him to realize that I'm too drunk to drive and to worry about how I'm getting home.

I'm not more than five paces along before I sense his absence. I turn and he's gone.

Fuck. Fuckfuckfuck. I consider calling L'Wren but it's too humiliating; her expectations for tonight might have been even higher than mine. I pull out my phone and order a ride. Nine minutes away. *Shit.*

Mosquitoes halo my head and I slap one against my neck, another on my arm. I'll be eaten alive out here. I walk back to the entrance to the building, hoping I might be able to wait in the lobby. The door is locked. Of course. I imagine the cringing embarrassment of ringing Oliver's doorbell again to ask if I could wait inside. That would really be the perfect ending to this horrible night. I lean back against the glass door, tears stinging the edges of my eyes. Seconds pass like minutes and there is a light tap on the glass. I pull away and see that it is Raleigh, in workout leggings and a powder-pink sports bra. The evening could in fact get worse.

She opens the door and glances at the phone in my hand. "Do you need a ride?"

"No," I say, the flames of my anger completely doused by the woman I thought was my friend. A woman I had invited into my home and comforted. That I shared secrets with.

"I'm so sorry," Raleigh says. "I know that was awkward. But if it makes you feel any better, we mostly just talk."

Mostly. I will myself not to cry. "What do you want?"

"We can still be friends. This doesn't have to change anything."

I want to laugh. This changes everything. "I don't think so, Raleigh. We were barely even friends to begin with."

"I didn't think anything was going to happen between us. But we were both so . . . lonely. That morning we went running we realized how much we both needed it, as a lifeline. So we take long runs sometimes."

"Raleigh. Oliver and I are still married." I see the car on my app slowly wending its way to me and decide to walk to the corner to meet it. Anything to get away.

"That's really unfair, Diana. The only reason you want him is because someone else does. Why can't you just admit that it's over between you two?"

"Are you serious? We're going through a hard time and you just made it so much harder. If you were really a friend, you would have chosen someone else's husband."

She looks wounded. "Well, I don't want you doing anything with my story. Whatever you're doing with those interviews, it's not art."

She's unbelievable. I never even asked. "Like I give a shit, Raleigh. Stay away from me."

"Does Oliver know?"

"Know what?"

"Does he know about your interviews?"

"Good night, Raleigh."

"So he doesn't know. Hmm. Just a piece of advice. I'd keep that all to yourself. Because one thing about Oliver? I can't see him getting back together with a woman who makes porn."

"Oh, Raleigh." I turn away and give her the finger, hand held high above my head as I walk off.

My head throbs and tears prick my eyes. I stumble toward the headlights of my Lyft as it heads directly for me, and for a long moment I'm not sure whether the driver spots me emerging from the darkness or not.

Chapter 24

My phone buzzes for a fifth time and this time I grab it, in case it's Oliver or the school or anything Emmy-related. I scroll through the texts, none of them from Oliver. They're from L'Wren and two other carpool moms at Emmy's school. I quickly dial L'Wren.

"Oh, honey, why haven't you picked up? I've been calling you all morning."

"Is everything okay? Are you okay?"

"Oh lord. Where do I start?"

"You're scaring me, L'Wren."

"Maybe I should just come over."

Soon L'Wren is at my door wearing faux-leather leggings and her usual oversize sunglasses. She lowers them to reveal a black eye.

"Oh my god. What happened?"

"I went full-on Jerry Springer in the carpool line. I couldn't help myself. Raleigh never saw it coming."

"You attacked Raleigh in the carpool line?"

"Attack? Noooo. No." She shakes her head. "I slapped her."

"L'Wren!"

"She thinks she can move in on my BFF's husband like some kind of Real Housewife? No way. Not today. Nope." She smooths the fabric of her shirt.

I study her face, so earnest and full of fury. L'Wren, defender of all creatures, stray and scrawny and shit-kicked, picked a fight in front of school, sticking up for me. "L'Wren, I can't believe . . ." As I open my mouth to speak, the whole scene plays before my eyes in vivid, perfectly placed panels: L'Wren emerges from her minivan with a head full of steam. I picture a kitten tucked under one arm and her purse slung over the other, as Raleigh appears in the next frame.

It's ten A.M., and I'm still in my pajamas, and L'Wren is in my living room with a black eye and now we're both laughing so hard I'm sure at least one of us will pee.

"What happened after you slapped her?"

L'Wren is on her feet to demonstrate. "Raleigh tries to tackle me and you know, she comes after me with these long nails and swats at my face. And I've been doing that capoeira/boxing/modern dance hybrid class for the last two years with Marcos? With the abs? So I use an uppercut jazz hand and then I kind of shove her against my car."

My hand covers my mouth. "No! What about the black eye?"

"Oh. She did get a good one in. Yeah. She sure did. With her elbow right to my face." L'Wren delicately fingers the skin around her eye. "I'm heading to the derm now for some filler since I already have the bruising. But I wish you'd been there, Diana. I know it was wrong, but it felt so damn good. There was a red handprint on her face! It was beautiful."

I pull L'Wren into a hug. "Thank you."

She pulls back. "You fuck with *you,* you fuck with *me!* I've been saying it for years."

I think about correcting her motto, but I'm too full of gratitude. "Something like that." I smile, suddenly unsure how I got lucky enough to have a friend like this.

For the next several weeks, time moves in slow-motion circles, like I'm falling out of circulation. Some days, my smiles are genuine and not just for Emmy. But other days, I start crying while eating a piece of toast. Some nights, I go to bed early and some nights I stay up and leave Oliver cringey late-night messages about going back to therapy. He doesn't call back, committing to the idea that we both need "space." Dinner is also out of the question, as if just being near me will remind him too much of our failures. I talk to Alicia every day and she encourages me to keep making art—she promises me that creating something will get me through. I keep interviewing women for Dirty Diana and realize I no longer have to go looking for people to talk to me. Every day someone new reaches out by emailing the contact @Dirty Diana address I posted on the site.

Some evenings, I lie on the bed and listen to other women's stories of love and longing and desire, and I think about Oliver and try to rewind the tape to how we got here. One Monday morning at the office, I find out he quit the Friday before, without mentioning it to me. But instead of feeling blindsided, I think of how numb he's been, too, for so long. We'd quietly, slowly let each other drift so far away.

Oliver never calls, but he does text. About things like pickup times and camp forms. I text him questions about the fuse box and ask again about therapy. He answers the easy questions and avoids the hard ones. But I ask him out to dinner again anyway.

.   .   .

One Saturday morning, I have two texts: one from Alicia and one from Oliver. Alicia reminds me that I promised to meet with a friend of hers who loves the site. I ask if we can push it a week or two, but she urges me to show up.

Then I check Oliver's text.

Sorry to bother you, but Emmy swears you told her she could have cupcakes for breakfast on Saturdays.

Nice try, Ems.

Thought so.

Three dots disappear then reappear. Then he adds:

How are you?

Good.

How do I answer that question?

Just enjoying my Saturday. But missing Emmy and her bald-faced lies.

She is . . . inventive . . . Are you at the house?

Do you really want to know or are you just bored?

Both.

Doing laundry. Running errands. Nothing too exciting.

At least there's less laundry to do now?

Sure . . . But I never minded the laundry.

Right.

I assume that'll be the end of our thread. But when I set my phone on the kitchen counter, it vibrates again.

I'm sorry about all this. It's weird, right?

Very.

His three dots appear. Then disappear. Then after a long few moments:

Maybe I'm having a midlife crisis?

Have you bought a tiny but obscenely expensive sports car?

No.

Before I can stop myself, my fingers fly over the keys.

A Hummer?

Do they still make those?? (Note to self: google vintage Hummers . . .)

Have you joined a dojo?

No . . . Not yet?

Nope. It's not a midlife crisis. I promise.

I pause, and then add:

You're just saying what you want.

Took me long enough.

Ha ha.

I slip my phone in my bag and a minute later it buzzes again.

Are you free for dinner?

I don't hesitate.

Yes. Tonight?

More dots appear and then nothing, until:

Okay.

As I hurry to get ready to meet Alicia's friend, Oliver's text thread plays over and over in my mind. What if he wants to meet to ask for a divorce in person? But why over dinner? What if he's reaching out to have a real conversation? What if there's a version of us where we do tell each other what we really want? Is it too late for that? Alicia sent me a time and place to meet her friend for coffee, but as I'm parking the car I have a sudden pang about how I'll find her. I scroll back through her texts but don't find a name.

I text Alicia.

What's this friend's name? Does she know what I look like?

I wait, staring at my phone. Nothing. It's almost time so I head into the café. There's no one sitting alone or seeming like they're waiting on anyone, so I find a table where I can watch the door. I order a coffee and check my phone, willing Alicia to text me back. Nothing.

When the bell above the door chimes, I glance up from my phone and see a slim, broad-shouldered guy enter. He's got tousled hair and a slow, easy walk and he reminds me of someone I once knew.

He walks toward me, and I keep telling myself he's a facsimile, because the original couldn't possibly be here. The original is somewhere else, somewhere lost to me.

Then he's standing in front of me, and I'm looking up at him. "Jasper."

He sits down opposite me and leans forward, his elbows on his knees. He looks me in the eyes and smiles.

"Diana," he says. "Thanks for taking the meeting."

Acknowledgments

___

All of our enormous thanks to:

Alia Hanna Habib and Anna Worrall, the *truly dynamic* duo of our duos. Thank you for leading us through every twist and turn with your brilliance, patience, and humor; to the Gernert Company team, especially David Gernert, Sophie Pugh-Sellers, and Ellen Coughtrey; and to Rebecca Gardner for taking *Diana* on the road in such a spectacular way.

To Whitney Frick, whose every note, meeting, and kick-ass editorial map leaves us feeling inspired and *so lucky*—THANK YOU!; and to Rose Fox, Cindy Berman, Laurie McGee, and the entire team at Dial for making a publishing house a true home.

To Lynne Drew and the HarperCollins UK team—what a dream to be in your excellent hands!

To Carin Besser, for solving puzzles with poetry, and for making this book—and everything—better.

To Demi Moore, for bringing Diana to life and for being our forever inspiration.

To Rob Herting and everyone at QCode, for being amazing champions from the very beginning.

To Emma Forrest for your immense friendship and for always talking life and sexcapades with us.

To Jen Pastiloff, for equal parts support and inspiration.

To the Ladies of Ladies' Night—Aisha, Inara, Liz, and Rina—for being there for us every step of the way. See you in the corner suite.

To Kara, Nami, and Loren—something magical happened on 12th Street and the magic is you.

To our endlessly supportive families and in-laws: Lana, Sandi, Toni, Matt, Bobby, Todd, Babs, Mikey, Dewitt, Lynette, Deanna, Blair, Gaby, Bob, Gerry, Kerry, Peter, Kelly, Paul, and Jen—thank you for rooting us on to every deadline and beyond.

To the Top Five of all time: Primo, Waylon, Ellis, Roman, and Odessa; and to Ben and Brian, for your love and intimacy.

And to best friends.

PHOTO CREDIT: CHRISTOPHER ZEBO

PHOTO CREDIT: SYDNEY SHEEHAN

Lifelong best friends Jen Besser and Shana Feste met as eleven-year-olds in California and have been collaborating ever since, beginning with writing, directing, producing, and starring in many regrettable middle-school talent shows. *Dirty Diana* first launched as a podcast starring Demi Moore, debuted at #1 on Apple, was nominated for Podcast of the Year, and won the Ambie Award for Best Fiction, Screenwriting. Feste is the award-winning screenwriter and director of several feature films, including *Country Strong* and *Run Sweetheart Run*. Besser is a fiction editor and publisher. They now live thousands of miles apart and talk every day. *Dirty Diana* is their debut novel.

Instagram: @jenandshana

Books Driven by the Heart

Sign up for our newsletter
and find more you'll love:

thedialpress.com